KISSING LILY

Sam swerved into an exit marked with a welcome to Texas sign.

"Whoa!" said Lily, clutching the edge of her seat. "What are you doing?"

He didn't know. His hands had decided to turn into the rest area, not him. Sam pulled into the first open parking space, and his foot stepped on the brake. "Stopping."

"Why? Are you going to get a Texas map?"

Sam didn't bother to answer. He opened his door, got out and was at the passenger door before Lily could get her seat belt undone. He opened the door, unhooked the seat belt and hauled her out of the car.

"Was it something I said?" she asked, faking innocence. She had rattled the big, bad detective. He looked positively fierce. Lily grinned at him.

"Young ladies shouldn't tease their elders."

"No? What are you going to do? Spank—oomph." Sam jerked her against him. She barely had time to register how neatly her body fit his before his mouth planted itself firmly on hers. . . .

Books by Dixie Kane

DREAMING OF YOU

CHASING LILY

Published by Kensington Publishing Corp.

CHASING LILY

Dixie Kane

ZEBRA BOOKS
KENSINGTON PUBLISHING CORP.
http://www.kensingtonbooks.com

ZEBRA BOOKS are published by

Kensington Publishing Corp.
850 Third Avenue
New York, NY 10022

For Mavis Cheeks, writer, neighbor, friend.

Copyright © 2007 by Hannah Howell

All Kensington Titles, Imprints, and Distributed Lines are available at special quantity discounts for bulk purchases for sales promotions, premiums, fund-raising, educational, or institutional use.

Special book excerpts or customized printings can also be created to fit specific needs. For details, write or phone the office of the Kensington Special Sales Manager: Kensington Publishing Corp., 850 Third Avenue, New York, NY 10022, Attn: Special Sales Department. Phone: 1-800-221-2647.

Zebra and the Z logo Reg. U.S. Pat. & TM Off.

First Printing: May 2007
10 9 8 7 6 5 4 3 2 1

Printed in the United States of America

Prologue

Thursday, May 8, 2003
Cook County Jail
Chicago, Illinois

C. Frederick Merritt, attorney-at-law, hastily stood up when the steel door to the windowless room opened. His client shuffled in, his usual arrogant stride hampered by the shackles around his ankles. The guard unlocked the shackles and the handcuffs and exited the room, closing the door behind him.

"Mr. Accardo. Arraignment is set for tomorrow at ten o'clock. Judge Greylord's courtroom. I've already filed a motion to set bail. It will be heard at the same time, I'm sure."

August "Gus" Accardo sat down at the scarred wooden table. "One more night in this place?" He growled the question.

C. Frederick Merritt tugged at the collar of his shirt. "Best I could do. Dockets are crowded this time of year. Crime stats always jump when the weather warms up."

"Yeah. Punks." Gus sighed. "About that other matter we discussed . . . ?"

"The Alabama job? Your instructions have been carried out."

A faint smile touched Gus's lips. "Good."

Friday, May 9, 2003
State Office Building
Springfield, Illinois

State Senator Tony Santori looked up from the proof of his latest print ad as George Neill, his campaign manager, entered his office.

"Your uncle's out on bail. They cut him loose this morning."

Santori leaned back in his chair. "That was to be expected. Never believe that old saw about crime not paying. Crime pays very well. Uncle Gus has millions. More than enough to grease the wheels of justice."

"You sure you don't want to tap him for a campaign contribution?" asked George.

"After years of distancing myself from that branch of the family? I think not."

"Too bad. We could use a few more dollars for our media campaign."

"Forget about it. Even without the negative publicity, any money from Gus would have strings you couldn't begin to imagine." Santori smiled grimly. "Besides, Mama would never forgive me. You know how she feels about her brother."

"Yeah. Mama Santori is the best tough-on-crime endorsement we've got."

"Exactly. I'm not doing anything to upset Mama. Which brings up that other little problem . . . ?"

"They left for Alabama two days ago. You can count on them to handle it."

Santori steepled his fingers. "Oh, I will. Believe me, I will."

Friday, May 9, 2003
Hunter and Sons, Investigations
Chicago, Illinois

Sam Hunter stared out his office window, watching the sail boats on Lake Michigan. He heard the door open, but he didn't bother turning around. He knew who had entered without knocking. "Well? Did you fire her? Has she left the building?"

"Yeah. That's the last one, Sam. From now on, you do your own firing."

Reluctantly, Sam turned and met his brother's gaze. "I can't. They always cry." He shuddered. "I hate crying women. I could take the tears if they'd be quiet about it, but I can't stand those awful snuffling sounds they make."

Sauntering to Sam's desk, Phil sat down in Sam's chair. "Change the rule about fraternization with clients and clerical staff, why don't you? Maybe if you weren't forbidden fruit, you wouldn't have women lusting after you." His brother looked him over, shaking his head. "I swear, I do not get your appeal for the fair sex. What is it about you that has women falling in love with you at first sight?"

"It wasn't love, and it wasn't that quick. It never is, no matter what they say. This one had worked here for at least five months before she snuck up on me in the copy room."

"Yeah. Lucky we extended the probationary period from three months to six months. That and the rule against fraternization ought to keep you out of any long-term trouble with the help."

Sam sighed again. A put-upon sigh.

"I don't get it," Phil repeated. "I'm better looking than you are. More charming. Younger. I'm the one looking for a special woman, a woman to fall in love with, so—"

"Not me."

"—why didn't Sally Lou harass me?"

"Maybe because love had nothing to do with what she wanted from me in the copy room." Sam shuddered at the memory. "I swear that girl has more than two hands. Did you call the employment agency?"

"I did. And I told them we wanted someone with at least twenty-five years' experience. If we're lucky, they won't send anyone under fifty."

"Isn't that kind of requirement flirting with age discrimination?"

"Maybe. But it's that, or you take another chance on being sexually harassed. Choose your politically incorrect position."

"No contest. Age discrimination it is."

Phil cocked his head to one side. "When are you going to do it?"

"What? Get old?"

"Fall in love again. Don't you think it's time?"

"You'll be waiting for that until hell freezes over. Been there, done that. Ain't gonna do it again. What do you think I am, stupid?"

Phil grinned at him. "I refuse to answer that." He stood and sauntered to the door. "Oh, by the way, Dad's gone. He took the Explorer."

"Gone? Gone where?"

"Where do you think? Alabama."

Monday, May 12, 2003
Redmond residence
Mobile, Alabama

Arthur Redmond stuck his coffee cup out from behind the newspaper. His wife, Pauline, known to family and friends as Polly, filled his cup, then sat on the breakfast nook bench opposite him.

Polly looked at the clock on the kitchen wall. "It's almost eight o'clock. Lily should be picking up her grandmother right about now. They wanted to get on the road by nine. Do you really think this will work?"

Arthur looked up from the *Mobile Register*. "It had better work. The last thing we need is for Mother to continue with her outlandish plan. I don't know what's gotten into her."

"Oh, Arthur. I know what's wrong. She's lonely. She and your father were married for over forty years. Lillian has been a widow for less than two years. No wonder she's still searching for something to fill the void."

"She could take up knitting," Arthur said.

"Not your mother. Knitting is too . . . mundane for her."

"Don't I know it. Thank goodness Lily takes after you and not her. We took a real chance, naming our daughter after Lillian. If she hadn't been the spitting image of Lillian's baby pictures . . ."

Polly smiled wistfully. "Now that she's grown, Lily looks just like Lillian looked when she was the toast of Hollywood."

"Physically, yes, but Lily doesn't have that wild streak Mother has. Lily has never given us a moment's trouble. We couldn't ask for a better daughter."

"No, we couldn't. Lily is a real old-fashioned good girl." Polly's eyes misted. "Has it struck you yet? She won't be our little girl much longer. She's going to be a wife."

"Now, Polly. You knew Lily would get married one of these days."

Sniffing, Polly nodded. "To tell you the truth, I thought she would have walked down the aisle before now. It's hard to believe our daughter is almost twenty-five. She and Dexter need to set a date."

"Yes," Arthur agreed. "But I think Dexter was wise to wait a few years before proposing. You can't blame the boy for giving Lily time to get any nonsense out of her system."

Pauline sniffed. "Lily doesn't have even a smidgen of nonsense in her system. She never does anything the least bit nonsensical. Our daughter always does exactly what we expect her to do."

"Amen," said Arthur. "Lily knows exactly what we expect of her this time. If anyone can make Mother give up her plan, it's Lily."

One

There was a man in her grandmother's bed.

He was on his back, his right hand flung over his head, his fingers curled around the iron bedpost. His other hand rested on the summer blanket that was pulled up under his chin. The man had coal black hair, tousled from sleep. One black lock had fallen onto his forehead, inviting someone to smooth it into place. Lily Redmond's hand reached out, seemingly of its own volition, before she came to her senses and jerked it back.

He was asleep.

Or dead.

Lily took a step closer, close enough to see the rhythmic movement of his chest as he inhaled and exhaled. Not dead. She let out the breath she hadn't realized she'd been holding.

Not dead, and not old.

If she'd thought about it, which she most certainly had not, Lily would have thought any man Lillian invited into her bed would be old. Older. Lillian was sixty-three. This man appeared to be in his thirties. Not old, and not handsome, either. His nose looked as if it had been broken more than once, and his face was shadowed with morning stubble. Lily's heart began to beat a little faster.

There was something about him. . . . Even asleep, he exuded intoxicating amounts of testosterone. Lily took another step closer to the bed. As she gazed at the man, she was aware that her body was reacting to him in a most inappropriate way. Having her heart rate speed up was one thing—that could be the result of shock. But the heat pooling between her legs, the way her nipples were becoming sensitized—those reactions could only be because she was attracted to him. On some purely physiological level.

A man who could elicit that kind of sexual response when he was asleep was beyond dangerous—he was downright terrifying. Staring at him, Lily could understand why her grandmother had gone and taken a man thirty years her junior into her bed. Almost.

But not quite. What would people think once they found out Lillian had a boy toy? Lily sucked in a breath. Forget about people. Wait until the family heard about Lillian taking a lover who was half her age. They would—

Lily saw the handcuffs.

The man's right hand was handcuffed to her grandmother's iron bedstead.

Handcuffs? Before Lily could wrap her mind around the idea of her grandmother and handcuffs, the man's eyes snapped open. He had green eyes. Lily had always coveted green eyes. With her flame red hair, she ought to have had eyes like his. But, no. Her eyes were brown. Not even an interesting brown, with flecks of gold or green or blue. Plain old Mississippi mud brown.

With a start, Lily realized this particular pair of green eyes was glaring. At her. She took two steps back.

"About time you got here, Red. Unlock these cuffs. Now. I think she left the key over there somewhere." He jerked his chin in the direction of her grandmother's dressing table.

Lily bristled. The man did not seem to realize he was in no position to be snapping orders. "Who are you? What have you done with my grandmother?"

He snorted. "Ask what she did to me, why don't you? Your grandmother pretended to be a sweet southern lady, invited me in, offered me tea and cake. A bed for the night. Then she did this to me." He yanked on the cuff, making it clang against the iron bedpost.

Lily sucked in a breath. This was worse than she'd thought. Lillian had taken an *unwilling* lover. "Why would she handcuff you? No, don't tell me. Where did she go?"

"I don't know why she cuffed me. It was around five o'clock this morning. I was sleeping soundly, too soundly now that I think about it. She must have drugged my tea. Are you going to get that key, or not?" He swung his legs—his bare legs—to the floor. The blanket slithered off as he stood. He had on a pair of black knit boxers. Nothing else.

Lily's mouth dropped open. He had the kind of body she'd seen only in television commercials for body-building machines. An appreciative sigh floated out of her open mouth. Okay. She got it. After one look at his sleek, hard muscles, Lily couldn't blame her grandmother for handcuffing this particular man to her bed. He had to be the sexiest man she'd ever—

The man's words registered. "My grandmother does not use drugs. And she doesn't own a pair of handcuffs. Where did she go?" Lily asked the question again, although now that at least a few of her brain cells had fought free of the pheromone fog, she had a pretty good idea of where Lillian had gone.

"Damned if I know. Maybe she left you a note. I don't know where she got the cuffs—they sure as hell aren't mine." The man held out his uncuffed hand, palm up. "The key?"

"I'm not turning you loose. Not until I call the police." Lily eyed the telephone on the bedside table. If she got close enough to pick up the phone, she'd be close enough for the man to grab her with his free hand. She almost took a step in his direction before her good sense returned. Lily took two steps back. "I'll use the phone in the kitchen."

With a nonchalant shrug, the man sat down on the edge of the bed, stretched out his long legs and crossed them at the ankles. He stifled a yawn with the back of his free hand. "Calling the police is a good idea. I want to press charges against your grandmother."

Lily halted her retreat. "Charges?"

"Assault. Battery. False imprisonment." He jangled the handcuffs against the bedpost. "That will do for starters. I may think of others once the cops get here. Go ahead and call. You can use this phone. I don't bite."

"Who *are* you? Why did Lillian handcuff you?"

"Sam Hunter. I asked her that very question, but she didn't explain. All she said was that her granddaughter would be here at eight o'clock to unlock the cuffs. After she left, I went back to sleep— probably because of whatever she put in the tea. And she did put something in the tea, Red. I know when I've been drugged."

Lily wrinkled her brow. "Grandmother does have sleeping pills. The doctor gave them to her when my grandfather died. To help her sleep, he said. She wouldn't take them. She thinks doctors

overmedicate senior citizens. I suppose she could
have put sleeping pills in your tea. But why would
she?" Lily's hands curled into fists. "Did you threaten
her?"

He gave her a disgusted look. "No. Are you
going to unlock these cuffs, or not?" Sam got to his
feet again. He tugged on the bed, and the heavy
iron bedstead moved a fraction of an inch.

"Stop that! You'll scar the floor."

"Then get the key."

Lily dithered. She didn't know whether she
should let him go, or leave him safely locked to the
bed until she figured out why her grandmother
had done such a thing. "In a minute."

"Now. I need to use the bathroom."

She thought fast. If Lillian had been afraid of
Sam, she wouldn't have invited him to spend the
night. But why had she given him her bed? There
were two perfectly good guest rooms right down
the hall. Surely Lillian didn't have men lashed to
those beds, too.

"Not yet. I'm going to look for Lillian before I
do anything else. Sit down and cross your legs."

"I don't have much choice," Sam grumbled, but
he followed her suggestion. "Hurry up."

Lily quickly checked the other two bedrooms.
Both were empty, although Lillian's everyday robe
and slippers were in the second guest room. Lily
noted that the beds in the guest rooms both had
solid wooden headboards—not suitable for cuff-
ing a person. That must be why Lillian had given
the man—Sam—her bed. Making a hasty survey of
the rest of the house, Lily found nothing to indi-
cate why her grandmother had done what Sam
claimed she had done.

Lillian was gone. Lily swallowed a most unlady-
like curse. Her grandmother had known she
would be coming to pick her up at eight o'clock.

She could have taped a note on the door. A short
note, nothing elaborate. Something along the
lines of, "Lily, don't be alarmed, but I left a man
handcuffed to my bed. Unlock him, will you
please?"

But no. Lillian had let her favorite granddaughter walk in on a strange, almost naked man with no
warning. Lily's tummy got that hollow, sinking
feeling her grandmother's actions often induced.
It was just possible that Lillian had left a man in
her bed to tempt her granddaughter into doing
something outrageous.

Like what, Grandmother? Jump the sexy stranger
handcuffed to the bedpost? Lily wrinkled her nose.
Not a chance. Not her. That was not her style, and
Lillian knew it. Not to mention that she was engaged
to be married, to Dexter Beauregard Jackson, III,
her childhood sweetheart and a scion of Mobile
society. An engaged woman did not fool around
with a strange man, no matter how sexy he was.

Lily knew what Lillian would say to that. She'd
ask, her blue eyes wide, "Why not, dear? I did."

Ending her imaginary argument with her grandmother before she lost it, Lily returned to the mas-
ter bedroom. Doing her best to ignore the *Playgirl*
worthy picture Sam made as he lay sprawled on
the bed, Lily walked to the dressing table. A small
key was in the china tray where Lillian kept her
jewelry when she took it off at night. Picking up
the key, Lily put it in the pocket of her shorts. "I'll
let you go after you've answered a few questions.
First, why did you come to see my grandmother?"

Sam was staring at her feet. Lily was wearing
crisp white shorts, a lemon yellow tee shirt and
sandals. Her toenails were painted hot pink, a
shade Lily adored but couldn't wear any closer to
her hair than the tips of her toes.

Raising his gaze slowly, Sam lingered a long

while at breast level. Finding his gaze unnerving, Lily almost crossed her arms over her chest.

When his eyes finally met hers, he seemed a little dazed. "You sure do look like her. She wore an outfit like that in *Tahiti Temptress.*" Sam yawned and shook his head as if to clear it. "I'm still groggy from that tea she fed me. What did you ask me? Oh, yeah. Why I came to see your grandmother. I was looking for my father. When Dad left Chicago last Friday, he said he was going to see Lillian Redmond, formerly known as Lillian Leigh, movie actress, in Fair Hope, Alabama."

"Chicago? My grandmother doesn't know anyone in Chicago." Lily's eyes widened. "Except—"

"Gus Accardo," Sam finished for her. He scratched the stubble on his chin.

"She hasn't seen him since 1958. Gus Accardo is your father? I thought you said your name was Hunter." Lily stuffed her hand in her pocket and clutched the key, not at all sure that she should release the son of a notorious gangster.

"My name is Hunter. Accardo is no relation of mine."

"You know who he is."

"Everyone in Chicago knows who Gus Accardo is. He's one of Illinois' homegrown hoodlums. Gus is currently in Cook County Jail awaiting trial for extortion." Sam moved into a sitting position and yawned again. "God. I'm still groggy. Like I said, Gus is in jail. Unless he's out on bail. Now that I think about it, his hotshot lawyers must have sprung him loose by now."

"Did Mr. Accardo send you? To shut Grandmother up?" A few months ago, Lillian had announced her intention to write her memoirs, concentrating on her time in Hollywood. That time included Lillian's brief but colorful stint as a movie starlet and her shocking relationship with Gus

Accardo. Lillian's career and her affair with Gus had both ended abruptly when the head of the movie studio where she worked had been murdered.

Because of his underworld connections, Gus Accardo would have been the favored suspect if Lillian hadn't given him an alibi for the night of the murder. The whole night. Lily felt her cheeks grow hot, thinking about what Lillian and Gus must have been doing that long summer night forty-five years ago.

"I don't work for mobsters. But the word on the street is that Gus doesn't want that old murder case reopened. Rumors that he got away with murder might prejudice the jury pool for his current crime. My father intended to come here to offer his services to your grandmother." Sam eyed her curiously. "Your cheeks are the same color as an overripe tomato. Was it something I said?"

Silently cursing her inability to control blood flow to her face, Lily ignored the question. "Accardo's after my grandmother? I knew it. I just knew it. Daddy was right. Grandmother should never have stirred up that old scandal. Services? What kind of services?"

"Body guard. It's a branch of the family business. Hunter and Sons, Investigators and Security Consultants."

"You're a private eye?"

"Investigator and security consultant."

"Same thing. You can't be very good at it. You let my grandmother get the drop on you." Lily smiled smugly when Sam's cheekbones reddened. She wasn't the only one who couldn't control certain physiological reactions.

Apparently she struck a nerve—Sam glowered at her. "I wasn't expecting any trouble. Not from a widow in her sixties."

"Do you have any identification?"

"In my coat pocket. Behind the door." There was a dark brown sport coat hanging on the hook on the back of the bedroom door. A pair of tan slacks and a white knit shirt were draped on Lillian's rocking chair.

Lily inched her way toward the door, careful not to get within grabbing distance of Sam. He might say he was an investigator, but he knew Gus Accardo. And, sexy or not, the more she thought about it, the more Sam looked like a hoodlum to her. Not the mastermind kind of criminal—more the enforcer type. Big. Lots of muscle. Add the broken nose and the well-defined muscles and anyone would think twice before getting close to him.

Patting the coat, Lily found a wallet in the breast pocket. She took it out and opened it. An Illinois driver's license identified Sam Spade Hunter, 6'3", 180 pounds, black hair, blue eyes, born August 5, 1970. The wallet also contained a private investigator's license, a couple of credit cards and a healthy amount of cash.

"Sam Spade?" Lily asked.

"Yeah. Naming sons after fictional detectives is a family tradition started by my grandfather. Dad is Archie Goodwin Hunter. My kid brother is Philip Marlowe Hunter. Are you going to let me go? Or should I be the one to call the cops?" His hand hovered over the telephone on the bedside table.

"No." Lily thought fast. She was ninety-nine percent sure she knew where her grandmother had gone. She had to get rid of Sam so she could go after Lillian and stop her before she got into any more trouble. Lily took the handcuff key from the pocket of her shorts and unlocked the cuff. She stepped away from Sam. Quickly.

Sam rubbed his wrist and stretched. "Bathroom?"

"Down the hall, first door on the left."

He picked up his clothes and walked out of the bedroom. As soon as Sam had closed the bathroom door, Lily hurried to the study. A search revealed at least two things were missing—her grandmother's address book and the accordion folder where Lillian had kept her Hollywood memorabilia.

Just as she'd thought. Her grandmother was on her way to California to relive her scandalous past.

What now? She could call her father. Or her mother. Her father would swear. Her mother would shriek, maybe even faint. They both had freaked when Lillian had announced she intended to write about her past. If they found out Lillian had run away to California again . . . Well, that didn't bear thinking about.

Lily's parents were understandably concerned—Lillian said they were obsessed—with propriety. Since the family business was banking, appearances *were* important. No one wanted a scandalous banker. How many times growing up had she heard her father say that?

She ought to call Dexter. Lily glanced at her watch. He would be at the bank by now—Dexter made it a point to be the first executive at the Redmond State Bank every morning. Sitting down at the escritoire, Lily let her hand drift over the telephone, but she didn't pick up the receiver.

She did not want to call her fiancé.

Not because Lillian's abrupt departure would shock him, although it would. Dexter knew about Lillian's past. His family had lived next door to her grandparents for years, until her grandfather had retired and he and Lillian had moved to Fair Hope, across the bay from Mobile.

Lily had resolved not to talk to Dexter again until she had figured out exactly what she wanted to say to him. The trip with her grandmother should have given her plenty of time to do that.

And she could have counted on plenty of advice from Lillian, too, if she had confided her misgivings to her grandmother.

And she probably would have. Lillian was the only relative who might understand her unexpected second thoughts. She didn't. Lily had known since she was eleven years old that she would marry Dexter Beauregard Jackson, III, someday. But ever since he'd finally proposed, she'd been feeling . . . unsettled. Maybe because he'd waited so long to propose.

Her mother and father thought Dexter would have asked her to marry him years sooner but for Lillian's youthful indiscretions. Because Lily had her grandmother's red hair, fair skin and classic features, some people—at times, even her own mother and father—thought Lily must have inherited what they referred to in hushed tones as Lillian's wild streak.

Lillian had run away from Mobile when she was seventeen. Dexter had waited seven years past Lily's seventeenth birthday before asking her to marry him. Lily had a strong suspicion that he had waited to see if blood would tell. Dexter was the cautious type.

If Dexter knew Lillian was on her way to Hollywood, and that she intended to go after her. . . . Lily's hand dropped into her lap. Even if she wanted to, she couldn't call Dexter. Chasing after Lillian was her job, not his.

Her family had entrusted her with the task of dissuading Lillian from exposing her youthful indiscretion to the public eye once again. They may not have anticipated that Lillian would run off, but that did not mean Lily had to go running back to her parents for new instructions. She was a grown woman, a woman on the verge of leaving home for good. It was time for her to take control of her own life. Her life and Lillian's, too. That meant keeping the people who knew about her grandmother's latest escapade to a minimum.

With a decisive nod, Lily made up her mind. She would find Lillian and bring her home before anyone realized her grandmother had forgone the Magic Kingdom for La La Land.

Luckily, her father had given her two weeks off—she was a teller at the family bank—so that she could take Lillian to Disney World and talk her out of writing about her past. All she had to do was call home occasionally and pretend that she and Lillian were in Orlando. She could do that. Lily had an unfortunate tendency to blush whenever she told even the teeniest fib. But she could lie long distance like a trooper.

Lily turned on the notebook computer resting on the desk. Her grandmother had bought the computer a couple of months ago, around the time she'd decided to write her memoirs. Lillian hadn't gotten the hang of the new technology yet. She'd signed up for a computer course at the senior citizen center, but that hadn't started yet. In the meantime, Lillian had continued using a pen and notebook for her literary efforts.

Lily had transferred the entries in Lillian's address book to the computer several weeks ago, though. She booted up the computer and opened the address book file. As soon as it appeared on the screen, she hit the print button. Several of Lillian's California cronies were listed in the book, she remembered. A couple of them no longer lived in or around Los Angeles.

While waiting for the printer to finish, Lily heard the front door open. Sam was leaving. Good. She felt her face grow hot, remembering her reaction to him. That couldn't have been attraction. Belatedly, Lily remembered that the body reacted to danger in much the same way as it did to sex. She had been shocked, and her body had gone into flight or fight mode, that's all. With good reason. It wasn't every day she found a strange man cuffed to a bedpost. Maybe Sam would be gone before—

Sam yelled, "Goddammit to hell!"

Lily got up and stuck her head out the study door. Sam was standing in the open front door. He was dressed in the clothes she'd seen in Lillian's bedroom. "Didn't your mother ever tell you not to swear in the presence of a lady?"

He looked at her over his shoulder. He'd shaved, too. Without the stubble, he still managed to look disreputable. The scar on his chin had something to do with that, she supposed.

Scowling, Sam pointed out the open front door. "Don't talk to me about manners, Red. Your grandmother is on her way to becoming a career criminal. That sneaky old broad stole my car."

"Broad?" Lily tossed her head, sending her hair swirling around her shoulders. "My grandmother is *not* a broad. She's a lady. A true southern lady. Even if she did slip a teensy weensy bit in Hollywood. People seem to do that in California—go a little wild, I mean."

"Fine. That wild woman—excuse me, that wild *lady*—took my car."

"She did not. Lillian has a car. Why would she take yours?"

"How would I know?"

"You're supposed to be a detective," muttered Lily, stalking out of the study and into the hall. "Why do you think she took it?"

He rolled his eyes. "She's gone. The car is gone. And my suitcase is here." Sam pointed to the suitcase next to the front door.

Lily had almost tripped over it earlier. She'd

thought it was Lillian's. Brushing by Sam, Lily walked out the front door, across the wide porch, and down five steps to the brick path leading to the detached garage at the side of the house. "My grandmother doesn't steal cars. Someone else must have done it."

Sam followed. "You know what criminals say, even when they're caught red-handed?"

Glancing over her shoulder, Lily said, "No. Why would I? I don't consort with criminals. What do they say?"

"Some other dude did it—it's a favorite defense."

They reached the garage, and Sam opened the doors. Lillian's white Cadillac was there, right where it was supposed to be.

Both rear tires were flat.

Sam knelt by the right rear tire. "Now we know why your grandmother took my rental car. She didn't want to take time to call the auto club. She must have wanted to get away from here before you showed up."

A tremor of unease slid down Lily's spine. *Two* flat tires? That seemed sinister somehow. "How would she get two flats at the same time?"

Sam ran his hand around the treads. "It doesn't look like the tires have been slashed. Someone must have let the air out."

"Slashed? *Slashed?*" More than sinister. Downright scary. Lily squatted next to Sam and stared at the tire. "Someone let the air out? Who would do a thing like that? Did you do it?"

"No, Red. That's not the way I operate. Looks to me like someone who wanted your grandmother to stay put. At least for a while." Sam stood and looked around the yard. "You can't see the street from here."

"That's why Grandmother and Grandpa moved to Fair Hope from Mobile. Large lots, lots of trees and shrubs. Privacy. And Granddad wanted a house on the water. He liked to fish." The grassy lawn behind the house, studded with oak trees and bordered with camellia and gardenia bushes, sloped down to Mobile Bay. Her grandfather's rowboat was still tied to the wooden dock that jutted out into the bay.

Lily got to her feet and brushed off her hands. "Someone came into my grandmother's garage and let the air out of her tires. That's scary."

"Red. Get past it. Your grandmother is all right. She left here before dawn in my car. Whoever did this wasn't expecting her to go anywhere—not until she got the tires fixed."

"Do you really think she's okay?"

"For now. But I need to find her, the sooner, the better." He held out his hand. "Give me your car keys."

"Keys?" Lily's silver Honda Civic was parked in the driveway, and the keys were in the ignition. She put her hands behind her back. She looked at Sam's hand. "Why do you want my keys?"

"You owe me a car."

"I do not. I need my car. I'm going—" Lily stopped. The last thing she wanted to do was tell Sam what she intended.

"No, you're not. You go home and stay there. I'll go after your grandmother. Archie is probably on her tail even as we speak."

"Archie?"

"My father. I told you his name. Archie Goodwin Hunter."

"What is going on? Why would your father be following my grandmother?" Lily winced, hearing the shrill tone in her voice.

Sam sighed. "I told you that, too. Pay attention, Red. Dad planned to offer his services to your grandmother."

"Then why didn't he?"

"I don't know. He should have gotten here before I did. Archie left Chicago last Friday, driving his new Ford Explorer. When I found out where he'd gone, I came after him. I flew to Mobile yesterday, rented a car and came here last night looking for him. Either he got delayed along the way, or—and this is more likely—he didn't want me to catch up with him."

"Why not? Doesn't he like you?"

"He doesn't like me telling him what to do. Can't say that I blame him, but he is getting close to retirement age."

"Lillian is my grandmother, not yours. If she needs help, it should come from me, not a stranger. I've got to go after her."

"No, you don't. I'm the professional here. I'll do it. Don't worry, Red. I promise you that nothing bad will happen to your grandmother, not with Hunter and Sons on the job. Did you leave your car keys in the house?" Sam headed for the front door.

Lily hurried after him. He could say he was a private eye, but she had only his word for that. His word and a private investigator's license. But everyone knew that licenses could be forged. She had to get rid of Sam so she could figure out what to do about Lillian.

Lily was fast getting in over her head. She didn't know anything about sinister tire flatteners or private eyes who called themselves security consultants. "You can call the rental company and have them bring you another car. Or I'll drive you to the airport, and you can rent one there."

Sam ignored her. He entered the house and went directly to the study. Lily had to scurry to keep up with him. "What were you printing?" he asked.

"Nothing."

"I heard the printer. Did she leave you a note?"

"Who?"

"Your grandmother, Red. Lillian Redmond. You know where she's gone, don't you? What's your name, anyway? I can't keep calling you Red."

Lily pushed a stray red lock of hair out of her eyes. "You don't have to call me anything. We won't be together much longer. Hey! That's private."

Holding Lily at arm's length with one hand on her chest, Sam took the pages from the printer and scanned them. "An address book. Good idea." He folded the papers and stuffed them in his coat pocket. "The message light on the answering machine is on. Did you play the messages?"

"No." Lily bit her lip. She hadn't even thought of the answering machine.

Sam hit the button. "No new messages," said the mechanical voice. He pushed the replay button.

A muffled voice said, "If you want to have a future, forget about your past."

Lily gasped. Her heartbeat shifted into high gear. Two flat tires *and* a threatening message? Lillian really was in danger. "I've got to find my grandmother. Right now."

Sam hit another button on the telephone. Lily heard ringing, then a click. "You have reached the Gibbons Costume Shop. Business hours are from nine to five, Monday through Saturday."

"What did you do?" she asked.

"Redial button. Who is Gibbons?"

"I don't know." Lily did know, but she wasn't going to tell him. He was the detective. Let him figure it out for himself.

Catherine Gibbons had been the wardrobe mistress at Winthrop Brothers Studio when Lillian had been an actress. Her grandmother had introduced her to Catherine years ago, when Lily had moved to New Orleans to attend Tulane. Cathy was the only one of Lillian's California cronies she'd met. But she knew the names of the others— the ones in Lillian's address book—because she'd helped Lillian address Christmas cards to them for years.

And she'd read all the newspaper accounts of the murder and the ensuing scandal.

Sam pulled the address book pages out of his pocket. "Let's see what we have here. Gaines, Gerard. Ah, here it is. Gibbons, Catherine. New Orleans, Louisiana." He put the pages back in his pocket. "Now. Keys." Sam held out his hand.

"The keys to my car? No. I need my car. Rent another one."

Sam backed her against the desk, then quickly and efficiently patted her down. "Where are they?"

Pressing her lips together, Lily shook her head and refused to answer him.

"You left your keys in your car, didn't you?" Sam turned and walked to the front door, picking up his suitcase on his way out. "You're too trusting, Red. It's going to get you in trouble."

Lily raced after him. "Where are you going? What are you going to do?"

"I told you. I'm going after your grandmother. And my father." Sam looked down the long driveway, lined with huge old oaks that screened the house from view of the residential street. "I don't know how I missed him last night. I have a feeling he was close by. Do me a favor, Red. If he shows up, tell him I'm on my way to New Orleans."

He had a nerve, asking her for favors. Lily danced around Sam's back, trying to get to her car before he did. She didn't make it. "Why? Why did he come to Alabama all the way from Chicago?"

"Archie has a personal interest in your grandmother's story." Sam opened the driver's side door and snagged the keys out of the ignition. He walked to the back of the car and opened the trunk. Taking her suitcase out, he set it on the driveway. Sam put his suitcase in the trunk and slammed it shut.

"Hey! Leave my suitcase alone. What kind of personal interest?"

Brushing past her, Sam got in the car, started the engine and lowered the window. "Didn't Granny ever tell you the story of Eric Winthrop's murder? I sure heard it often enough growing up."

"She told me, but not until I was grown. It's not exactly a bedtime story. What did your father have to do with it?"

"Archie was Eric Winthrop's bodyguard." With that, Sam started the engine and drove off.

He didn't bother to wave good-bye.

TWO

A huge billboard informed drivers on Interstate 10 West to take the next exit if they were headed for the Riviera Outlet Mall in Gonzales, Louisiana.

Lillian Redmond noted the sign but ignored the exit. She adored shopping, but she did not have time for frivolous activities on this trip. She was on a mission, a mission involving truth and justice. And the avoidance of boredom.

She might be sixty-three years old, but she was not ready to sit on her porch and rock away what was left of her life.

Glancing in the rearview mirror, Lillian noted that the dark green Ford Explorer was still behind her. Not immediately behind her car—the driver of the Ford usually kept one or two vehicles between them. She'd first noticed the SUV in the French Quarter. The narrow streets made it hard to miss an automobile that big. She had seen the SUV again on the twelve-mile bridge over the Bonnet Carre spillway, another spot where concealment was difficult.

Who was following her? The man who'd left the message on her answering machine? Or whoever had let the air out of her tires, forcing her to steal—borrow a car?

It couldn't be that nice young man she'd left handcuffed to her bed. Sam wouldn't have had time to catch up with her. And she had his car. It might be his father, however. Sam had said Archie had left Chicago by car Friday last. She wished she'd thought to ask Sam what kind of car Archie drove, but she hadn't. All her concentration had been on finding a way to keep Sam from delaying her planned departure from Fair Hope.

Lillian was close to hoping that Archie was the pursuer in the Ford Explorer. As much as she had wanted to do this on her own, she was fast coming to the conclusion that she needed help. She almost wished she'd brought Lily with her. But her granddaughter never would have agreed to come along. That would have required Lily to be disobedient, and the child didn't have a rebellious bone in her body.

Lillian had barely begun her investigation, and she had already concluded that finding a murderer—especially a successful murderer—would require intelligence, intuition and luck. And the occasional lie. Lily was smart as a whip, but she lacked experience. And she couldn't tell even a little white lie without turning beet red. Lillian nodded, satisfied that she had been right to leave her granddaughter behind.

Still, when Sam had turned up on her doorstep, she could have asked him for help. Or she could have waited for Archie. Sam had insisted that he must be close by. Lillian brushed a lock of red hair out of her eyes. She might have done just that if she had been positive they wanted to help her. It was just as likely that they wanted to stop her.

Someone did.

Lillian glanced in the rearview mirror again.

The Explorer was too far back for her to get a good look at the man behind the wheel. Mentally shrugging, Lillian put her pursuer out of her mind and concentrated on what she'd learned from Cathy Gibbons that morning.

Cathy had started working at Winthrop Studios in the forties, when Eric's and Thomas's father had been head of the studio he'd founded in 1927. She knew everyone who had ever worked there for any length of time, a fact that had made it easy for her to tick off a list of people who might have wanted Eric Winthrop dead. Cathy had started with Eric's fiancée, Madeline Morrow. Then there were his two ex-wives, several of the women he had victimized on his casting couch, plus all the writers, directors and actors Eric had screwed over one way or another.

Eric Winthrop had not been a nice man.

Lillian had known that from personal experience, but that hadn't kept her from being shocked at the number of possible suspects. If she was ever going to get to the bottom of Eric's demise, she had to shorten the list somehow. Who had been at the studio that night?

Cathy told her she had left around eight the night Eric was murdered. According to the medical examiner, the time of death had been somewhere between nine o'clock and midnight. Cathy recalled her assistant had stayed late that night working on costume designs for Madeline's next movie, an historical drama set in the Regency period. He might have seen something—and he might not have reported what he'd seen to the police. The man, Bobby Kaminski, had been a recent émigré from Poland and feared the police.

Cathy had stayed in touch with him—they exchanged Christmas cards every year—and she'd given Lillian his address. He lived in a small town in Arizona, not far from the Grand Canyon. Lillian had added him to her list of people to visit on her way west.

But Cathy's assistant wasn't her next stop. She had to see Max Segal in Houston before that. Segal had been in charge of the makeup department at Winthrop Bros. Studio during the fifties. After Max, Lillian planned to visit David Epstein, the man who had directed two of her three movies. David had retired years ago and now lived in Cloudcroft, New Mexico.

Lillian continued down the highway humming to herself. She glanced at the dashboard clock. Almost noon. Lily had met Sam by now. A satisfied grin curved her lips. Sam's arrival had been unexpected, but fortuitous. Someone needed to push Lily out of her comfortable rut. A runaway grandmother and a sexy stranger might be just the ticket to get Lily on the road to adventure.

It was past time for Lily to kick up her heels and have a little naughty fun. In a few months her favorite granddaughter would be walking down the aisle, getting married to that clone of her father. Lillian loved her son, but he was not the adventurous type. After that one slip in college, Arthur had been the epitome of propriety. A more boring man Lillian could not imagine. Except for Dexter Beauregard Jackson, III. What was Lily thinking?

Just because Lily and Dexter had known each other practically since they were in diapers was no reason for them to get married. But both sets of parents had decided when Lily and Dexter were children that they were a match made in heaven. Lillian snorted. A match made in their mamas' kitchens was more like it. The fathers went along with the plan because they both owned stock in the Redmond bank and Dexter was being groomed to take Arthur's place when he retired. It was positively medieval—an arranged marriage in this day and age.

To think that a granddaughter of hers would have meekly agreed to marry the likes of Dexter Beauregard Jackson! Oh, on the surface, he seemed like a good catch. And he might very well be, for a woman who would be satisfied with a completely predictable life.

Predictable and *boring*.

If she had brought Lily along with her, Lillian would have spent a good part of the trip asking her some very pointed questions about her reasons for accepting Dexter's proposal. After seeing Sam, Lillian had decided it would be much better if Lily asked herself why she had agreed to marry Dexter. When there were men like Sam Hunter running around loose, no woman should settle for a Dexter. Sam was the kind of man who could tempt a nun to forget her vows, exactly the kind of man to show Lily what she was missing.

The fuel light on the dashboard caught Lillian's attention. She had to stop for gas, and soon. It was possible the Ford wasn't following her, only traveling in the same direction. If she stopped, the Ford might keep on going. Lillian saw a Chevron sign at the next exit and pulled off the highway.

Her heart began beating a little faster when she realized that the Ford Explorer had followed her into the gas station, stopping at the pump directly behind her. Lillian got out of the rental car. Time to settle this once and for all. She walked to the SUV.

The car door opened, and a man got out. A mature man, with a liberal sprinkling of gray throughout his black hair. He wore a suit, navy, a crisp white shirt and a navy-and-maroon-striped tie. Deep laugh lines bracketed his blue eyes. Lillian's eyes widened in recognition. "Archie Hunter. I thought it might be you. Why are you following me?"

"You remember me?" He looked surprised. And pleased.

"Of course I remember you. There's nothing wrong with my memory. You were Eric Winthrop's bodyguard."

"That's right. I didn't do such a good job of guarding his body, did I?" Archie took her hand in his and gave it a firm shake.

How ridiculous. Archie blamed himself for Eric's death. Lillian asked, "As I recall, Eric had sent you away that night. If you weren't there, you couldn't have saved him." Archie was still holding her hand, she noticed. She didn't attempt to pull her hand free.

"Eric was waiting for someone. Someone who made him sweat. I should have insisted on staying with him."

Lillian narrowed her eyes. As far as she'd known, Gus had been the only person able to make Eric nervous. "How do you know that he was waiting for someone? I never heard that before. Did he tell you?"

"No. If he had, I would have told the police. I didn't know. I had a hunch. But I was too young back then to trust my hunches."

"How old were you in 1958? Nineteen?"

"Twenty-one."

"Working for Winthrop must have been your first job."

"My second. I worked with my father in Chicago first. He had a detective agency. After a few months with my old man, I thought I couldn't work for him—Dad was the bossy sort—so I went west to seek my fortune. After the murder, I had to crawl back and beg him to take me on again."

"Did he?"

"Not right away. He suggested that I join the police force and save us both the aggravation of him trying to teach me how to be a detective. I did that. I rejoined my father in the family business a few years later. By then, I was old enough to recognize how much smarter he'd gotten during my years on the force." Archie handed her a card.

Lillian took the card and read it out loud. "Hunter and Sons, Investigations and Security Consultations." She glanced at Archie. "The Hunter is your father?"

"Dad passed on a few years back. I'm the Hunter now."

"How many sons do you have?"

"Two. You've met one of them, I believe. Isn't that his car you're driving?"

"Yes. I didn't hurt Sam." She smiled, remembering Sam's sleepy outrage when she'd closed the cuff on his wrist. "Well. Maybe his pride."

"He'll get over that." Archie slanted a curious glance her way. "What did you do to him?"

"Let's just say I convinced him to stay and wait for my granddaughter. I thought it would be a good idea for Lily to meet a man like your son."

Archie's eyes widened. Whether from shock or admiration, Lillian couldn't tell. Shaking his head, he said, "Sam is not usually so agreeable, especially when it comes to meeting young women. He tends to get a trifle skittish around nubile young misses. I don't think I want to know how you managed that."

"All right. I won't tell you. I will say that young people often underestimate their elders. Why were you following me? You were following me, weren't you?"

"Yes. I came to Alabama to offer you my services, but Sam showed up on your doorstep before I got around to it."

"You didn't want to see your son?"

"I didn't want him to see me. Plus, I had my eye on a dark blue Mercedes with Illinois plates. I ran across it when I got to your neighborhood. There were two people in the car. Both men, I think. But the windows were tinted, and I couldn't be sure."

"Someone visiting from up north?"

"They didn't get out of the car, not while I watched. Which was for a couple of hours. And that's not all. At dusk, I parked my car a few blocks away and took a stroll through your neighborhood. I circled your house on foot. Lots of trees and shrubs to hide behind, Lillian. Your house is not exactly secure."

"Archie. I live in Fair Hope, Alabama, not Chicago. No one locks their doors in Fair Hope. It's not necessary."

"Maybe it is. For you, anyway. Now that you've set out to solve Eric Winthrop's murder."

"How do you know that's what I intend to do?"

"Lillian. Everyone knows what you're up to. You haven't been exactly discreet."

"I suppose not. Once you hit sixty, discretion is one of the first things to go—and one of the few things whose absence I do not miss in the slightest. To tell the truth, Archie, I really thought no one would pay me any mind—people do tend to ignore little old ladies. I see now that I was wrong about that."

"Yes, you were." He gave her an admiring once-over. "Little old lady? You look exactly like you did in 1958."

"Flatterer. Keep it up, Archie. I love flattery. Always have."

"Not flattery, at all, Lillian. The simple truth. I know you intend to find Eric's murderer—you've made that plain. What I'm not sure about is why? After all these years?"

"Because whoever killed Eric has gotten away

with it long enough." A search for justice wasn't the only reason, not even the primary reason, but Lillian wasn't ready to share her motives with Archie. Not yet. Even if she did have the feeling that he, if anyone, would understand completely.

"That's true. But it looks like you and I are not the only ones who remember Eric's murder. When I was lurking about in your yard, I saw a young man sneak into your garage. I got close enough to hear air whooshing out of tires."

"Two tires on my car were flat this morning. That's why I took Sam's rental car. Do you think the man you saw was one of the men in the Mercedes?"

"Possibly. I tried to follow him when he left your house, but he moved too fast for me. Agility fades almost as fast as discretion, have you noticed?" At Lillian's rueful nod, Archie grinned sympathetically. "The Mercedes followed you from Fair Hope. It kept going when you pulled into the gas station. I expect they'll be waiting for you down the highway."

"I didn't notice a Mercedes. I did see your SUV."

"Only because I wanted you to. I wasn't trying to hide from you. They are. Do you want to lose them?"

Lillian gave the question some thought, then nodded decisively. "Why, yes, Archie. I believe I do."

"Then leave the car here and come with me."

"I will. It's your son's rental car, you know. Should we just abandon it?"

Grinning, Archie escorted her to the SUV and opened the passenger door. "I'll call the rental company and tell them where it is."

Lillian nodded. "All right."

After he made the call to Hertz, Archie transferred Lillian's luggage to his vehicle. He started the SUV and pulled out of the gas station. "Be ready to duck when I tell you to—which will be when I spot the Mercedes."

"Duck?"

"Yeah. I don't want to take a chance on those goons seeing you with me."

Lillian smiled at Archie. "Why, Archie, that's so sweet of you. Protecting me from Gus's goons."

"Don't do that."

"What?"

"Smile at me like that. It makes me want to—"

"What?"

"There they are. Duck."

Lillian bent over quickly, resting her head on her knees. Archie had been dazzled by her smile. It had been a long time since a handsome man reacted to her smile that way. She grinned at her knees. This ride promised to be a lot more exciting than anything Disney World offered.

Around eleven o'clock Monday morning Sam passed the New Orleans city limits sign. He took the Orleans Street exit off the interstate and drove into the French Quarter. While navigating the narrow one-way streets searching for a parking place, Sam thought about Red. He grinned at the memory of Lillian Redmond's granddaughter in his rearview mirror. Red had been jumping up and down yelling at him. He hadn't been able to make out what she was saying, but her expression had let him know she wasn't bidding him a fond farewell. The redhead had been royally pissed.

The grin faded. Well. So was he. What was it with senior citizens? First, Lillian Redmond, a woman in her sixties, had decided to relive her scandalous youth by writing the story of her time in Hollywood. Then his father, only a few months shy of being eligible for Medicare, had made up his mind to help her. Without discussing his plan with his sons, Archie had taken off in his SUV, riding to the rescue of a woman he'd known briefly more than forty years ago.

Archie had told Sam and Phil the story of Lillian Leigh from the time they were old enough to appreciate the appeal of sex and violence. Lillian had arrived in Hollywood in 1957, the same year Archie had quit his job at the family firm—it had been Hunter and Son back in those days—and gone west to seek his fortune.

Eric Winthrop had hired Archie as his bodyguard only weeks before he put the sexy southern redhead under contract. Archie had been there from Lillian's first screen test until the day she left California for good.

During her brief career, Lillian had been cast in three black-and-white films, the kind film buffs called film *noir*. Back then, according to Archie, they'd been known as B movies. Lillian had played three variations of the femme fatale. And very well, too. Sam had seen all of her films more than once, thanks to Archie's ongoing fascination with Lillian and her part in ending his job in Hollywood.

On screen Lillian Leigh had been temptation incarnate, the "bad" girl for whom a man would give up everything, including his honor. Off screen, according to Archie, she'd been more wide-eyed innocent than world-weary vamp. Lillian Leigh had been some woman, according to his father.

Some woman was right. Sam winced. If Archie and Phil ever found out that he'd let a sixty-three-year-old woman chain him to a bedpost, he'd never live it down.

Lillian's Hollywood career might have ended decades ago, but the lady could still act. She'd played the gracious southern lady to the hilt, and he'd fallen for her performance, hook, line and sinker.

He'd arrived at her house at nine, after searching the surrounding streets for a sign of Archie's SUV.

Sam hadn't found Archie, but he had gotten a good look at a dark sedan with Illinois plates parked several blocks away. Could have been coincidence, he supposed. But the heavily tinted windows suggested something sinister. That was why he'd accepted Lillian's invitation to spend the night at her house. He had thought she might need his help before the night was over.

Over tea and cake Lillian had answered all his questions. Yes, she remembered Archie Hunter. No, she hadn't seen him, not in forty-five years. She'd told him she and her granddaughter were leaving for Orlando in the morning, and that the purpose of the trip was to distract her from her literary efforts. She'd laughed at that, telling him she hadn't meant to get everyone all stirred up. Lillian had at least implied that she was willing to be distracted.

Before he could pin down her travel plans, Sam had yawned in her face. That should have given him a clue all was not as it seemed. True, it had been a long day, but Sam was used to long days. He didn't usually get sleepy at nine o'clock at night. He'd apologized, of course, and he'd asked Lillian to continue her story.

She had told him the story would wait until morning. Then Lillian had insisted that he stay the night, and she'd showed him to the bedroom. At the time, it had made sense for him to remain where Archie was bound to turn up sooner or later. So he'd accepted what he'd assumed was an example of southern hospitality. Sam had retrieved his suitcase from the rental car, taken a quick shower and climbed into bed. He'd slept well, too, until around five o'clock in the morning. That was when Lillian had crept into the bedroom and cuffed him to the bedpost. The snap of the cuffs had waked him. When he'd protested, Lillian had patted him on the cheek and told him her granddaughter would be along in a few hours.

And Red had arrived, right on schedule. At least he'd gotten the better of one of the Redmond women. He grinned again, thinking about the way she'd looked when he'd opened his eyes and stared at her. Shock had been written all over her expressive face. She'd thought her grandmother had brought a stud home for the night.

Red was something to look at, all right. As he continued his quest for a parking space, Sam let himself play the description game Archie had taught him and Phil when they were kids. "Look," Archie would say, pointing to someone they'd never seen before. "Now. Look away and tell me what you saw."

Long, long legs. Full, round breasts. Masses of red curls reaching her shoulders. Fair skin, dusted with freckles across a turned-up nose. And big, brown eyes. Bedroom eyes—

Sam stopped. Bedroom eyes? Where had that come from? He couldn't be thinking about bedding a woman he'd just met, a woman he would never see again. A picture of Red flat on her back, with her red hair spread on a pillow, formed in his mind.

Well. Damn. Apparently he could be thinking of Red that way. Sam forced the vision out of his mind. It had been seven years since he'd felt that kind of instant attraction for a woman. He thought he'd learned his lesson.

Sam thought about it for a few minutes, then breathed a sigh of relief. He *had* learned his lesson. Red hadn't been the attraction—it was Lillian Leigh. Sam had fallen in lust with the sexy movie star when he was fifteen. Coming face-to-face with

Lillian's lookalike had sparked the attraction. So it wasn't lust at first sight, after all. He'd seen Lillian many, many times before today, on the silver screen and in his horny teenage dreams.

Sam forced his thoughts away from Lillian Redmond's granddaughter and back to the issue at hand. Where was his father?

Archie never had showed up at Lillian's. That didn't mean he hadn't been nearby. Sam knew his dad. He would have taken great pleasure in eluding his son's efforts to find him and send him back to Chicago. And if Archie had been in the neighborhood early that morning, he would have followed Lillian.

Sam reached for the cell phone on the car seat next to him. It took him a second or two before realized the phone wasn't his. His phone was in the rental car Lillian had stolen. This one had to be Red's. Sam dialed Archie's number. The recorded message advised him that the cellular customer he was calling was not available.

Sam dialed another number. His brother answered on the first ring. "Phil. Have you heard from Dad?"

"Not a peep. I tried calling him a few times, but he either has his cell phone turned off, or he's let the battery run down again. You didn't find him with the lady in Alabama?"

"No. I think they're both on the road to California."

"Together?"

"I don't know for sure. I never saw Dad last night. But they have to be traveling west. Do you have Dad's file on the Winthrop case?"

"Nope. I looked for it, at home and at the office. It's gone. Dad must have it with him."

"Figures. Well. I'm pretty sure I know where Mrs. Redmond will be making her first stop—New

Orleans. She called a number there yesterday—a costume shop owned by a woman named Cathy Gibbons. Sound familiar?"

"Sure," Phil answered. "Winthrop Studio's wardrobe mistress. Never thought memorizing the players at Dad's old job would come in handy, did you?"

"Only as a memory exercise." The memory game was another of Archie's instruction methods. "Guess Dad is smarter than we give him credit for."

"Smart. Or lucky. Who could have predicted that Lillian Leigh would go after Eric Winthrop's killer after all these years?"

"Not me. I don't have a crystal ball. Call me if you hear from him. I've got a new number." Sam rattled off the number of Red's cell phone. Before Phil could ask why he had a new phone, he added, "I've also got a tag for you to check out."

After repeating the number, Phil asked, "Where'd you pick that one up?"

"Off a dark blue or black Mercedes with tinted windows parked not far from Mrs. Redmond's house last night. Could be coincidence, but—"

"—you got an itch. You and your itch."

"Hey. It works. Sometimes. Hold on a minute, I just found a parking place." Sam shoehorned the Honda into a tight space, then picked up the cell phone again. "Phil? You still there?"

"Yeah. Anything else?"

"Not at the moment. Call me if you hear from Dad. Better yet, have him call me."

"Okay. I'll get back to you on the license number."

Sam ended the call and got out of the car. It had taken a little over two hours for Sam to drive from Fair Hope to New Orleans, another half an hour to find the address on Royal Street and a parking place around the corner on St. Ann. Hoping Lillian would still be there, he walked to the costume shop. A sign on the shop door said, "Closed for lunch. Back at one."

With a frustrated groan, Sam looked around. There was a restaurant across the street. His stomach rumbled, reminding him he'd skipped breakfast. Sam ambled across the street, entered the restaurant and took a seat at a table in front of the window. He could see the door to the costume shop. A waiter brought him a menu and a tabloid-size newspaper.

"Seen this week's *Gambit*?" the waiter asked, laying the newspaper on the table.

"No. Thanks." Sam ordered a shrimp po' boy and settled down to wait.

He'd finished his sandwich and was working on a piece of pecan pie and a cup of coffee when a couple entered. Out of habit, Sam made a mental note of their appearances. Woman, late twenties or early thirties, blond, blue eyes, 5'7" or 8", 120 pounds. Wearing beige slacks, white blouse, navy blazer—overdressed for the French Quarter if she was a tourist. Sam turned his attention to the male. Younger, late teens or early twenties, brown hair cut short, hazel eyes. Medium height, muscular build. Dressed like a college student in running shoes, faded jeans and a navy knit shirt. They took the table next to his. The blonde ordered a salad, and the college boy ordered a hamburger.

"This is not working," said the blonde. She slammed an object onto the small table.

Sam recognized a handheld G.P.S. satellite monitor, used to track personnel or vehicles—provided the person or vehicle had been outfitted with an electronic bug. Hunter and Sons had several similar devices. Picking up the *Gambit*, he opened the tabloid-size paper and, pretending to read, shamelessly eavesdropped.

"Sure it is. We found their car, didn't we? Right where this said it would be." He took the monitor from the blonde.

"Yes," she hissed. "We found the car. But we didn't find her. We haven't *seen* her, or her granddaughter. I've never seen either one of them. You're the one who went to the bank."

"Yeah. That worked, didn't it? I found out the cute little redhead was taking Granny on a trip, didn't I?"

"To Florida. They were supposed to be going to Florida. This is not Florida. How can we be sure they're in the Honda? Maybe they took a taxi to the airport and flew to Orlando. Or Los Angeles. I want to see them."

"Come on, Desiree. Calm down. The Honda didn't get from Fair Hope to New Orleans all by itself. The old broad's got no reason to go to Florida. We know that. Orlando was a red herring."

"Yeah? If she planned all along to go west, why would she need to pretend they were going to Disney World?"

"She must think you-know-who is after her."

"Maybe he is. He probably follows people the old-fashioned way, without stupid toys."

College boy held the monitor in front of the blonde's—Desiree's—face. "This is not a toy. It is a highly accurate and sophisticated piece of electronic surveillance equipment. We found their car. We'll find them as soon as they return to it. We sure as hell know they didn't take the Caddy, not with two flat tires. They're around here somewhere—we know that because we followed them here. Probably having lunch." He looked around the restaurant. "Don't worry, Desiree. We're not going to lose Lil—"

The blonde put her fingers on his lips. "—the

target. How many times do I have to tell you? No names. We don't know who is listening."

Behind his newspaper, Sam held up his coffee cup, signaling for a refill.

Interesting. The buttoned-up blonde and her boyfriend were following Lillian. They had bugged Lily's car. They were the ones who had put Lillian's Cadillac out of commission. That much was obvious. But who were they working for? Not Gus. One of his wannabe successors? He'd have to call Phil and get him to put out feelers. Who else might want to shut Lillian up?

Sam glanced out the window. The costume shop across the street was now open for business. And who was standing on the sidewalk outside the shop but Red.

The blonde's companion saw her at the same time. "Hey, look. There's the granddaughter. I told you they would show up sooner or later. See her? She's going into that costume shop across the street."

"I see her," said Desiree. "I wonder where she left Granny. And why would she need a costume?"

"Should we ask her?" He half rose from his chair.

"Not yet. Let's wait and see if Granny joins her."

Sam finished his coffee and got up, casually strolling by the table where Desiree and the young man sat.

Once Sam was outside the restaurant, he crossed the street and entered the costume shop. Red was talking to a gray-haired woman.

"Here's the parking receipt. I really appreciate this, Cathy."

"No problem, Lily. I'll take good care of Lillian's car." She noticed Sam, standing behind Lily. "May I help you, sir?"

"I sure hope so. Tell me when you last saw Lillian Redmond."

Red—Lily glanced over her shoulder. "Oh. It's you."

"Yeah. It's me." Sam nodded to Cathy. "Mrs. Gibbons. I'm Sam Hunter, Archie Hunter's son."

"Well, now. This is turning into a regular reunion," said Cathy. "Excuse me while I check on a customer. She's in a dressing room trying on a Cleopatra costume. I think I heard a scream—she may have gotten tangled up with the asp."

Sam watched as Cathy bustled to the back of the shop, then turned to Red. "How did you get here so fast?"

"I was highly motivated. I want my car back."

"It's close by."

"I know. I saw it. You parked on St. Ann." Lily held out her hand. "Give me the keys to my car."

"No."

"Fine. I don't need them. I have another set." She dangled a key chain under his nose. Turning her back on him, she called out, "Cathy? I'm leaving now. Thanks for all your help."

Cathy stuck her head out of the dressing room. "You call me, Lily, you hear? As soon as you find your grandmother. And don't worry about Lillian's car. I'll take good care of it."

"I know you will." Lily waved at Cathy and headed for the door.

A group of tourists entered. Sam took the opportunity to take Lily by the arm and steer her into a corner of the shop, next to the storefront window. "Lily. Your name is Lily. Short for Lillian?"

"No." She looked at his hand on her elbow.

"But you were named after her."

"Yes." Red gave an experimental tug, but Sam held on.

"Why do you want your car? Are you going home?"

"That is none of your business." She tried to jerk her arm away, but Sam held on. "Let me go."

"Listen to me, Red. Your car is bugged. You'll be followed."

"Bugged?" Her brown eyes widened, then narrowed. "Oh, sure. Like I'd believe anything you say, you car thief."

"I'm telling you the truth. Two people in that restaurant shop across the street have been following your car with a G.P.S. tracker. They're waiting for you right now, waiting for you to lead them to your grandmother. Don't look."

Red peeked around a manikin dressed in a gorilla costume and looked out the window. "The blond woman and the studly college boy with her?"

Sam pulled her away from the window. "Yeah. I told you not to look. You think he's studly?"

"In a Schwarzenegger kind of way. They didn't see me—they weren't even looking this way. For all I know, you're making this whole thing up. I want my car, and I want my cell phone."

"Tough. I'm not giving you your keys or your car. Haven't you got the picture yet, Red? There are bad guys after your grandmother. Once they find out she's gotten away, you'll be their only lead. They'll come after you, Red. You need protection."

"I do not. What I need is my car. I hated driving Lillian's Cadillac. It's too big. If you don't let me go, I'm going to scream." Sam dropped her arm, and Lily opened the door and left the costume shop.

Sam waited until Lily was around the corner on St. Ann Street before he went after her. He didn't want Desiree and her buddy to see them together. Once Lily was out of sight of the restaurant, Sam exited the shop and caught up with her. "Any idea where your grandmother might go next?"

"No."

"You're a lousy liar, Red." He took her by the hand.

"Come on, let's get the Cadillac and be on our way. I'll drive."

"I'm not going anywhere with you. And I'm not leaving my car in New Orleans." She tried digging in her heels. "If you don't let me go, I'm going to scream."

"You said that before."

"This time I mean it." Lily opened her mouth wide.

Sam let her go again. "All right, Red. What's your plan?"

"I'm going to get in *my* car and leave."

"If you take the Honda, you'll be followed by Desiree and her boyfriend."

"Desiree? I know you made that up. No one is named Desiree. Outside of an erotic novel, that is."

"That's what the boyfriend called her. She didn't call him by name. From what I overheard, I think she's the brains and he's the muscle. Are you sure you want to lead them to Lillian? And what do you know about erotic novels?"

With a toss of her head, Lily sent her red hair swirling around her shoulders. "I see no reason to answer your questions."

"Listen, Red. Leave the Honda where it is. Where did you park the Cadillac?"

"Why do you want to know? Planning on stealing it?"

"I didn't steal your car. I borrowed it. Lucky for you that I did. You never would have figured out you were being tailed."

They reached the Honda where he'd parked it.

She unlocked the door and got in. "Good-bye, Mr. Hunter." She locked the door and started the engine.

Sam remained on the sidewalk. He should let her go on alone. What did he care if Desiree and her boyfriend were following her? They were after the grandmother, not the granddaughter. Yeah. Let her go. He could get a plane back to Chicago. Archie would call in sooner or later. There was absolutely no reason for him to go chasing after Lily and her grandmother.

Like hell there wasn't.

Sam hailed a passing cab just as Lily managed to extricate the Honda from the tight parking space. He got in and tapped the driver on the shoulder. "See that silver Honda at the next red light?"

"Yeah."

Sam sighed. "Follow that car."

The driver's head whipped around. "You're kidding me. I've been driving a hack for almost twenty years and no one ever asked me. . . . You really want me to follow—"

"Yeah. I do."

Three

Lily had seen Sam flag down a taxi as she pulled away from the curb in the Quarter. The same yellow cab had been visible in her rearview mirror ever since. The taxi did not take the exit to the New Orleans airport as she had assumed it would. It appeared that Sam was not bent on catching the next flight back to Chicago.

Sam Spade Hunter was following her.

Lily ground her teeth. Of all the nerve. First he stole her car; then he tried to scare her into going home, and now he was following her. Sam Hunter was an outlandish liar—making up that unbelievable story about her car being bugged, pointing to two innocent tourists sitting in the window of a Quarter restaurant and telling her they were after Lillian. Ha! There had been only one car behind her since she left the French Quarter—his taxi.

She would just ignore him.

Sam couldn't follow her all the way to Houston in a taxi. That would cost a fortune. He'd probably give up as soon as they reached the New Orleans city limits.

He didn't.

Having Sam chasing after her kept her from thinking about important things, like what she was going to do when she caught up with Lillian. Or what she should do about Dexter. All she could think about was Sam. The way he had looked that morning, a poster boy for masculine temptation. The way his breath had tickled her neck like the precursor to a kiss when he'd whispered to her in the costume shop. The way his hand had felt hot and demanding on her bare skin.

Lily turned on the radio, found a golden oldies station and sang along with the Supremes and the Beatles for a few miles. The noise drowned out thoughts of Sam. By the time Lily reached the outskirts of Baton Rouge, she hadn't forgotten Sam and his taxi, but they didn't dominate her thoughts any longer. She had other things on her mind.

She was hungry. It was after three o'clock in the afternoon, and she had eaten nothing but a banana for breakfast—hours and hours ago. Her stomach was past growling—angry snarls were coming from her midsection. Lily took the Bluebonnet Exit off Interstate 10 and turned into the Mall of Louisiana parking lot. She had to stop and eat.

It wouldn't hurt to take a short food break. Cathy had told her Lillian was on her way to see Max Segal, the former head of the makeup department at Winthrop Brothers Studios. Segal was in a nursing home in Sugar Land, Texas, a suburb of Houston.

According to Cathy, Lillian had left New Orleans around ten o'clock. Factoring in stops for food and fuel, Lily figured the earliest Lillian could get to Houston was four or five o'clock, at the peak of rush hour traffic. Lillian hated driving in heavy traffic, and Houston traffic had to be worse than Mobile's. Lily was betting that after being up and on the road since five that morning, Lillian would opt to find a motel, rest and freshen up before visiting Max the next morning. Lily planned to be at the nursing home at the crack of dawn, waiting for her grandmother to show up.

She had to spend some time before then rehearsing what she intended to say to her grandmother. She would have to come up with some very good reasons for Lillian to turn around and go home. The fact that Lillian had attracted the attention of people who left threatening messages on answering machines and others who disabled cars should have been enough to keep her grandmother in Fair Hope.

But since Lillian had ignored both the message and the flat tires, Lily knew she would have do more than point out the danger. Lillian would insist she thrived on danger. Overcoming her grandmother's adventurous bent would require intense concentration, and Lily's brain cells—the ones that weren't beginning to think about Sam again—were fixated on food.

Lily found a place to park close to the Dillard's entrance. Once inside the mall, she headed for the Food Court on the upper level. She was in line at the Chinese restaurant when Sam caught up with her. Pretending not to see him, Lily ordered shrimp lo mein and an egg roll, and found a table. Sam sat down across from her. Not deigning to look at him, Lily dipped her egg roll in sweet and sour sauce. "If you don't stop following me, I'm going to—"

"—scream. Yeah, I know. You said that before." Sam laid a small metallic object on the table.

"—call the police. What's that?" she asked around a mouthful of egg roll.

"A G.P.S. transmitter. It was attached to your bumper."

Lily picked up the object and turned it around in her hand. The thing looked harmless to her.

"Attached how?" She put it down and took another bite of egg roll.

"Magnet." He leaned back in his chair. "I told you your car was bugged."

Lily glanced at the device. "That could be yours."

"It isn't. You're being followed, Red."

"I know that. I saw you in the rearview mirror. How much does a taxi from New Orleans to Baton Rouge cost?"

"Never mind. I wasn't the only one on your tail."

"You're the only one I saw."

"Right. Because they were tracking you with a G.P.S. monitor." Sam picked up the transmitter. "As long as you had this on your car, they didn't need to stay close behind. You were leading them straight to your grandmother."

"I was not," Lily insisted. She looked at the thing Sam was holding, feeling a slight niggle of doubt. What if he was telling the truth, and that whatever-he-called-it had allowed some unknown people to follow her? Lily met Sam's gaze. His unreadable gaze. Sam Spade Hunter was either telling the truth, or he was a consummate liar. She opted for liar. "I don't think 'they' exist. I think you made them up to scare me."

"Is it working? Never mind. I can see you're not afraid. You should be, though. Trust me, Red. I don't know who those two are, or who sent them, but they are real. I overheard them talking at the restaurant across from the costume shop. They tracked your car to New Orleans, and you can be sure they've followed you this far."

"Have you ever considered writing fantasy? I know you're making this whole thing up. You're the one who wants to find out where Lillian is going next, not some mysterious couple."

"Who knew you and your grandmother were leaving on a trip?"

After a short pause, during which Sam waited impassively, Lily decided it was easier to answer his questions than to ignore him. "My parents knew, of course. Dexter. Other people I work with."

"Dexter?"

"Dexter Beauregard Jackson, the Third. My fiancé." Lily moved her left hand to her lap, but not quick enough to keep Sam from seeing that her ring finger was bare.

He only raised a brow. "Where do you work?"

"At the Redmond State Bank. I'm a teller."

"Daddy's bank?"

"Yes. Well. Daddy's and Dexter's daddy's bank. My great-grandfather founded it. Dexter's grandfather bought stock in it. Why would someone bug my car? How could they know I was going to take Lilian— Oh." Lily wasn't quite ready to swallow Sam's story whole, but parts of it were beginning to make a weird kind of sense.

"Oh? Oh, what?"

"Last Friday. The bank was crowded—people getting money for the weekend. Dexter tried to talk me into taking grandmother's car to Orlando." Lily remembered one man in particular. A young man, someone she hadn't recognized. She'd kept her eye on him, as much as she'd been able to between customers. He'd hung around the counter where the deposit slips and other forms were kept. Now that she thought about it, she'd never seen the man transact any business.

"Red?" Sam waved his hand under her nose. "Where did you go?"

Blinking, Lily pushed Sam's hand away. "That man in the restaurant—the one with the blonde. I think I've seen him before."

"When? Where?"

"Last Friday, at the bank. He might have overheard Dexter talking about our trip. We—Lillian and I—had reservations at Disney World. Dexter thought we'd be more comfortable in the Cadillac. I told him we had decided my Honda was perfectly comfortable. I don't like driving a big car, and Lillian doesn't like driving on interstates. Usually. But even if it was the same man, and he did eavesdrop on our conversation, how would he have known which car was mine?"

"Easy. He followed you from the bank. Would you have noticed if anyone followed you home?"

Lily would have liked to say yes, but the truth was, she might not have noticed Sam was following her if he hadn't been in a bright yellow taxi. Lily shrugged her shoulders.

Her noncommittal gesture didn't fool Sam. "You wouldn't have noticed," he said decisively. "Where was your car over the weekend?"

"At home. I park in our driveway. Mom and Dad keep their cars in the garage. Spring Hill is an old neighborhood, and most houses don't even have a garage."

Sam's eyebrows shot up. "You still live with your parents? Never mind. Okay. Here's what happened. Someone came to the bank for the express purpose of finding out about you and Lillian."

"Who would think a bank would be the place to do that?"

"What's the name of the bank, Red?"

"Redmond State Bank. Oh."

"Yeah. Oh. The guy from the restaurant heard you talking about your trip. He and his girlfriend followed you home and planted the bug Friday night— it doesn't take but a second to attach a magnetized transmitter to a car's bumper. Then they waited for you to leave town. Why did you wait until Monday?"

"Grandmother had a garden club meeting at her

house on Saturday." Big city detective thought she was some kind of immature baby, did he? So she lived at home and worked for her father? So what? "So do you."

"No, Red. I never have garden club meetings at my house."

"I meant so do you work for your father. What's wrong with that?"

"Did I say anything?"

"No. But you looked . . . superior."

"I don't think you're inferior, Red. Naive, yes. Inexperienced, too. But not inferior. What about Sunday? Why didn't you leave on Sunday?"

"Church. We couldn't have left until afternoon. Lillian wanted to get an early start. Now I know why. I'm not naive. I'm almost twenty-five." She would have liked to add that she had plenty of experience, but that would be a lie. And lying made her blush.

"That old? Pay attention, Red. The blonde and her buddy must have flattened the tires on the Caddy so you wouldn't change your mind and take that car instead. How did you get the tires fixed, by the way?"

"Lillian has an air compressor—Grandad always kept one in the car. I used it to put air in the tires. I drove to a gas station and had them checked, and they were okay. I bought two cans of that flat-fixer stuff, just in case." Lily raised a smug brow. No matter what Sam thought of her abilities, she had managed to catch up with him, and she had retrieved her car.

"So I was right. Someone just let the air out. Whoever Desiree and her buddy are working for must have told them to inflict minimal damage."

Both Lily's brows sank into a worried frown. "You really think that couple you saw in New Orleans is following me?"

"I really do. Look, Red. Maybe the reason they

haven't done any real harm up until now is because they thought you and Lillian were going to Florida. Now that they've figured out that Lillian is headed west, they may start playing rough."

"You don't know that they're the ones who let the air out of Grandmother's tires. If they wanted to know where we were going, why didn't they just put one of those things on the Cadillac?" She pointed to the metal object on the table.

Sam shrugged. "Who knows? Maybe they only had one transmitter. Or maybe thought it would be easier to run a Honda Civic off the road."

"Run me off the road? Stop it."

"Stop what?"

"Trying to scare me."

He leaned across the table and scowled at her. "I'm not trying to frighten you, although that's not a bad idea. I'd like to scare you all the way back to Alabama."

"Humph. You don't scare me, and I'm not going home. Not until I find Lillian." Pushing her plate away, Lily stood up.

"Finished already?"

"I seem to have lost my appetite. I'm leaving."

Sam stood up, too. "I'm going with you. No arguments, Red. You need me." He took her by the arm.

His touch sent tingles from her fingertips to her shoulder. Startled by her reaction, Lily jerked her arm free. She said, "I have to go to the ladies' room."

With a sigh of resignation, Sam let her go. "All right, but hurry up. I'd like to get out of here before the odd couple shows up."

Lily wound her way through the tables to the corridor where the rest rooms were located. The ladies' room was empty. She breathed a sigh of relief. All Sam's talk of nefarious strangers flattening tires and tracking cars by satellite had made her—not scared exactly, but definitely jumpy. Added to that, every time he got close she started having unusual and unseemly urges. She had the strangest desire to grab Sam by his lapels and kiss him on his mouth.

Lily dallied as long as she dared in an attempt to get the unfamiliar impulses under control. When she exited the stall, the room was no longer empty. A tall blond woman was standing at the sink, washing her hands. A young man stood in front of the door to the hallway. Lily recognized them. They were the couple Sam had pointed out to her in New Orleans. And now that she was close to him, she was sure he was the same man who'd been in the bank on Friday.

The tiny hairs on the back of her neck rose.

Lily thought about screaming, but her throat had tightened up. Clearing it, she asked, "Is there a problem with the plumbing?"

"Not that I know of," said the woman, turning off the faucet and taking a paper towel from the holder.

"Then why is there a man in the ladies' room?"

"We want to have a talk with you," the blonde replied. She tossed the paper towel into the trash. "In private."

Lily looked from her to the man. Leaning against the door, he grinned at her. It was not a friendly grin. "Who are you? What do you want?"

"Never mind who we are," the woman said. "You know what we want. Where's Granny?"

"I don't know what you're talking about. Have you lost your grandmother?"

"No, honey. We've lost *your* grandmother. And if we don't find her, we're in big trouble. So much trouble that we'll do anything we need to do to find her again. Now, talk, and talk fast."

Lily shook her head. She wouldn't tell them anything.

"Chad."

The man moved away from the door and grabbed Lily with enough force that she dropped her purse. He held her with her back to him, one arm around her waist, the other circling her shoulders. She couldn't move. "Hey! Let me go!"

They were facing the mirror. The mirror reflected the man holding her in an obscene parody of a lover's embrace.

Lily couldn't believe what was happening. She was being mugged in a public rest room.

The woman picked up Lily's purse and rummaged through it. She found the computer printout of Lillian's address book right away. "What have we here? A list of addresses? Granny's buddies?" Dropping Lily's purse onto the tile floor, Desiree shoved the papers into her tote bag and moved to stand in front of the door to the hallway. "That could come in handy. But you're even more handy. Tell us where Lillian is going."

Lily pressed her lips tightly together and shook her head. She wasn't going to tell them anything.

"Chad."

That was the second time Desiree—it had to be her—had used the man's name. She had to tell Sam—

Chad kept one arm around her waist and pulled her closer, so close that she could feel his hard thighs pushing against her bottom. He moved his other hand to cup her left breast. "Nice tits, Cupcake," he said, winking at her in the mirror.

Then he found her nipple and pinched. Hard.

Tears filled her eyes, blinding her. Lily tried to twist out of his grip, but Chad held her in place. "Let me go," she gasped, stunned. No one had ever intentionally hurt her, not since she was six years old and Mary Alice McAllister had pushed her off the monkey bars.

Chad kept his hand on her breast, kneading. He

put his thick, wet lips close to her ear and began whispering. "Soft. I like soft. Yin and yang, you know? Soft and hard. Keep on wiggling, Cupcake. You're making me hard. When I get hard, I get real friendly." He nipped her earlobe.

"No!" said Lily, twisting her head in a futile attempt to escape his mouth.

Chad pinched her breast again. "Go ahead, Cupcake," he said out loud. "I kinda like it when a woman fights me. Makes things interesting." He rotated his hips, rubbing his erection against her.

Eying Chad's hand on Lily's breast, Desiree said cooly, "What Chad likes is to hurt women. Unless you want his attentions to get even more disgustingly personal, I suggest that you talk. Now."

Chad moved his hand from her breast to her throat. He squeezed, all the while whispering sick obscenities in her ear. "Didja ever do it in a public place, Cupcake? Wanna give it a whirl? I bet Desiree would like to watch."

Chad smirked at Desiree.

"This has gone on long enough," said Desiree. "Stop choking her and let her answer, Chad."

Chad loosened his grip on her throat. "Where is Lillian?" he asked.

"I don't know where my grandmother is," Lily gasped, clawing at the hand tightening around her throat once more.

Someone tried to open the rest room door. Desiree leaned against the door and held it closed. "Sorry. The restroom is closed for repairs," she said.

"Red? Are you in there?"

Lily screamed. With Chad's fingers wrapped around her throat, the scream came out as a croak.

Sam must have heard her anyway because the door was shoved open, and he surged into the small space.

Desiree jumped out of his way, then ran out the open door.

Lily could see Chad's reflection in the mirror. He looked confused, as if he didn't know what to do in the face of Desiree's desertion.

"Let her go. Now." Sam snarled the words.

Chad shoved Lily at Sam.

The momentum sent her crashing into Sam's chest, knocking him against the wall. Lily clung to Sam, afraid if she let go she would fall to the floor.

"I'm out of here," said Chad. "So long, Cupcake."

Lily wound her arms around Sam's neck and held on. Sam had come. She was safe. But she couldn't stop shaking.

"Let me go, Red. I need to go after those—"

"No!" Lily pressed closer and held on tight. "Don't leave me!"

When Lily had crashed into his chest, Sam's arms had gone around her waist automatically. Feeling her tremble, he tightened his grip. "Okay, Red. Settle down, honey. The bad guys are gone."

"Oh, Sam," she whimpered, somehow managing to wiggle even closer. "I'm so glad you followed me."

"Yeah. Me, too." Sam made a conscious effort to let go of her. Having an armful of Lily Redmond felt way better than was good for Hunter and Sons' no fraternization policy. It wasn't doing his own personal rule against quicky involvements any good, either. "Let go, Red. We need to get out of here."

She raised her head off his shoulder. Her brown eyes were suspiciously moist. "What if they're waiting for us in the parking lot?"

"Not a chance. They'll be as far away from here as they can get."

"How do you know that?"

"I'm a professional, remember? Rats like that

never hang around the scene of the crime." He tried unwinding her arms from around his neck.

She let go, sliding her hands from his neck to his shoulders to his chest. "Sam?" She looked at him, her brown eyes shiny with unshed tears.

Sam swallowed a groan. She was going to cry. A crying woman made him crazy. "What?" he asked, his tone curt.

"Th-thank you. I don't know what would have happened if you hadn't come after me. He—" She buried her face in her hands. "Oh, Sam, it was awful."

"Did that son of a bitch hurt you?" Sam asked through clenched teeth. Lily had been out of his sight for only a few minutes, not long enough for anything really bad to have happened. But long enough for some asshole to terrorize her. He reached for her again and hugged her close. Women were to be protected, not victimized. A man who used his superior strength to hurt instead of protect wasn't a man at all.

"Y-yes."

"What did he do to you?"

"He pinched me. And he b-bit my ear, after whispering awful things—"

"He pinched you?" Sam smiled, relieved. That didn't sound so bad. The couple were still inflicting minimal damage. "Where? On your bottom?" Sam's hand slid from Red's waist to her bottom. He intended to give her a comforting pat, but his hand had other plans. Sam cupped her round bottom.

"No. M-my breast. He s-said I had nice tits, and then he pinched me. Hard. It h-hurt. And he whispered in my ear. He said he was going to do awful things to me, and then he bit my ear."

Sam pried his hand away from her tush. He pushed Lily's hair behind her ears. "Which ear?"

"This one." She pointed to her left ear.

Leaning closer, Sam examined her ear. "Your

lobe is a little red, but he didn't break the skin. You won't have to get a tetanus shot." Before he realized what he was going to do, Sam kissed the redness.

Lily jerked her head away. "Did you just kiss my ear?"

"Yeah. I did. I—uh—I thought it might be soothing. Or something."

"Oh. Soothing." She rubbed her ear. "I suppose it was. Oh, Sam. I didn't believe you, but you were telling the truth. They were following me. I am so sorry I didn't believe you. They wanted me to tell them where Lillian's g-going."

"You'll be all right, Red. I won't let them hurt you again. I promise." Sam's arms went around her again. Lily snuggled closer. He thought he heard a snuffling sound.

Holding her away from him, Sam warily examined her eyes. She blinked, and a single tear slid down her cheek. He dropped his hands to his sides. "Hey. Don't cry, Red. It's all over. You're okay." He gave her an awkward pat on the shoulder.

Lily blinked rapidly, and a few more tears fell. "I'm mad. I always tear up when I get mad. It's not the same as crying." She sniffed, then wiped her nose with the back of her hand. "It's not!"

"Okay. You're not crying. I believe you. Do you have to make those sounds?"

"Yes." Lily snuffled. "I need a tissue."

"Sorry. All out."

Lily walked to the sink, pulled a paper towel out of the dispenser and blew her nose. "There. No more noises."

"Good." Sam picked Lily's purse up off the floor and handed it to her. "Feeling better?"

"I think so." She breathed out a shaky sigh. "Sam? Would you hold me again?"

"Why?"

"I need another hug." Lily stepped in front of

him and wound her arms around his waist, resting her head on his chest. "You're a good hugger."

Sam put his hands behind his back. His hands might want to grab, his arms might want to hold, his tongue might itch to—never mind what his tongue wanted. He wasn't a callow youth, overwhelmed by hormones. Sam Spade Hunter was a grown man, a man in charge of his body parts. All of them.

No more hugs, no more pats, no more kisses. "Later, Red. We need to get out of here before—"

A woman entered the rest room. "Well. Really. Can't you find somewhere else to do that?"

"Sorry, ma'am. My wife wasn't feeling well. She was in here so long, I got concerned. But she's better now. Aren't you, sweetheart?"

Lily nodded, her cheeks bright red.

Sam hustled her out of the ladies' room. "Do you need a drink? Water?"

"No. I'm all right now. I'm sorry I was such a baby in there. I really can take care of myself. Most of the time. But I wasn't expecting two people to accost me in a ladies' room."

"Hey. Don't beat yourself up. I understand. You're not used to dealing with people like Desiree and college boy."

"His name is Chad. I forgot to tell you that. She called him Chad. Twice." She stepped onto the escalator and looked around. "I recognized him, Sam. Chad *was* at the bank last Friday. What do you think they'll do now?"

"Hard to say. Without the transmitter on your car, they won't be able to follow you. Even if they happen to see the Honda and try following you without the monitor, once they see you're on your way back to Mobile—"

"I'm not going back to Mobile."

"Yeah, you are. Now that you see the kind of people after your grandmother—"

"Exactly. Now that I know how much danger she's in, I've got even more reason to find her." Lily stepped off the escalator and headed for Dillard's, walking fast. "I'm going to find Lillian and save her from everyone who is after her."

Sam chased after her. "Wait up, Red. What's up with you? Five minutes ago you were a quivering wreck. Now you're Wonder Woman? Stop and think for a minute. You're not up to dealing with Desiree and Chad."

"I know I wasn't this time. They took me by surprise. Next time I'll be ready for them."

"Red. There isn't going to be a next time. I'll take care of Chad and Desiree."

Lily stopped suddenly. "Ohmigosh. Lillian's addresses. Desiree has them. She took the list out of my purse."

"That won't help them much, unless—"

"Unless what?"

"Unless they have a list of the people who worked at Winthrop Studios forty-five years ago."

"Oh." Lily sounded relieved. She exited the department store and headed for her car. "What are the chances of that?"

"Slim to none, I'd say. Depends on who they're working for. Hold up a minute." Sam took the G.P.S. transmitter out of his pocket, bent down and stuck it on the rear bumper of a Dodge pickup truck with an empty gun rack in the back window. "That should take care of Chad and Desiree."

"Aren't they working for Gus Accardo?"

Sam stood up. "I don't think so. Gus isn't what you would call an equal opportunity employer. I've never heard of him using a female enforcer."

"The sexist pig. What about Chad? He likes to hurt people. That would qualify him as an enforcer, wouldn't it?"

"Not if he's a psycho. Professional muscle men usually are in it for the money, not for pleasure."

Lily shuddered. "Chad was enjoying himself."

"Aw, hell. You're trembling again." Sam gritted his teeth. He was not going to hug her. "You can't do this, Red. You're too soft for this kind of action."

"That's what Chad said. That I was soft." Lily stopped in front of her Honda and rummaged in her purse. She pulled out the car keys, then looked him straight in the eyes. "Maybe you're right, you and Chad. Maybe I am too . . . inexperienced to do this alone. I guess there's no shame in needing a little help. Okay. I'll hire you."

"Not necessary. I've got a personal interest in this caper. My father, remember? You don't have to pay me to go after Lillian."

"Oh, Sam. Thank you. That's so sweet of you." Lily opened the passenger door and handed him the keys. "Here. You can drive."

"Drive where? I'm not going back to Mobile."

"Neither am I." She got in the car and closed the door. "We're going to Houston."

Sam stared at her through the closed window. Red had her chin up, and she was staring straight ahead, refusing to look at him. He shook his head. She was something. Two rats had cornered her, hurt her, made her cry—made her mad. But they hadn't stopped her.

If Chad and Desiree hadn't been enough to make Red run back home to Mommy and Daddy, he didn't stand a chance. With a resigned sigh, Sam walked around the car and climbed into the driver's seat. He ought to be glad. At least she had condescended to let him drive.

"You said we're going to Houston. Why Houston?"

"Because that's where Max Segal is. Mr. Segal is in a nursing home in a suburb of Houston. Sugar

Land, to be precise. I'm almost positive that will be Lillian's next stop."

Sam started the car. "Makes sense, Segal being the head of Winthrop's makeup department. It looks like your grandmother intends to talk with everyone who might have been around the studio the night of the murder."

"How did you know who Segal was?"

"Archie. He had me and my brother memorize the names of everyone involved in the murder investigation."

"Why on earth would he do that?"

"When we were growing up, Dad had us play these games—the description game, the memory game. At the time, Phil and I thought memorizing the players in the Winthrop murder case was just another one of those junior detective exercises he put us through. Now I'm beginning to wonder . . . Maybe Dad always meant to solve the murder some day. Your grandmother just gave him the excuse he needed to get off his arse and do it."

"Well, I hope he hurries up and does it soon. Once the murder is solved, Lillian won't have any reason to gallivant across country."

"Phil said Archie took the Winthrop file with him when he left Chicago."

"He had a file? So did Lillian. I looked for it this morning, but it was gone. Do you think—between the two of them—that they really could figure out who killed Eric Winthrop?"

"I don't know. Solving a murder after forty-five years isn't going to be easy. For all we know, the murderer may be dead by now."

"Well. Someone is trying to stop her. I wonder where Lillian and your father are now. I hope your father is close to Lillian. In case there are more people like Chad and Desiree after her."

"So do I, Red. So do I. How far is it to Houston?"

"I'm not sure. I think it's about a four hour drive from Baton Rouge."

Sam twisted his wrist and looked at his watch. "It's after four, so we'll get there around eight. Your grandmother could be there already."

"I doubt it. Grandmother has to stop every couple of hours and walk around for a few minutes. Arthritis."

"Even so, she'll get there before we do."

"Maybe not. She's been on the road since five this morning, and she'll get to Houston at the peak of rush hour. She hates driving in traffic. I think she'll be too frazzled to see her old makeup man tonight. Lillian will want to see Max looking her best. And her best is very, very good."

"You're right about that. She aged well. Very few wrinkles, and her hair is still that Titian red."

"Well. I probably shouldn't tell you, but Lillian dyes her hair. She's not really vain, not about anything but her hair, that is. Lillian would never consider anything as drastic as cosmetic surgery, for instance. Grandmother says every age is beautiful in a different way. But she hates gray hair. When her gray roots start to show, she hates looking in the mirror—she says it makes her feel old."

"Archie says the same thing, but he isn't completely gray. Just a touch around the temples," said Sam.

"Lillian never minded when my grandfather went gray—and he went completely gray before he was fifty. She said it made him look even more distinguished."

"How do you feel about the passing years, Red? Are you worried about getting old?"

"I haven't thought too much about it, to tell you the truth. But I don't see that worrying about it would do much good. If I age as well as Lillian and my mother, I don't think I'll mind getting old." She settled into her seat and gazed out the window at the passing scenery.

"Guess not. You've got good genes." Sam dragged his gaze from Lily's profile and concentrated on driving.

It was going to be a long trip.

Four

Chad Boyd drove the van out of Baton Rouge over the Mississippi River Bridge, then exited at the first rest stop. "We'll wait here until the Honda starts moving again."

"Fine," said Desiree. "That will give me time to look over the list of addresses I got from Lily." She pulled the crumpled list out of her tote bag and smoothed it. Most of the addresses on the first couple of pages were in Fair Hope or Mobile. She had turned to the third page when Chad spoke.

"Who do you think the guy was?"

Desiree looked up. "Her fiancé?"

"That wasn't him. I saw Cupcake's boyfriend at the bank the day I found out she was supposedly taking Lillian Redmond to Florida. Blond guy, slender build."

Her brow furrowed, Desiree thought for a moment, then snapped her fingers. "Whoever he is, I've seen him before. He was at that restaurant in New Orleans where we had lunch. And he followed Lily into the costume shop. He didn't come out with her, though. Who could he be?"

Chad chuckled. "Well, well, well. Little Miss Cupcake must be cheating on her fiancé. I thought the guy at the bank looked too lame to satisfy a hot number like her."

"Her name is not Cupcake, Chad. No woman is named Cupcake. Her name is Lily. Lily Redmond. When her car starts moving again, I want you to get close enough so that we can see if that man is traveling with her. He could be a problem." Desiree glanced at her watch. "What's taking her so long? She should be on the road by now."

Chad checked the monitor. "Here she comes." He started the van and pulled out of the rest area onto the interstate.

Not until they reached the Atchafalaya Swamp did Chad get the van close enough to the transmitter to tell there was a problem. "Shit."

"What?" asked Desiree, leaning forward and peering through the windshield. "The Honda must be in front of that pickup."

"There's nothing in front of the pickup." Chad hit the steering wheel with his hand. "Fuck. The transmitter is on the pickup. The mall guy must have taken it off Cupcake's car and put it on the Dodge."

"How would he know to do that?" asked Desiree.

"If he was in the restaurant, he heard us talking about the G.P.S. monitor." Chad slammed his hand on the steering wheel.

"Why weren't they together then?" asked Desiree.

"I don't know. Maybe they planned to meet up in New Orleans."

She sighed. "Pay attention, Chad. I told you. They didn't leave the shop together. I would have noticed."

"So? They had a lovers' quarrel or something."

"Or maybe he's following her, too. I don't like this. Who can he be?"

"Maybe he's a cop."

Desiree started. "Cop? No. We can't have cops. Santori will fire both of us if we get the police involved."

"Okay, okay. Don't get your panties in a twist. He doesn't have to be a cop. He didn't look like a cop. And he didn't flash a badge in the rest room."

"No, he didn't. Maybe he works for Accardo. Santori warned us that his uncle might have people after Lillian, too."

"How would Cupcake hook up with a mobster? A sweet, innocent little thing like her?" Chad grinned.

Chad's smarmy grin gave Desiree the creeps. Why she had gotten stuck with him and his van and his electronics, she did not know. There had been a last minute change of plans. Literally last minute. She'd had her foot in the door of the airport bus when Chad, armed with a letter from the man himself, had tapped her on the shoulder. "How do I know? Her grandmother managed to get involved with Gus. Maybe Lily inherited a craving for crooks from her."

"I'd like to satisfy her cravings." Chad made a sucking noise with his thick lips, then winked at her.

Ugh, thought Desiree. "Forget about her. We've got to find Lillian. Fast."

Passing the pickup, Chad said, "Damn. The boss isn't going to be happy that we lost Lillian."

Rolling her eyes, Desiree said, "*You* lost Lillian, not me. Why anyone thought electronics was the way to go is beyond me. And you've got the van stuffed with all that useless equipment."

"Parabolic mikes and pinhole video cameras are not useless. All we have to do is get close to them, and we'll hear and see everything."

"Uh huh. Tell me, Chad. How are we going to get close, now that your bug is on the wrong car?"

"Geez Louise. The boss is going to be royally pissed," Chad muttered.

"No, he's not." Desiree chewed on her bottom lip. She had taken on this job to prove to Santori that she could handle a delicate assignment. And handle it alone. She could have, too. The job required persuasion, verbal persuasion. She could have put the right spin on it, without letting air out of tires or putting bugs on someone's car. Desiree looked at Chad. Where had Santori found him? She had never seen him around the office or at campaign headquarters. If Chad screwed up, it would reflect on her. She was not going to let him and his questionable methods end her chances of being promoted to Santori's senior staff. "We're not going to tell him we've lost the Redmond woman. I'll find her."

"How?"

Desiree tapped her temple with her fingers. "I'll use my brain. All I have to do is think like the old lady is thinking. Where is she going?"

"Not to Disney World, that's for sure. If they'd gone to Florida, we could have gone back to Chicago. Course, then I wouldn't have gotten to play with Cupcake." Chad grinned his scary grin.

Desiree did not grin back. It was time she reminded him who gave the orders on this trip. "Listen, Chad. No more games. Keep your pants zipped and your mind on the job. Our job, in case it's slipped your mind, is to find Lillian Redmond and convince her not to write her memoirs. And the convincing is to be done with words, not violence.

"Right. I know that. But Cupcake—Lily wasn't used to rough handling. And that's all I did. I didn't hurt her. If we catch up with her again, that's one way to get her to talk."

"*If* we catch up with her again. It's not the only way. Besides, I don't think she has any more idea where Lillian Redmond is than we do."

"We'll find the old lady. Sooner or later. Cupcake is going after her grandmother, right? They're both going west. California is west. They're headed for Hollywood."

"Yes, Chad. I think we can be sure that Lillian is headed for California."

Her sarcasm went right over his head, or maybe through it. Chad shot Desiree a triumphant look. "So what's the problem? We'll go to Hollywood, hang around the Winthrop studios until she shows up."

"No. We need to find Lillian before then. Find her and stop her before anyone from the press figures out what's going on. Santori wants us to handle this discreetly."

"Yeah." Chad looked disappointed.

"Come on, buddy boy. You're never going to get far in politics if you end up with a criminal record."

Chad opened his mouth, then closed it. "I don't intend to get caught."

"No crook ever intends to get caught."

"I am not a crook." Chad did a creditable imitation of Richard Nixon, then spoiled it by cackling like a fool. "Unless I get to play with Cupcake—then I'll pretend to be a crook if that's what turns her on."

Desiree let him laugh at his own joke, then said, "Back to the problem at hand. Lillian's not in any hurry, not if she's taking time to make stops along the way."

"How do you know she's making stops?" asked Chad.

"I don't think little Lily would have showed up at that costume shop if Granny hadn't gone there first. That's why she had this." Desiree held up the computer printout of Lillian's address book. "I think Lillian gave her granddaughter the slip, just like she said. We didn't see the old lady in New Orleans or at the mall in Baton Rouge. If Lily hadn't followed her in the Honda, we'd still be in Fair Hope, waiting for your tracker to track something."

Chad curled his thick upper lip. "So how are *you* going to track Granny down? Do you have a crystal ball?"

"No. Like I told you, I've got a brain." Desiree looked behind her seat. "And a list of everyone the police interviewed after Winthrop's murder. All I have to do is check those names against the list I got from Lily."

She reached in the back of the van for an attache case, opened it and took out the list of names and addresses gleaned from the police reports of the Winthrop murder investigation. Santori had provided the list, but he hadn't explained how or when he'd gotten it.

Desiree looked over the two lists. "Okay. I was right. See here? Cathy Gibbons is on the old lady's list with an address in the Quarter." She pointed to the other list. "Gibbons was the wardrobe mistress at Winthrop Brothers Studios at the time of the murder. She must own the costume shop."

"I get it. All you have to do is check for names on both lists?"

"Yeah. There may be other people she plans to visit on her way to California." Desiree skimmed the lists. "Here we go. Winthrop Studios' former head of the makeup department has an address in Sugar Land, Texas."

"Sugar Land? Where's that?" asked Chad.

"I'll check the atlas in a minute. First, I'm going to make sure there aren't any other matches between here and Texas."

When Desiree satisfied herself that the next match led to Sugar Land, she took the atlas from the passenger door pocket and opened it to the state of Texas. "I found it. Sugar Land is a suburb of Houston."

"So. Our next stop is Houston?"

"You got it. If we're lucky, we'll get there before Lily and her boyfriend. If we're really lucky, we might even arrive at the same time as Lillian."

Chad stepped on the gas. "I'll get us there."

"Not too fast. The last thing we need is to get pulled over for speeding."

Pointing to the radar detector on the dash, Chad said, "Won't happen, doll. Electronics rule."

"I thought we'd never get over that bridge," said Sam. "Who would have thought a town the size of Baton Rouge would have bumper-to-bumper traffic at four o'clock? The interstate was a parking lot back there."

Lily had thought Sam was going to remain silent all the way to Houston. He hadn't said a word since they had left the mall. If he talked, she'd have something to think about besides how close he was. She almost wished that she'd done as Sam wanted and taken Lillian's Cadillac. Sitting shoulder to shoulder with Sam in the confines of the Honda was only increasing her awareness of him.

Slanting a look his way, Lily sighed. Sam was a hero. That went a long way toward explaining his attraction. She hadn't met all that many heros. How could she ever have wanted to get away from him? If he hadn't come to her rescue, Chad would have done more disgusting things to her. And now Sam was going to help her find Lillian.

"Thank you," she said, blinking away the sudden moisture filming her vision.

Sam did not respond.

"I said 'thank you.'" Louder, this time.

"Yeah. I heard you. What for?"

"You saved my life."

"No, I didn't. I'm almost positive they wouldn't

have killed you." He glanced at her, then quickly looked away. "Red. Don't look at me like that."

"Like what?"

"All gooey-eyed. I've seen that look before. I know what it means."

Lily blinked. "Gratitude?"

"You can call it that if you want. Whatever you call it, stop."

"Stop what? I don't know what you're talking about. No one ever rescued me before. Naturally, I'm grateful."

"Did you ever need rescuing before?"

"Well, no. But—"

"Keep it that way. Stay out of trouble."

"Hey—are you blaming me for getting mugged in the ladies' room? That was not my fault."

"If you had listened to me and stayed at home, it wouldn't have happened."

"Why are you so grumpy all of a sudden?"

Sam clenched his jaw. "We have a rule against fraternization."

Lily wasn't sure she'd heard him right. "What?"

"Hunter and Sons. We have a rule. No fooling around with the staff or the clients. Keep that in mind."

"Sam. You're not making any sense."

"Listen, Red. We're going to be in close quarters for a few days. And we may run into other situations that get the adrenaline flowing. You're already feeling—what did you call it? Grateful. Don't start thinking it's more than that."

"Sam, I *really* do not know what—"

A cell phone chirped. "That's your phone," said Sam. "It's in my jacket pocket."

Sam had thrown his jacket into the backseat when he'd gotten in the car. Lily reached for it, found the phone and answered. "Hello? Grandmother?"

"No. Sorry. Philip Hunter here. Who's this?"

"Lily Redmond. Do you want to talk to Sam?"

"Lily—any relation to Lillian?"

"She's my grandmother."

"You and Sam are together? How did that happen?"

"It's a long story. Shall I put him on?"

"In a minute. Right now, I want to talk to you. No, that's not it. I want you to talk to me. I'm a sucker for a southern accent. Do you like Sam?"

"Yes," Lily said warily.

Phil chuckled. "That's what I like—the way you can take a word like 'yes' and turn it into multisyllables. Yay-yes. So. Are you at all attracted to my big brother?"

"What? No." Startled, Lily slanted a look at Sam. He was scowling. "Why would you even ask something like that?"

"Sam's been alone for a long time—hasn't had a relationship last longer than a couple of weeks in years." Phil lowered his voice. "Between you and me, Lily, I don't get it. Sam's got a lot to offer, don't you think?"

Lily hesitated, aware that Sam was listening to every word. "I think I could agree with that."

"Yeah. And it's not like he's unattractive. It is true that I got the good looks in the family, but Sam's not ugly. And several women of my acquaintance have assured me that Sam is a hottie even if he isn't pretty-boy handsome."

"Hmmm ummm."

"You agree with that. Good. That's a start. You never know what may happen next, what with you and Sam traveling together, getting in and out of trouble . . . Has there been any trouble yet?"

"Some. I got mugged in the ladies' room at the Mall of Louisiana—that's in Baton Rouge. Sam saved me."

"That's my big brother. A real, live hero. But a lonely hero. He needs a good woman to love him. I hope you . . ."

Lily waited a beat, but Phil didn't go on. "Phil? You hope I what?"

Sam stuck out his hand. "Give me the phone, Red. Now."

She handed it over. Phil must have been teasing her. If Sam was alone, it had to be his choice. Lily had no doubt that Sam could have all the female companionship he wanted—look how she'd reacted to him the first time she'd seen him. And Sam had been asleep at the time.

Lily made herself stop speculating about Sam and his relationships or lack thereof. It was none of her business. But whatever he was talking to Phil about might be. She listened.

"I want you to check out a couple of names: Chad and Desiree, no last names. Desiree is blond, pushing thirty, 5'8", 125 pounds. Chad is 5'10", sandy brown hair cut short, muscular build, early twenties. I want to know who they are and who they're working for." After a pause, Sam continued, "They bugged Lily's car. G.P.S. tracker. Then they cornered Lily and tried to get her to tell them where Lillian was."

Sam gave Phil a few more instructions, then ended the call. He handed the cell phone to Lily.

She took the phone and stuck it in her purse. "Your brother sounds nice."

"He is nice. The whole family is nice. Archie is with Lillian, by the way, so you can stop worrying about her."

"Oh, good. How did your brother find that out?"

"Dad called Phil. For some reason, Dad will talk to Phil, but not to me."

"Maybe your father is concerned about the family business."

"Dad knows Phil can handle things. More likely he's calling Phil because he's got him checking on things."

"What kind of things?" asked Lily.

"License plates. Gus Accardo has someone chasing after your grandmother driving a dark blue Mercedes."

"Chad and Desiree?"

"No. The Mercedes followed Lillian out of Fair Hope this morning. Once Dad and Lillian hooked up, Dad gave them the slip."

"Them? How many are there?"

"I don't know. I'd guess at least two. Probably no more than three."

"*Three* gangsters are after my grandmother? In addition to Chad and Desiree? Ohmigosh. Maybe we should call the police."

"Which police? We don't know for sure what state your grandmother is in. And if we did know where she was, what would we tell the cops? That some people who may or may not be criminals may be following your grandmother?" Sam looked at her and must have seen how worried she was. In a gentler voice, he said, "Don't worry about Lillian, Red. Dad will take care of your grandmother. Archie believes protecting women, children and small animals is a man's job—a job he's very good at."

"So are you. You followed me all the way from Fair Hope to protect me from the likes of Chad and Desiree."

"Listen, Red. I'm on this trip for one reason, and one reason only. I'm chasing after my father, not you. If I could get rid of you, I would," Sam said. "I'm going to try and call Dad. Where's the cell phone?"

Smarting from Sam's dismissal, Lily retrieved the phone from her purse. "What's his number?"

Sam told her, and she punched in the number. "'The cellular phone customer is not available,'"

Lily quoted. "Your father has the phone turned off. Why would he do that?"

"Probably because he knows if I talk to him, I'm going to tell him to go home. Why don't you try Lillian?"

"She doesn't have a cell phone."

"She's got mine. It was in the rental car." Sam rattled off another number.

"No answer," Lily said after letting the phone ring six times. "Grandmother doesn't want to talk to me any more than Archie wants to talk to you. She thinks I'm going to try to convince her into leaving her past where it belongs. In the past."

"That is why you were going to take her to Florida, right?"

"Yes. But now I don't care what she does, as long as she doesn't get hurt. I want Lillian to be safe. I don't like all these people following her."

"We're following her."

"But we're not going to hurt her."

Lily stayed quiet for a few miles, staring out the passenger window. She couldn't stop thinking about how Sam had warned her against fraternization. He must think she had designs on him. Humph. Conceited. That's what he was.

But why had Philip asked if she was attracted to Sam? If she didn't know better, she'd think Sam's younger brother was matchmaking, and that Sam had somehow anticipated that he would do that. Maybe Phil made a habit of trying to push women at Sam. She ought to have told him he was wasting his time—she wasn't in the market for a man. She had Dexter.

True, she was having second thoughts about her engagement. Also true—she had experienced a few peculiar emotions since meeting Sam. But none of those feelings meant she was on the verge of falling in love with Sam.

Okay, so Sam was sexy. She'd noticed that right away. She would have to be as lifeless as a rock not to have noticed. But he was more than sexy. Sam was a hero, a rescuer, a man who thought women were to be protected. A dreamy sigh escaped her lips.

Lily gave a guilty start. She should not be sighing over Sam. She had never sighed over Dexter, but then the most Dexter had ever saved her from was being dateless on a Saturday night. Dexter was not a hero.

That wasn't fair. Dexter might be a hero if he ever was in a situation that called for heroics. She spent a few minutes imagining Dexter as a superhero, a few more trying to come up with a situation where Dexter would have to rescue her.

A bank robbery?

But at the last staff meeting dealing with bank security, Dexter had emphasized the wisdom of complying with a robber's demands. Don't fight back, he'd said. Leave the heroics to the bank guards and the police.

Adjusting the air-conditioning vent so that it didn't blow on her bare knees, Lily said, "Your brother told me you've been without a significant other for years. Is that true?"

Sam sighed. "Yeah."

"Why? Aren't you at the age where most men start thinking about settling down? Don't you want to get married and have a family?"

"I've been married. Once was enough."

"You were married? How long? When? Who was she? What happened?"

"Two years. I was twenty-five when I got married—too young to know what I was doing, as it turned out."

"I'm twenty-five. Almost. But then, girls mature faster than boys. Tell me about your wife."

"Ex-wife. Eleanor Elizabeth Hatcher. Daughter

of Judge Jerome Hatcher. I met her when I did some work for her father. Met her on Tuesday, married her on Sunday."

"Oh. One of those marry in haste, repent in leisure things?"

"The repent part was hasty, too. At least for Elly. The reality of being a young man's wife instead of her daddy's darling hit her hard. She wanted the lifestyle of the rich and powerful, and I couldn't give it to her."

"The marriage lasted how long?"

"She went home to Daddy after six months. He was the one who told her to hold off on the divorce for at least a year. The judge thought a quickie divorce to end a quicker marriage would be vulgar." Sam gave her a sideways glance. "That's when I stopped believing in love at first sight."

Lily returned his look. Was that some kind of warning? Did Sam think she had fallen in love with him the first time she saw him. Ha. "I don't remember the first time I saw Dexter. I've known him since the day I was born. He gave me my first real kiss at my sweet sixteen party. He took me to my senior prom. I suppose we fell in love gradually, one day at a time." She couldn't quite keep the touch of vinegar from creeping into her voice when she added, "But he waited seven years after my senior prom to propose."

"How long have you been engaged?"

"Two weeks last Sunday."

"Ah. That's why you don't have a ring yet."

"I'm not getting a ring. Dexter thinks diamonds are a poor investment. He gave me a certificate of deposit for an engagement present."

"A C.D.? Huh. That's . . . different."

"Yes. It is."

"You wanted a ring."

With a sigh, Lily admitted it. "I did. I wanted a

diamond solitaire, square cut, with a gold band. Not platinum or white gold. Yellow gold."

"Did Dexter know that?" asked Sam.

"I showed him pictures often enough."

"How many carats?"

"What?"

"How big a diamond?"

"Size doesn't matter. An engagement ring is a symbol, not an investment. Of something that's supposed to last forever."

"Maybe you should tell him that."

"Do you think so? That was one of the things I was going to discuss with Lillian. Why haven't you married again? Phil said you hadn't had a relationship that lasted longer than two or three weeks in years."

"Phil should keep his mouth shut."

"He seemed to think that I—uh, that you—that is, he asked—" Lily stopped herself. Phil had been teasing when he'd brought up the possibility she might fall in love with Sam. Sam would think she was a gullible fool if she mentioned it.

Sam didn't wait long before he prodded. "Phil thought you. . . ?"

"Oh, nothing important."

"Phil asked you if you could fall in love with me."

Lily stared at Sam. "No, he didn't. He asked me if I was at all attracted to you. I assumed he was teasing. Why would you think he'd ask me if I'd fallen in love with you? No one falls in love with someone they've just met." Belatedly, Lily remembered that Sam had fallen for his wife just that fast. "I mean, I know some people do. Fall in love at first sight. You did. But I couldn't do that."

"No one can. People who believe in love at first sight are fooling themselves. Love doesn't happen that fast."

"I thought you said it happened to you."

"I told myself I loved Elly—and I told her the same thing—for one reason and one reason only. I wanted to get in her panties."

"Well. That's crude."

"That's honest, Red. I know better now. I don't lie to get what I want, especially not to myself. One episode of self-delusion was enough. I have a rule—I never ask a woman out until I've know her for at least six months." He signaled a lane change and passed a Wal-Mart truck. "Make that two rules. If I ever get married again, it's going to be to a woman I've known a minimum of six years. But Phil can't get that through his head. My little brother is ready to settle down as soon as he finds the right woman, but he's got some crazy idea that I should go first. I keep reminding him that I did get married first. Now it's his turn."

"Six years?"

"That's right."

Lily loosened the seat belt and turned sideways in her seat.

"Yeah. What? Why are you staring at me?"

"I'm trying to decide if you would be worth waiting six years for. That's an awfully long engagement."

"The engagement wouldn't be for six years. I meant I wouldn't start thinking about proposing unless I'd known the woman in question for six years."

"Isn't that kind of risky? What if she met someone else while she was waiting for you to propose?" Lily frowned. What if she'd met someone else while she'd been waiting for Dexter to pop the question? Someone who made her feel all jiggly inside, the way she'd felt when she'd seen Sam in his boxers. Lily decided to save further speculation on that subject until later. Much later. "Don't bother answering. That six-year thing is just another way of saying you're never going to get married again, right?"

"You got it. Next time you talk to Phil explain it to him, will you? What else did my little brother say?"

"Phil said women classify you as a hottie. And I did have an unusual reaction to you this morning. I'm not sure why. You're not all that good looking, you know. If your nose wasn't so crooked, maybe, but between that and that scar on your chin—how did you get that? In a knife fight with a bad guy?"

"I fell off my tricycle when I was five."

"No. Really?" Lily giggled.

"Why would I lie about that?"

"I don't know. To make yourself . . . more—"

"More what?"

"Exciting, dangerous. Women are attracted to dangerous men. Or so I've heard. Mostly from Lillian, come to think of it. The broken nose and the scar make you look like you're acquainted with danger."

"I have been in a tight spot a time or two. It's not something I enjoy. Nor do I recommend it to others."

"Dangerous or not, you are sexy, and you do have that hero thing working for you, but—"

"You think I'm sexy?"

"Oh, yes," Lily said earnestly. "I noticed that about you right away."

"What hero thing?"

"You saved me. You must have saved other women before me. Haven't you?"

"Define 'saved.'"

"Rescued. Protected. Made safe. I would think that's in a day's work for a security consultant and private investigator."

"Doing my job does not make me a hero," said Sam. He looked uncomfortable.

"Define 'hero.'"

"Someone who risks his, or her, life for another person or for a just cause."

"I have never risked my life for anyone or anything."

"Maybe not yet. But you would. I can kind of understand how a woman might mistake hero worship for something stronger. I got the warm fuzzies thinking about how you saved me from Chad and Desiree." She reached over and patted him on the knee. "Not to worry, Sam. Forewarned is forearmed, as my daddy likes to say. I won't mistake gratitude for anything stronger. Isn't that why you warned me about Hunter and Sons' fraternization policy? You were afraid I was going to fall in love with you? At first sight?"

"It crossed my mind."

"Is that why you have the rule? Because it's happened to you before?"

Sam snorted. "More than once. But it isn't love they fall in. Love has nothing to do with it. Lust. Women harass me. Sexually."

"You're a victim of sexual harassment?"

"All the time."

"How awful for you," Lily said, feigning sympathy. "Bless your heart."

"It is awful. And a nuisance. That's the reason for the rule against fraternization."

"You're big on rules, aren't you?"

"Yeah. I believe in rules. Rules are what separate the good guys from the bad guys."

Sam was a good guy. He fought bad guys for a living. How noble was that? Sam Hunter was a man of action, a man who did what needed to be done. Even breaking the rules if he had to—he had stolen her car, after all. But he had saved her from the bad guys. And he was taking her along with him, even though he thought she ought to go home.

Lily felt her insides go mushy again.

Uh oh.

She'd been doing just fine, teasing Sam about

being sexy and dangerous. Then he had to go and say something that reminded her she was sitting next to a real, live hero. Lily leaned back and closed her eyes. If she couldn't see him, she wouldn't think about him.

Lily could see him with her eyes closed. She could smell him, too. He smelled of soap and after-shave and something that let her know it was Sam next to her. Her eyes popped open. This was serious. She was sitting next to a man she'd known less than twenty-four hours—less than *twelve* hours—thinking that she might be falling in love with him.

Lily shook her head. She refused to be in love with him. After knowing him less than twenty-four hours? Something else was going on. Her worry about Lillian, her shock at being manhandled by Chad, her doubts about Dexter, not to mention Sam's straight-faced claim that she would only be following a long line of women who'd harassed him. All that would have anyone off balance and thinking about sex.

Not just sex. Sex with Sam. But did she really want to be one of the crowd of women trying in vain to tempt him into a long-term relationship? She did not.

Lily knew that women in her family tended to do foolish things when they got the hots for some man. Lillian had an affair—maybe only a one-night stand—with a crook. Lily's mother had gotten pregnant when she was nineteen, and she and Daddy had been forced to marry years before they had planned. Lily's parents didn't know she knew that, but she had found their marriage license when she was fifteen. She could do the math. Lily thought her parents' slip went a long way toward explaining their need for propriety. It also made them more human.

Over the years, Lily had wondered from time to

time what foolish thing she might do if she ever felt love or lust, or whatever emotion had motivated her mother and grandmother into doing something reckless. She had thought she wouldn't have to worry about that once Dexter had finally gotten around to asking her to marry him. Being engaged should have made her immune to temptation.

It hadn't. Partly because of the way Dexter had done it in front of their parents, and the fact that he had given her a bank account, not an engagement ring. Lily let a covetous glance slide over Sam. But mostly because now she understood what Lillian had meant when she'd extolled the appeal of dangerous men.

Sam Hunter ought to be locked up, for the safety and sanity of the entire female population.

Lily couldn't take her eyes off of Sam. He had grooves bracketing his mouth, and laugh lines radiated from the corners of his eyes. Squinting, she thought she could see a few gray hairs. He was older than her. Thirty-three, according to his driver's license. And he thought she was a baby because she lived with her parents and worked for her father. And because she shed a few tears when she was scared or angry.

That was it—she'd found exactly the defense she needed. Sexy or not, Sam Hunter was too old for her. She could not possibly think she wanted a man who treated her like a baby.

"We have to get another car," said Sam, rolling his shoulders. "This one is too small."

Baby car for baby girl. That's what he meant. "Not for me. My car is just the right size for me."

And Dexter was the right man for her. Not some practically middle-aged private detective who planned on waiting six years before falling in love.

Five

Sam met Lily's gaze in the rearview mirror. She returned his gaze briefly, then looked away. Lily had lost that gooey-eyed look, and damned if he didn't miss it. For some reason, when Red looked at him that way with her big, brown eyes, he didn't want to run and hide. Her admiring glance had made him feel powerful. Brave.

Horny as hell.

Sam's arms ached and his palms itched, and not because he'd been driving for miles and miles. His appendages wanted to grab Lily and hold on. No two ways about it—he had to come up with a way to keep his hands off Red.

Fast.

His mind went blank. What was up with that? His hands and arms now had minds of their own, so the brain in his head was shutting down? Clutching the steering wheel until his knuckles turned white, Sam tried again. There had to be something about Lily causing his brain cells to freeze up. Once he figured out what that something was, he'd be on the road to recovery.

Maybe it was subliminal. All those years of watching movies in which Lily's grandmother played sexy ladies on the make had planted some kind of insidious seed in his subconscious. When he'd come face-to-face with Lillian Leigh's look-alike, he'd been programmed to go into seduce-me-baby mode.

Nah. That couldn't be it. He couldn't be tying himself in knots because Lily was the spitting image of her grandmother in her movie actress heyday.

Or could he?

Sam remembered something Archie had told him shortly after Mary died. Grieving for the loss of his wife, Archie had punished himself for every slight, every missed anniversary, every forgotten birthday. There hadn't been all that many. But Archie's most heinous fault in his own mind was that for years he had lusted in his heart for Lillian Leigh.

At the time, Sam had pointed out that since Mary had never guessed that Archie occasionally daydreamed about a sexy and unattainable movie star, Archie's guilty pleasure couldn't have caused her a moment's pain. Privately, Sam had thought that even if his mother had known about Archie and Lillian, she would have reacted with laughter, not tears. And probably confessed that she felt much the same way about Sean Connery.

Sexy and unattainable.

Was that what was making him react to Lily? Could be, he decided. All those other women— the ones who professed their love for him within hours of being introduced to him—may have been sexy, but he hadn't noticed. They had been much too attainable. Or, to quote his brother, too easy. No challenge. According to Phil, half the fun of the man-woman thing was the chase. The other half being the catch.

With her flame red hair, her bedroom eyes and her knock-'em-dead figure, Red definitely qualified as sexy. Lily could match her grandmother's sensual appeal with no trouble at all. Hers might even be more potent because she seemed totally unaware of how men reacted to her. Sam had seen male heads turn and stare at her everywhere—in the French Quarter, at the mall.

But Red wasn't an image on a silver screen, as Lillian had been to Archie. Lily was flesh and blood, and she was sitting next to him. She was as attainable as hell, if he wanted to reach out and grab.

Sam clenched the steering wheel. He couldn't do that. He had never been a grabber. Men who grabbed women were assholes. Like Chad. Archie would hit him upside the head if he ever treated a woman that way. Phil would kick him in the butt.

By the standards of Hunter men, then, Lily *was* unattainable. So, no problem. He'd lust after her in his heart, but he would keep his hands off her. He could do that. Just to prove it, for a few miles Sam allowed himself to indulge in a lusty fantasy involving him, Red and a hot tub.

"Sam!" Lily screeched.

"What?"

"You almost hit that truck."

"I saw it." In the nick of time. A few seconds more, and he would have driven the Honda under the eighteen-wheeler. Sam quickly revised his rules. No grabbing and no lusting while behind the wheel.

Concentrating on driving kept Sam's brain occupied for several more miles. But then, apparently jump-started by his hot-tub fantasizing, his mind joined his body parts in obsessing about Lily. They wouldn't be in a car forever. Sometime, somewhere, they would stop. Unless they caught up with Lillian and Archie soon, there were nights at motels in their future. That fact almost blossomed into an even more erotic daydream. Sam nipped that one in the bud before he ran the car off the road.

It might be a different story if Red made the first move—if she grabbed first, so to speak. Sam slanted a hopeful glance sideways. Lily's eyes were closed. She wasn't even looking at him.

After that brief show of admiration, Lily had made it clear she wasn't interested in him. Perverse as it seemed, that had to be the reason he was attracted to her. He'd gotten so used to women coming on to him, the first one he met who kept her distance had become the only one he wanted.

Badly.

If Red was feeling the same strong primal urges he was, she was doing a much better job of concealing her emotions. The first time she had set eyes on him, he'd been helpless. Handcuffed to a bed. Almost naked.

Sam had been ambushed by the water cooler and cornered in the copy room often enough when he'd been fully dressed. It wouldn't have surprised him if Red had taken a liberty or two. No such luck—she had been reluctant to come close enough to unlock the cuffs. And she had wanted him to leave her alone at her grandmother's house as soon as possible.

She hadn't been any more impressed with him in New Orleans. Lily had questioned his professional opinion—she'd thought he'd made up the story that she was being followed. She hadn't been pleased that he wanted to accompany her. In their short acquaintance, there was only one bright moment—Red hadn't kept her distance in the mall rest room. She'd clung to him like the proverbial vine.

But only after Chad had shoved her straight into his waiting arms.

His reward for rescuing her? Lily had given him that one unguarded look of sheer adoration.

One lousy look.

Which she had attributed to gratitude.

Which probably had been gratitude.

Hell, Lily Redmond was engaged. That should add another layer to her unattainability. Sam snuck another quick peek at her. Was she really going to marry a dork? A guy who thought a certificate of deposit was better than a diamond?

C.D. aside, Dexter did have at least one thing going for him. Dexter had known Lily since birth. They had a history together, a long history. That kind of familiarity had to be the best foundation for a lasting relationship.

Not that he was looking for any relationship that lasted longer than a few days. And nights. Sam slanted another expectant glance at Lily.

Red did not look as if she was contemplating jumping his bones. If the thought had ever crossed her mind, she seemed to have gotten over it. Why did she have the ability to resist him? What gave her immunity? If he knew, he could bottle it and use it to fend off all the unwelcome and incomprehensible attention from other women—women he didn't want.

What kind of joke was fate playing on him? Lily Redmond—the first woman since Elly who'd made his libido sit up and beg—was the one woman who found him resistible.

Maybe it wasn't a joke. Maybe it was punishment for ignoring the gift the gods had given him—the one that made him the honey pot and women the bees.

Grinding his teeth together in frustration, Sam

forced his mind back to the subject of the car. The small car meant Lily was only centimeters away from him. Close enough that her bare knee occasionally grazed his thigh. Close enough that the A/C blew her scent straight up his nose.

Much too close for comfort.

Clenching the steering wheel, Sam said, "We need a bigger car." He had in mind a stretch limo, with Lily in the backseat, far, far away from him.

"We do? Why?"

"We have hundreds of miles to go. My neck is stiff, and my butt is going numb."

"I'll give you a shoulder massage." Lily unfastened her seat belt and started to climb into the backseat.

Sam took one hand off the wheel and held her in place. "Put your seat belt back on." The palm of the hand he'd put on her shoulder itched like crazy. His hand wanted to move from her left shoulder to her right because his arm wanted to pull her across the gear shift and into his lap. If she got in the backseat, he would stop the car and join her. "Sit, Red. I mean it."

"But—"

"I don't want a shoulder massage. I don't want you touching me." Sam managed to force his hand to let go of her shoulder.

"Why on earth not?"

"I don't like being touched by—"

"By . . . ?"

"I don't like being touched." He would give his right arm to be touched by Red, to feel her hands on his shoulders, his back. Everywhere. That scared the hell out of him. He'd never even seen her—if you didn't count all those hours watching her look-alike grandmother—until that morning. Since then, he had chased Lily from

Mobile to New Orleans and from New Orleans to Baton Rouge.

Sam had never chased after a woman before. Not even Elly. There had been no need to chase her. She hadn't run from him. Elly had thrown herself in his arms the first time she'd seen him.

"Fine. I won't touch you." Lily refastened her seat belt. After a moment, she asked, "Do you want me to drive for a while? Are you getting tired?"

"No, I am not tired. I haven't been behind the wheel all that long. I got a break from driving when I took the taxi."

"But if your butt's getting numb, maybe we should stop and let you walk around for a while. Lillian has to do that."

"I don't need to stop and walk around. I am not sixty years old, Red."

"Yes, but you said—"

"Forget what I said. This car is fine. I'm fine."

"You don't sound fine," she mumbled.

"What?"

She raised her voice. "I said you don't sound fine. You sound pissed."

"Pissed? Aren't you a little young to be using words like that?"

"No. I'm sorry. I shouldn't have used 'pissed' in the presence of my elders. Shows a lack of respect."

"Elder? What's that supposed to mean? I'm what—eight or nine years older than you—"

"Exactly. You're my elder. I'll try not to offend again, using modern slang."

She thought he was too *old* for her? Hell, the last girl—woman—Phil had fired for him had been twenty. *She* hadn't thought he was elderly, not if her actions at the copy machine were anything to go by. If he hadn't been pissed before, he was now. He wasn't old. How old was Dexter the Dork?

Eighteen? "'Pissed' isn't modern slang. 'Pissed' has been around since the middle ages. Anglo-Saxons were pissed."

"Were they really? My. I didn't know that. I'm glad we had this little talk. One can learn so much from one's eld—"

Sam swerved into an exit marked with a welcome to Texas sign.

"Whoa!" said Lily, clutching the edge of her seat. "What are you doing?"

He didn't know. His hands had decided to turn into the rest area, not him. Sam pulled into the first open parking space, and his foot stepped on the brake. "Stopping."

"Why? Are you going to get a Texas map?"

Sam didn't bother to answer. He opened his door, got out and was at the passenger door before Lily could get her seat belt undone. He opened the door, unhooked the seat belt and hauled her out of the car.

"Was it something I said?" she asked, faking innocence. She had rattled the big, bad detective. He looked positively fierce. Lily grinned at him.

"Young ladies shouldn't tease their elders."

"No? What are you going to do? Spank—oomph." Sam jerked her against him. She barely had time to register how neatly her body fit his before his mouth planted itself firmly on hers.

Lily tried for one complete second to resist Sam's unexpected assault. And he was assaulting her, snatching her out of the car, grabbing her before she could catch her breath, and kissing her as though he was a starving man and she was prime rib. But the kind of punishment Sam was inflicting on her poor mouth didn't make her feel helpless or afraid.

She felt *desired*. Lily opened to him like a night jasmine unfurling its petals. She kissed him back.

Sam ended the kiss much too soon for Lily.

Her hands had ended up between them, and she could feel his heart wildly pounding underneath the palm of her right hand. Her pulse exactly matched the primitive rhythm of Sam's heartbeat. "Sam?" she said, not sure what she was asking for.

"In a minute," said Sam, trying to catch his breath. He was going to let go of Lily. Now. But his traitorous arms refused to let go of her, and his lips were puckering up in preparation for going back for another taste.

So much for being in control of his body parts.

Sucking in another breath, Sam tried to apologize. If he couldn't let her go, that seemed the least he could do. "Lily, I'm really sorry I grabbed you. First you get mauled by Chad, now by me. If you would back up a step, I think I would be able to let you go."

Lily didn't move an inch. Why should she? She was very happy right where she was. She reached up and stroked Sam's clenched jaw. "I don't want to back away. I don't feel mauled. I feel . . . zingy."

"Zingy?"

"Like I was an electrical appliance, and you were a power surge."

"Ah. Zingy. Yeah. I know the feeling." He rested his forehead on the top of her head. "This is bad. I never break the fraternization rule." And he had never grabbed. Not until today.

Lily slowly removed her hands from Sam's chest. "Well. Technically you haven't." She couldn't figure out what to do with her hands. Sam's arms had hers pinned to her sides. Lily knew exactly where she wanted to put her hands, but they were in a public place. She gave up and rested her hands on his waist. "I'm not an employee or a client."

"You're almost a client."

"What does that mean? How can I be almost—"
Sam kissed her again.

Lily wrapped her arms around Sam's waist and
held on while his lips did their magic one more
time. She wasn't sure exactly what was happening,
but whatever it was, she did not want it to stop, not
yet.

When Sam finally came up for air, he gasped, "I
mean it, Red. This is bad."

"Very bad," Lily agreed, nuzzling his neck. Sam
smelled good. He also was a good kisser—make
that an outstanding kisser. Lily's mouth tingled,
and electrical aftershocks were still zinging along
her nerve endings. She frowned. "Why is it bad?"

Sam had to think a for a full minute before he
could come up with an answer. He used the time
to let his hands explore Red's back from her nape
to her butt. "Uh. You're engaged. You shouldn't
be kissing another man," he said, making his tone
accusing.

Lily frowned. He was blaming her? That didn't
seem fair. But it didn't make her angry. Sam had
sounded desperate, not accusing. She'd never had a
man desperate over her before. In consideration
of that fact, Lily made her response mild. "Sam,
you didn't exactly give me a choice."

"Right. I didn't. My fault, entirely. Sorry, Red. I
don't know what came over me." Sam ordered his
hands to drop to his sides. They refused. "Whatever
it is, it's overcoming me again." With a groan, Sam
lowered his head and kissed Lily for the third time.

Lily savored the kiss for a minute or so, then
abruptly jerked her head back. She had suddenly
remembered who it was with his tongue in her
mouth: Sam Spade Hunter, the man she'd been
determined to resist. She got her hands between
them again and pushed. "Wait! Stop! I can't do
this. I can't fall in—I can't do this."

"Sure you can," Sam murmured, his lips next to her ear.

His breath on her neck made her forget her protest. "Can what?"

"Do this. You're doing fine." Sam kissed her one more time.

Lily felt as though she were sinking. No, not sinking, falling. Falling in love. Her eyes popped open. Sam's eyes were closed. She couldn't be falling in love with him. She had been in love with Dexter since she was sixteen. Maybe sooner.

Sam's mouth left her lips and grazed the side of her neck. Zing. She'd never felt zingy with Dexter. She couldn't remember ever wanting Dexter to strip her naked and take her in a public place. But that was exactly what she wanted Sam to do. Here. Now. In a busy rest area, a place where people stopped to get maps of Texas, close to a crowded highway.

But this couldn't be love. She knew what love was—it was knowing someone so well that you could finish their sentences for them. It was feeling comfortable and safe and . . . cherished. It wasn't this . . . mindless need for . . . she didn't know what.

Lily gave Sam a push. He didn't budge, and his hands were busy stroking her back, kneading her nape. If he kept touching her, kissing her, she would do something very foolish. She would not fall in love with Sam—that was out of the question—but she very well might fall in bed with him. "Sam? Maybe we shouldn't kiss anymore."

"We definitely shouldn't kiss anymore." When neither of them made a move to separate, Sam added, "We're in agreement. This isn't going to happen again."

"Never again." Lily pressed her body firmly against Sam's, just as an experiment. Only to see if they really did fit together like pieces of a one-of-a-kind puzzle.

They did.

Lily looked up and found herself staring at Sam's mouth. "On the other hand, maybe we should try one more kiss. Just to get it out of our systems."

Sam lowered his head. She could feel his hot breath on her lips. Lily closed her eyes in anticipation of another zing-inducing kiss.

Sam shoved her away.

"No. Not again. Kissing you was a mistake. A big mistake. For which I take full responsibility, of course. But it's not going to happen again. I never make the same mistake twice." He opened the car door and practically threw Lily inside.

He got in the car and started the engine. "Seat belt," he said, his voice hoarse.

Lily fastened the seat belt, then sat staring straight ahead. Hot tears of frustration welled in her eyes, but she blinked them away. She would never let Sam see her cry, even if the tears were angry tears. He'd think she was crying over him. He would be sure it was because she was in love with him, and he'd rejected her.

Nothing could be farther from the truth. She certainly was not the least little bit in love with him—how could she be? She'd only known him for—she looked at her watch. It was a little after six. She'd met Sam exactly ten hours ago. A person did not fall in love in ten hours, not even with Sam the-big-bad-wolf-in-hero's-clothing Hunter.

Not only was she not in love with him, but she hadn't really wanted Sam to kiss her again. Those first few kisses had caught her off guard. He wasn't *that* good a kisser—the surprise element had disoriented her, that's all. And those electrical shocks were probably due to hunger—all she'd had to eat all day was a banana and half an egg roll.

Sam had been right to stop. And he'd been right about it being a mistake. For her. She shouldn't be kissing anyone but Dexter. Lily tried to work up a little remorse, but something else kept intruding on her thoughts. She knew why she should not have enjoyed Sam's kisses. She wasn't clear on why Sam thought it had been a mistake for him.

"Sam. Why did you kiss me?"

Sam sighed. "To shut you up. To prove to you that I'm not middle-aged. I don't really know why, Red."

"Hunh. Well. I think I know why I kissed you back."

His head whipped around. "It wasn't love, Red. You were right about that. No one falls in love at first sight. Lust, maybe. But not love. I speak from experience."

"I know that. It wasn't love. Not lust, either."

"What was it then?"

"Curiosity." She looked in the rearview mirror—her smile had exactly the right amount of smugness.

"You were curious? About kissing?"

"No, silly. About kissing an older man. I must admit you are good at it—must be all those years of experience."

"Red. I am thirty-three. You are twenty-five. Eight years isn't that much older. How good?"

"I'm twenty-four. Very good. It might have been better if—" She stopped. "Maybe you don't want any constructive criticism."

"Too rough. I was too rough, right?"

"No. Being yanked out of the car and hauled against your chest was . . . exciting stuff. Powerful."

"Yeah. Right. What good is power if you can't control it?" He muttered the last bit.

That had her whipping her head around to stare at his profile. "Are you saying you kissed me because you couldn't help yourself?" That idea had her zinging all over again, and Sam wasn't even looking at her, much less touching her.

"No."

"Are you sure? Maybe it wasn't you after all. Maybe it's me. I never knew I might have that kind of power over men. One day with me, and they lose control."

"I did not lose control."

"You didn't? Oh, heck. I sort of liked the idea of being the kind of woman Lillian played in the movies—you know the type? A sultry siren who lures a man to her bed and, when she's done with him, tosses him aside. Lillian Leigh destroyed men like Godzilla destroys Tokyo."

"Would you like to destroy men?"

Lily gave that some thought, then shook her head. "Not all men. Just you."

"You've made a good start. Can we talk about something else? Better yet, how about a little quiet time?"

"You want me to shut up? Are you going to stop the car and kiss me again?"

"No. I told you. That was a mistake. It happened. I'm sorry it happened. It won't happen again."

"I don't think we can be sure of that. We're in awfully close quarters here—by the way, is that why you wanted a different car? A bigger one? So we wouldn't be so close?"

"Yeah. I lied about my butt going numb."

"I think you lied about the other thing, too. I think you did lose control. You're not the kind of man who grabs women and kisses them against their will. Are you?"

"No. But I did not lie. I didn't lose control. Not completely. And it wasn't against your will. You wanted me to kiss you. I was the one who stopped the kissing."

"That's true. You did stop." Lily paused for a full second. "But you didn't want to." When he worked his jaw, she quickly added, "But that's only my opinion. How many days do you think it will take us to get to California?"

"I don't know."

She leaned over and looked at the speedometer. "Let's see. We've come about 350 miles, and that sign we just passed said it's 120 miles to Houston." Lily sat back in her seat and did some math out loud. "So, about 500 miles from Fair Hope to Sugar Land. We're still not there, and it's getting dark. It's going to end up taking us eleven or twelve hours."

"Yeah? So what?"

"So it must be another 1500 miles or so to L.A. That's three more days we're going to be together. Three nights, too."

"Not if we catch up with Grandmother tonight. What's your point?"

"My point is, if we were all over each other after only ten hours, what's going to happen after twenty-four? Thirty-six? Forty—"

"Stop. I kissed you. I got it out of my system. Not going to happen again. No more kissing, no hanky-panky. From now on, this is strictly a business trip."

"Hanky-panky? What a quaint old-fashioned term. What does it mean?"

"You know what it means. We are not going to have sex, Red. No way, no how, no time."

Lily could hear her grandmother's voice whispering in her ear. She repeated Lillian's words out loud. "Why not?"

That had him sputtering. "What do you mean, why not? There are all kinds of reasons why not. We're practically strangers. You're engaged. I'm too old for you."

Lily giggled.

"What? Oh. I get it. You were jerking me around."

"Teasing. I was teasing you. I wanted you to talk to me. About what happened at the rest stop. We need to figure out why it happened."

"No, we don't. Why do you women always want to analyze everything to death?"

"Not everything. Just the important things."

"One kiss is not important."

"It was more than one kiss, and it *is* important. I've never kissed a man who was practically a stranger before. Do you realize we've only known each other since eight o'clock this morning?"

"Why is it so important?"

"Lillian always said I was a late bloomer—I think she said that because she thought I was so . . . boringly placid. She's always urged me to show some spunk."

"I never knew what that meant. What is spunk?"

"Courage. Nerve. I've always been pretty much a coward."

"I find that hard to believe. You came after Lillian, alone. You stood up to Chad and Desiree."

"I did not. They had me shaking in my sandals before Chad ever touched me."

"I didn't say you weren't afraid. Fear and bravery are not mutually exclusive, you know. You didn't tell them where Lillian was."

"Oh. No. I didn't. But then, I couldn't have since I don't know where she is, just where I think she might be tonight or tomorrow morning."

"You didn't tell them that."

"True. Not even when Chad—never mind. Maybe that's when I began to change. Then when you kissed me, I was brave enough to kiss you back, even though you had me quaking in my boots, too. A nice kind of quake, you understand. I'm not complaining."

"Change? From cowardly to spunky? Is that what you're talking about?"

"I think so. Grandmother said someday I'd break loose and have an adventure. This must be it. *You* must be it. You're my adventure."

"Listen to me, Red. You want to think of chasing Lillian as an adventure, fine. But don't include me in your plans."

"Why not? We're together, we're attracted and we've got a three or four days to—"

"Don't go there, Red. I'm not having a fling."

"Who said anything about a fling? I thought we might discuss what happened at the rest stop some more. Delve into the underlying reasons. Explore why we're attracted to each other after such a short acquaintance."

"Dexter."

"Who?"

"Dexter Beauregard Jackson, the Third. Your fiancé. The guy you're going to marry. Dexter the do—banker."

"Oh. Oh! Dexter. Yes. You're right. But don't you see? He's another reason why it's important for me to figure out why I kissed you. I don't think Dexter would like it if I made a habit of kissing strange men. What's a dough-banker? Oh, I get it. A man who banks dough. As opposed to *baking* it. Is that a Chicago term?"

"No, it isn't. Get back to the subject. If Dexter wouldn't like you kissing other men, he sure as hell wouldn't like it if you . . . did more than kiss."

"Are you talking about hanky-panky again?"

"I'm talking about us—you and me—having sex at the next motel we come to. Dexter wouldn't like it."

"I don't suppose he would. Why do you keep bringing sex up? You only kissed me."

"Kisses are step one. One step leads to another, and pretty soon—bam. Sex."

"I never realized . . . My, but I'm learning a lot on this trip."

"Get your tongue out of your cheek and listen to me, Red. I know and you know you are not going to cheat on your fiancé. You're not the type."

"Cheating? That's a tacky way to put it."

"How would you put it?"

"I am thinking—and only thinking—about exploring my sexuality, as I have every right to do. Since I know that might upset Dexter if he knew about it, if I did happen to decide on a brief affair, I just wouldn't mention it to him."

"In other words, if you cheat, you'll lie about it."

"Why would I have to tell him? He certainly hasn't told me about the women he's slept with over the years."

"Dexter fools around on you? How do you know?"

"Not because he tells me. Dexter has some consideration for my feelings. At least, I think that's why he doesn't tell me about his peccadillos. But other people do. In high school, he and Mary Alice McAllister did it in his father's Lincoln. In college—he went to Alabama, and I went to Tulane—he had a lot of girlfriends. I dated some, too, of course. But I never engaged in—what was that term you used? Oh, yes. Hanky-panky. I never did that."

"Never? Then why start now? After you're engaged."

"I don't know that I will. But 'forsaking all others' only applies after you're married, not before."

"That's quite a rationalization, Red. Given cheating a lot of thought, have you?"

"It wouldn't be cheating, and no, I haven't. Not until you kissed me silly. It really isn't fair of you to grab me like that and then pretend to be morally outraged about it."

"I'm not outraged, morally or otherwise. What happened back there was completely out of character. I never grab. I don't kiss strangers, and I don't have affairs with engaged women. Or married women."

"Now you tell me."

"I couldn't think at the time. You fogged my brain."

"Not on purpose. Fogged your brain, huh? So you couldn't think? Neither could I. I just felt."

After a long pause, Sam said, "Well? Are you going to tell me how you felt?"

"Aroused."

"Aroused?"

"Yes. Aroused and desired. I never felt so wanted."

"Never?"

"Never. You're not going to drive into a ditch, are you?"

Sam jerked on the wheel, and the wheels of the car returned to the pavement. "No more talking. It's dark now, and I need to concentrate on driving."

"What are we going to do when we get to Houston?"

"Try to find Archie and Lillian. The sooner we find them, the sooner—"

"We can go home." Lily sighed. "I don't want to go home. I want to see California, and everything in between here and there. I want to experience . . . stuff."

"Are you talking about sex again? Because if you are, I'm asking—no, I'm begging you to stop. It's been a long day, and I can't take any more."

"Sorry. I'll be quiet now." Lily closed her mouth and her eyes. She needed to think.

What was going on here? Teasing Sam, yes. But the more she talked about sex with him, the more appealing the idea became. Sam was the sexiest man she'd ever been this close to. And he had kissed her, so there was mutual attraction going on. It was about time her dormant hormones woke up. She couldn't stay a virgin forever. Waiting until the wedding night had never been her idea in the first place. But Dexter had always been afraid of . . . what? Her father and a shotgun? Being forced to marry her because he'd ruined her for other men?

Being forced to marry her when he didn't want to?

Lily sat up straighter. Now there was a thought. Why had Dexter waited so long to propose?

She slanted a look at Sam. He was staring straight ahead, concentrating on driving like he'd said he was going to do. Why shouldn't they have an affair? It seemed like an excellent plan to her.

But Sam was resisting the idea.

Must be that hero thing again. He probably thought he'd be taking advantage of her. Well. She could deal with that, or she wasn't Lillian Redmond's granddaughter. She would just have to convince him to do the wrong thing.

Six

Shortly before nine o'clock Monday night, Archie pulled out of the parking lot of the Briarwood Center in Sugar Land, Texas, just as a beige General Motors van turned in. He might not have paid it any attention but for the Illinois license plate. "That couple came a long way to visit," he said, memorizing the plate out of habit.

"So did we. For all the good it did us." Lillian sighed. "Poor Max. I know it's been forty-five years, but I keep thinking of people the way they were back then. Not Cathy, of course. I've seen her over the years. And I've seen Madeline in the movies and on television. But Max was *old.*"

Archie grinned. "So are we, Lillian. Although you don't look a day older than the last time we saw each other."

"Humph. I'd like to believe that, but I see myself in the mirror every morning. I know I look good for a woman of my age, but you look better. Men always age better than women. That gray at your temples gives you a certain air of distinction that you lacked when you were twenty. My hair isn't naturally red any longer, by the way. It's out of a bottle."

"It looks the same." After a brief pause, Archie chuckled. "We're a fine pair of flatterers."

"Forget about how we look. I don't feel old. Do you?"

"Only in the mornings. I creak a little before I get going."

"Oh, that. I creak, too. It's gotten worse since I've been sleeping alone." Lillian blushed. Sixty-three years old, married for forty-one years, and she *blushed*. She couldn't bring herself to look at Archie.

"Your husband died two years ago."

"Yes. How did you know that?"

"Oh, I've kept my eye on you over the years."

"Why on earth would you do that? Oh. I know." Disappointed, Lillian leaned her head against the headrest and closed her eyes. "You're one of *those* people."

"Who are *those* people?"

"The ones who think I lied about being with Gus that night. That includes the police, the press and most of my so-called Hollywood friends."

Archie's brows went up to his hairline. "Is that why you left? Because everyone thought you were lying?"

"I left because suddenly I was a fallen woman. Either I, a single lady, had spent the night having hot monkey sex with a gangster, or I had given a murderer a false alibi. Either way, I had lost my innocence."

"Hot monkey sex? Where did you get that? Your granddaughter?"

"Heavens, no. I heard it on *Sex and the City*. Lily would never use such language in my presence. Probably not in anyone's presence. Lily's parents have raised her to be prim and proper."

"You don't approve of prim and proper?"

"Not entirely. I agree that there is a place for prim and proper. And a time. But Lily's only twenty-four, too young to—never mind her. We were talking about me, and my loss of innocence. That's the ironic part of it. It was all right for me to play a gangster's moll or a femme fatale on screen, even though I was only eighteen and wet behind the ears as my granddaddy used to say. But life could not imitate art. Not in the fifties."

"Regrets, Lillian?"

"A few. Mostly I regret the things I didn't do, not the things I did. How about you?"

"At the time, I was very sorry that I had left Chicago to seek my fortune in Hollywood. When Eric was shot and killed on my watch, I felt like a failure. And a fool. But now that I'm older and wiser, I don't regret my time in California. I met a few good people, and I learned a valuable lesson or two. Were you sorry to leave your career behind?"

"No. I had begun to tire of the movie biz before Eric was killed. You did that very well."

"What?"

"Avoided my question. Did you think I was lying?"

"About being with Gus at the time of the murder? No. Oh, I'll admit I came up with a convoluted scenario involving knockout drops and Gus sneaking away in the middle of the night. I really wanted him to be the bad guy, you see. But I never thought you lied. It cost you too much to admit you had spent the night with Gus Accardo."

"Why, Archie. That's so sweet of you. Not many people do believe me, you know. I hate to say it, but a few members of my own family have their doubts."

"Your husband must have believed you."

"You would think so, wouldn't you? Alan did a creditable job of riding to my rescue—he came to California and took me home to Mobile. And he married me, even though I had been unfaithful to him."

"Unfaithful? How do you figure that? You weren't engaged to him when you and Gus . . ."

"No. I gave him back his ring before I left Mobile. But Alan always believed we would be married—sooner or later. And we were. For forty-one years—most of them happy. Still. I don't think he ever forgave me."

"I don't get it. There was nothing for him to forgive. He had no claim on you—"

"I know that. But I also know the way Alan's mind worked. Not that he ever threw my past up to me. He never said a word. I wish he had. One big, no holds barred fight might have cleared the air, once and for all."

"Now that's the way things should be done. You have a problem, you get it out in the open. Yell and scream for a minute or two if you have to. Then make up. Making up is the only reason to fight, in my opinion."

"Did you and your wife fight?"

"Not often. But when we did . . . oh, my. She was a terror, my Mary."

"How long has she been gone?"

"Five years this July. I miss her still."

"If we still had our spouses, we wouldn't feel so alone. And useless."

"Speak for yourself, woman. I'm not useless, not yet. Not that Sam and Phil aren't trying to push me out the door. But I'm not ready to retire. Maybe when a few grandchildren come along, I'll be of a different mind."

"Any hope of that?"

"Neither Phil nor Sam is in a serious relationship. Or so they say. However, they don't always keep me informed about their love lives." Archie snorted. "I get the feeling they think they might shock me."

"My grandchildren are all grown. I miss having babies around."

"You're wishing for great-grandchildren?"

"Oh, my. Great-grandmother? I hadn't thought about that. That sounds positively ancient. Maybe I don't want that, after all." Lillian smiled.

"How many grandchildren do you have?"

"Three. Lily is the oldest. My daughter—she and her husband live in Atlanta—has two sons, both still in college. They won't be having babies for a few more years. Of course, Lily is engaged, but—"

"But?"

"Dexter Beauregard Jackson is not the right man for her. I can't tell her that, of course. She has to find it out for herself."

"Find out what? What's wrong with him?"

"Nothing's wrong with *him*. He's a fine young man. But he's wrong for *her*. Dexter is a vice president at my son's bank. Good-looking, too. Blond, blue eyes, nice build. If you like lanky. Myself, I always liked a man with muscles. Not like those body builders, mind you. But a man who looked like a man. Like you. Like your son, Sam."

"Sam's been roughed up a few times. His nose—"

"Gives him character. Your son has a man's face. Dexter's so good looking he's almost pretty. But it's not his looks that worry me. Dexter is . . . bland. The boy hasn't got an exciting bone in his body. Not one. If Lily marries him, she'll die of boredom. I can't imagine a fate worse than that."

"You crave excitement, do you, Lillian?" Archie winked at her in the rearview mirror.

Archie was flirting with her. Lillian felt a thrill of

awareness she hadn't felt in a long, long time. "I did when I was young—younger than Lily is now. That's why I went to Hollywood. And why I've done a few other things since then. Lily has never done anything exciting. Not in her whole life. Not one thing."

"Are you telling me your granddaughter is bland, too?"

"If she is, she's no relation of mine. But she does a good imitation of bland. Because that's the way her parents want her to be. Bland, boring and good. Everyone always talks about the preacher's children—how they have to be better than anyone else. But, according to my son, a banker's child must be even more above reproach."

"Were you a good girl? Before you ran away from home?"

"I tried to be, Archie. I really did. And most of the time, I succeeded. But I wanted to see the world, at least some of it. I needed to get away from southern Alabama to find out who I was and where I was meant to be. And Lily needs to do that, too."

"How did you talk Sam into waiting for Lily?"

Lillian pursed her lips. She wasn't at all sure she should answer that. She didn't want to embarrass Sam.

"Lillian? You did want Lily to meet up with Sam, didn't you?"

She nodded. "Oh, yes."

"So, tell me. How did you convince Sam to give you his car and stay behind to meet your grand-daughter? Sam isn't keen on meeting women."

"Why not? He isn't gay, is he?"

"No. Gun shy. Sam went through a bad marriage a few years back. Don't think he's ready to try again."

"Oh, well. That's all right, then. He doesn't have

to fall in love with Lily. Lust will do. All I want is for Lily to experience a real man. Before she settles for Dexter."

"You talked Sam into breaking up your grand-daughter's engagement?"

"No, of course not. Lily's name never came up last night."

"Then why did he stay behind?"

"Well. I didn't exactly give him a choice."

Archie laughed. "What did you do? Tie him up?"

She shook her head. "That would have taken too long. And I didn't have any rope. I gave him a sleeping pill and handcuffed him to the bedpost."

Archie's head snapped around. "You did what?"

"Archie! Keep your eyes on the road. I didn't hurt Sam. I left the key on my dressing table. Lily was due at my house at eight this morning, and she's never late. Sam would only have been hand-cuffed for a couple of hours."

There was a long pause. Archie cleared his throat. "I think a change of subject is in order. Tell me about you and Accardo."

"What do you want to know?" Lily hedged. Archie sounded jealous, but that could be wishful thinking on her part. His tone could just as well have signaled disgust.

"What was the attraction? I know what he saw in you—that was obvious. Still is. But what did you see in him?" Archie's tone might be ambiguous, but the admiring look he gave her was clear as rain.

Jealousy, then. Lillian felt a surge of heat. With a happy sigh, she let herself remember what it had been like the first time she'd felt that kind of heat. "Gus was different from any man I'd ever met. Not that I'd met all that many men before I went to

California. Alan—my husband—was the first boy I dated. And I suppose he'll be the last."

"Oh, I don't think so. Go on."

The look Archie gave her made Lillian's temperature go up another degree or two. "Gus was a man, not a boy. He was exciting, dangerous. And he saved me from Eric's casting couch."

"That was a problem?"

"It could have been. Eric thought of the starlets the studio had under contract as a harem."

"With him as the sultan?"

"Exactly. About the time Eric decided I was going to be the next notch on his bedpost, he introduced me to Gus. Gus made it very clear that he intended to have me, and that he did not intend to share." Lillian felt a little echo of remembered excitement. Being wanted by two handsome, powerful men had been heady stuff for an eighteen-year-old from Mobile, Alabama.

"So Eric backed off."

"Yes. Gus was a money man, remember? Eric always kowtowed to the money men."

"Was Gus jealous of Eric?"

"I don't think so. He had no reason to be. I was well and truly smitten with him. Why do you ask? Are you looking for a motive?" She almost asked if his interest was more personal, but lost her nerve.

"Gus *is* the best suspect."

"Except for three things. No motive, no opportunity and no means."

"Oh, he had means and opportunity. He might not have pulled the trigger, but he could have told one of his goons to take Eric out. But according to the reports, the police couldn't find evidence that any of his goons were in town. No one else from Chicago was around at the time."

"No one but Renata Accardo. His sister had

been in Los Angeles for a few weeks, but she left before Gus and I . . . got close. Even if Gus could have imported a hit man, why would he? Gus loved being in the business, having admission to closed sets, hobnobbing with directors and actors and actresses. He was star struck. Eric's murder ended Gus's Hollywood adventure, just as it ended mine."

"That's a puzzle, all right," said Archie. "If Gus did have Eric killed, what was his motive?"

Lillian swallowed a yawn. "I don't know."

"Ready to find a hotel?" Archie asked.

"I suppose we'd better. A motel will do. There's a Marriott Courtyard at the next exit. I saw a sign."

Archie pulled into the drive in front of the lobby and got out of the car. He walked around to the passenger door and opened it. "Why don't you come in with me? I don't want to leave you out here all by yourself."

Lillian allowed Archie to assist her from the car. His hand on her elbow reminded her how long it had been since a man had touched her. She knew exactly what she wanted, and it wasn't a good night's rest. "Archie? Let's tell the desk clerk we'll only need one room."

"Fuck!" Chad pulled out of the nursing home parking lot too fast, then had to hit the brakes to avoid a collision with a gold Lexus.

"Watch it, Chad," snapped Desiree. "Your fancy electronics aren't going to help us if we get into an accident."

Chad glared at Desiree. The bitch was getting to him. Cool, never showing emotion except when she yelled at him. "We almost had them. If we'd gotten to the nursing home a few minutes earlier, we would have had them. How in hell did they get ahead of us?"

"We don't know that Lily and her boyfriend were Segal's other visitors."

"Who else? It wasn't the old lady. The receptionist said we just missed another couple who came to visit Segal. Lillian is traveling alone."

"Maybe she isn't. Maybe she picked up an escort along the way, just like her granddaughter did," said Desiree. "What is it with these Redmond women? They attract men like magnets," she muttered, pulling out the two lists of names.

Chad could have told her a thing or two about what made a female attractive. It wasn't only looks. Desiree had the looks. She also had stainless steel balls. No real man wanted a wannabe man in bed. Chad swallowed another curse, reminding himself that no matter what Desiree thought, he was the one in charge of their dirty tricks op. To keep her from suspecting, Chad sucked up. "At least we know you were right, Desiree. Lillian is visiting all her old Hollywood buddies, and Cupcake knows it. You ought to feel good about figuring that out."

Desiree tapped her temple with her forefinger. "I've got brains. We know something else—Segal didn't tell them doodley squat." With a finger on the computer printout of Lillian's address book, she said, "I know where they're going next, too. David Epstein, Lillian Leigh's old director, is listed with an address in Cloudcroft, New Mexico. With any luck, we'll catch up with them there."

"Them who? Lily and her man, or Lillian?"

"Doesn't matter. It would be better if we got to Lillian, but if we find Lily first, we'll get her to tell us where Granny is."

Chad grinned. "I'm looking forward to that. I'd like to have another go at her."

"Some other time, lover boy. No gratuitous violence, Chad. Senator Santori wants us to keep a low profile."

"How're you going to get Cupcake to spill the beans without causing her a little pain?"

"Threats should do the trick. If we can separate Lily from her bodyguard, I think we'll be able to convince her to talk."

"Yeah. So do I. She's soft. Not tough like you." Chad furrowed his brow. "So what we're going to do is make the girl squeal so we can find Lillian and stop her from talking."

"That's the plan."

Chad waited a few minutes, but as usual Desiree didn't bother to explain herself. "You haven't told me the whole plan. How are we supposed to shut the old lady up if we can't play rough?"

"There are ways of playing rough that don't involve violence, Chad."

She was using that snotty, I'm-smarter-than-you tone again. "Yeah? Like what, for instance?"

"You don't need to know. Let's just say that if I get Lillian Redmond alone for five minutes, I'll be able to convince her to go back home and find another hobby—at least until November. After that, it won't matter what she does."

"Santori must have something on the old broad."

Desiree shrugged.

Chad bit back a curse. He had every right to know exactly what was going on, and one way or another, he intended to find out. Santori was ambitious—Chad knew he didn't intend to end his political career in the governor's mansion. Tony Santori had his eye on the big prize—the White House. And Chad intended to be there with him, all the way to the top. Santori would owe him big time once he'd done what he'd been paid to do. Desiree thought she'd have a leg up, too. But she didn't know everything—she just thought she did.

To pass the time, Chad asked, "Why do you suppose Santori wants the old lady shut up?"

"God, Chad. How can you ask that? If I've told you once, I've told you a hundred times. The senator doesn't want his uncle's involvement in that old murder in the news while he's in the middle of campaigning for governor."

"Accardo makes the news pretty regular. What's different about this?" Chad grinned. Playing dumb with Desiree was a hoot and a half. The bitch really thought she was the smart one. Wouldn't she be surprised if she knew who was really calling the shots?

"It's the big M, stupid. Gus has never been charged with murder."

"A murder that happened in the dark ages. Who remembers?"

"Exactly. No one does remember. But if Lillian Leigh stirs it up again, everyone will remember. Voters will remember."

"Remember what? That Santori's mother is Gus's sister? They know that. And they know that Gus is a criminal."

"But Gus has never been associated with anything really bad, like drugs or murder. So he bribes a politician every now and then? Voters shrug that off—it may be a way of doing business in Chicago, but the Santoris have always lived in Springfield."

"Numbers and whore houses are Accardo's specialty, right?"

"Yes. Illegal gambling and prostitution are still considered victimless crimes by a lot of people. Even Accardo's loan-sharking business is more or less legit these days. Gus used his clout to get laws passed that allow him to charge almost the same interest rates as he did before. And Santori voted against the amendment to the usury laws, remember?"

"Yeah, and he passed up any hope of getting donations from loan companies. Sometimes I think Santori takes his white hat a little too seriously."

"With an uncle like August Accardo, he's got to be purer than pure. Santori knows what he's doing."

"Yeah. Accardo usually knows what he's doing, too. Where was old Gus's clout when he got arrested for extortion?"

"Arrested. Not convicted. And I doubt that he will be. Not for threatening an alderman who was trying to bribe him. He'll probably have the charges against him dismissed before we get back to Chicago—months before the election."

"How long before we get back to Chi Town?"

"What's the matter, Chad? Are you homesick?"

"I'm sick of riding around in this van." *With you,* he added silently. When he'd been recruited for this trip, he'd had some idea that he and Desiree might end up between the sheets. True, she had a few years on him, but she wasn't so old that anything was sagging yet. A little small up top, but she had a nice, firm ass. A man could learn a few things from an older-woman, or so he'd heard. Up until now, he'd picked women who were young— not jail bait, but not old enough to know their way around.

Still, he'd been willing to give the older-woman thing a whirl. It had taken only one day on the road with her and that little fantasy had gone poof in a hurry. Desiree was all business. "You know what, Des? I'm beginning to think you don't trust me. I think I deserve to know the whole plan. What if something happened to you, and I had to carry on alone?"

"Nothing's going to happen to me. If I should

get struck by lightning, you can call the senator and ask him what to do next." Desiree smirked. "Santori's paying us to keep Lillian Redmond quiet until after the election. You don't need to know more than that."

Just for kicks, Chad decided to test her loyalty. "Have you ever thought maybe somebody else would pay us more?"

"Like who, for instance?"

"Like one of the senator's opponents."

"Forget about it. Santori's way ahead in all the polls."

"Then what is he so worried about? Everyone knows Gus is his uncle. And that Santori doesn't have anything to do with him. Hey—did Santori help Gus cover up the murder?"

Desiree gave him that superior look, the one that let him know she thought he had shit for brains. "Oh, yeah. Use your head, Chad. Santori is forty-four—he wasn't even born when the murder happened."

"It was that long ago?"

"Yes, Chad. Forty-five years ago, to be exact. In 1958 Santori's Uncle Gus had a fling with Lillian Leigh, a second-rate movie star. A murder happened. Gus Accardo was a suspect. Lillian gave him an alibi. End of story."

"But most people think the alibi was bogus, right?"

"Right."

"You think Gus paid for the alibi?"

Desiree shot him a suspicious look. "Where'd you get that idea?"

"I don't know. Why else would someone give a gangster an alibi? It had to be money or threats."

"Not necessarily. Like I told you, Lillian and Gus were an item back then. Maybe she did it out of love."

"Love. Yeah, right." Chad sneered. "What was Accardo doing in Hollywood, anyway?"

"The mob wanted in on the show biz action. Unfortunately, the man who gave them a foot in the door was the guy who got himself killed."

"Gus sure as hell blew that. I'm surprised the Chicago gang made him boss. Why doesn't Santori want the story told again? Like you said, it happened before he was born. If everyone already knows . . . ?"

"People have forgotten. *Voters* have forgotten. Santori doesn't want them reminded that his uncle got away with murder. It's bad enough Gus is on trial for extortion."

"I don't know. I think something else is going on. Something Mr. Santori doesn't want us to know about."

"He's told us all we need to know to do our job."

"Yeah? So what are we going to do next? I vote for getting a room."

"Not tonight. We know where Lillian is going next. I say we drive all night and get there before her."

"Drive all night?" Chad rolled his shoulders. "I've been behind this wheel for hours already. My back hurts."

"I'll drive for a while. You can take a nap in the back of the van. That is the reason for all those pillows back there, isn't it?" She didn't wait for an answer. "Keep driving, Chad. Next stop, Cloudcroft, New Mexico."

After driving for several hours in complete silence—Lily had her eyes closed—Sam pulled into a Holiday Inn a few miles outside of Houston. It was almost ten o'clock. Lily's estimate of travel time hadn't taken into account the traffic jam in

Baton Rouge or the unscheduled stop at the rest area in Orange. Before checking them in at the motel, Sam used Lily's cell phone to call the nursing home. While Lily pretended to sleep, Sam had a brief conversation with the person on duty.

Ending the call, he told Lily, "Visiting hours were over at nine. The receptionist let it slip that Mr. Segal had four visitors this evening—she seemed surprised that he had more people interested in visiting him."

That opened Red's eyes. *"Four* visitors? Who?"

"She wouldn't give me names. But they weren't together, and they weren't family. Two couples. The second couple asked about the first."

"Desiree and Chad asking about Lillian and Archie?"

Smart girl, Sam thought. "That's how I figure it."

"We missed Archie and Lillian. I really thought she wouldn't go to the nursing home until morning."

"Archie must have convinced her to get it over with tonight," said Sam.

"What are we going to do now?"

"Get a room. Tomorrow we'll visit the nursing home and see what Segal has to say about all his visitors. Then we'll decide where to go from here."

"A room? Did you change your mind?"

"What?"

"You said get *a* room. One room for the two of us." Lily gave him a sleepy smile that had his blood pressure soaring into the red zone.

"Figure of speech. I meant two rooms." He got out of the car and slammed the door a little harder than was strictly necessary. Why had he ever thought having Lily put the moves on him would be a good idea? She had already made him violate one of his rules. And she knew it. Lily might have been doing nothing more than getting even with him with all her suggestive talk, but she might be getting ready to try him on for size, too.

Sam didn't want to be Lily's wild adventure. He wasn't sure why not. A few nights together, and they'd both move on. But Lily was engaged. She shouldn't be thinking about flings and adventures. She sure as hell shouldn't be so eager to share her thoughts with him. Not when her thoughts included sharing a room and a bed.

It would almost serve her right if he took her . . . at her word. Almost. But he was older and presumably wiser, and he was certain Lily would regret a fling.

Midlife crisis—that's what was happening to him. Lily had pointed out that he was approaching middle-age. Yanking her out of the car and kissing her breathless had to be some kind of male menopause thing. He'd never manhandled a woman before in his life. Not that he hadn't been tempted to put his hands on a woman before— some of the women who claimed to be in love with him could have used a little shove. But he would have pushed them away, not grabbed and held on like he'd done with Lily.

All he had to do was get through the next few days. Once he was back in Chicago, he'd forget all about Red and her sexy southern drawl. She would forget about him even quicker.

Sam motioned for Lily to open her window. When she complied, he leaned down and said, "I'll check us in. Wait here."

"Sam, I don't like it that Chad and Desiree found Lillian and Archie. How did they manage that?"

"They found Max. We don't know that they found Archie and your grandmother. The receptionist said the older couple left a few minutes before the other two arrived."

"How did they find Max?"

"They've got the same address list we do. They must have a list of Winthrop Studio's employees, too." Sam straightened up. "I'll be back."

Lily waited, somewhat reassured now that she knew Chad and Desiree had apparently missed Archie and Lillian. But by only minutes. As if that wasn't enough to worry about, she also had to deal with Sam.

And those kisses.

There was something wrong with her. She shouldn't have reacted to a kiss like that—not when she'd just spent a good bit of time lecturing herself about the dangers of dangerous men like Sam. Her principles had melted like ice cream in August the second Sam's lips had touched hers.

What was different about Sam's kisses? Dexter was a good kisser. But his kisses didn't make her want to rip off her clothes and attack him. With only his wicked mouth, Sam had gotten her so worked up she'd been on the verge of pushing him into the backseat. Where she would have gotten both of them naked in the blink of an eye, and then—

Lily made herself close the curtain on that scenario. Her cheeks had gotten hot just thinking about what she'd wanted to do with Sam. Fanning herself with her hand, Lily thanked the Lord that Sam had insisted on separate rooms. If her wild streak was making a belated appearance, she needed all the help she could get to keep it under control.

Why should she ignore her urges?

Losing control sounded reckless, carefree, exciting. Lillian had certainly encouraged her to—

Sam tapped on the window, making her jump. "Our rooms are at the back. I'll drive us around."

He parked at the rear of the motel, then escorted Lily through a glass door into a carpeted hallway. He stopped in front of room one twenty-four. "This is your room." He inserted the card key in the door and let her enter. Dropping her suitcase inside the door, he said, "I'm next door. Room one twenty-six. Call me if you need anything."

"Adjoining rooms?" That meant a connecting door. A door either one of them could open. She could open it, and test her control or lack thereof. "Did you ask for that?"

"Yeah. With Chad and Desiree in the neighborhood, I wanted to be within shouting distance."

"They can't know where we are. You took that transmitter thingy off my car. We didn't need adjoining rooms."

Sam scowled. "What's the problem, Red? Too close for comfort? You want me to get another room?"

"No, of course not." She eyed the door connecting the two rooms. It was closed, of course. Locked, no doubt. But not with a key. Only a dead bolt separated her room from Sam's. "What about dinner?"

"What about it?"

"I'm starving. While I was waiting for you to check us in I noticed a Papacito's across the street in the next block. Do you like Mexican food? Aren't you hungry?"

"Call room service. I'm not getting back in that car." With that, he closed the door, almost slamming it in her face.

"Well. That was rude." Lily stalked across the room and picked up the telephone. She ordered a club sandwich and a glass of milk.

While she waited for her dinner, she got a night-shirt out of her suitcase and hung up the sundress she planned to wear the next day. Her dinner was delivered, and she ate every bite. A quick shower, and she was ready for bed.

Before she turned back the covers, Lily opened the curtains and looked at the Honda parked right outside her room. She had the duplicate set of car keys in her purse. She could wait until she was sure Sam was asleep, get in the car and leave him and his testosterone far, far behind.

That almost seemed like the smart thing to do. Lily had the feeling that if she and Sam were to-gether much longer, she was going to find out ex-actly what Lillian meant when she said a wild streak could be a good thing.

And as intriguing as being reckless seemed, there were bound to be consequences. Those might not be fun.

With a sigh, Lily reminded herself that the trip wasn't about her cutting loose and having a fling. It was about saving Lillian. She couldn't do that by herself—not with gangsters and Lord knew who else after her, too. Much as she didn't want to admit it, accepting help from a professional like Sam was the smart thing for her to do.

Lily dropped the curtain and flopped onto the bed. There had to be some way for her to make it through the next few days without making a com-plete fool of herself. Running away seemed a bit drastic, though. Cowardly, too. Now that she wasn't crowded in a car with him, she could view the situ-ation objectively.

She wasn't really in danger of falling in bed—or in love—with Sam. It had to be the unfamiliar situ-ation that was making her behave out of character.

She had never lost her grandmother until today. And what a day it had been—beginning with Sam handcuffed to Lillian's bed, followed in rapid succession by chasing him to New Orleans, meeting up with Chad and Desiree, and having Sam kiss her senseless at a rest stop in Orange, Texas. Any combination of two of those things would be enough to get a person off balance. She'd experienced them all in less than twenty-four hours.

As Sam had pointed out, Chad and Desiree were around somewhere. Somewhere close. She certainly didn't want to chance running into them alone. Lily yawned. As soon as she had a good night's sleep, she'd get her equilibrium back.

As Scarlet said, tomorrow *was* another day.

Seven

Sam ordered a burger, fries and a beer from room service, then tried calling his father. Archie's cell phone was on, but Archie wasn't answering. He called Phil, who also didn't answer. At least Phil had voice mail. Sam left a message, telling Phil what they had learned at the nursing home. He'd just finished the call when there was a knock at the door.

"Room service."

He had the waiter put the tray on the desk, signed the check and gave the man a tip.

He sat at the desk, ate his meal, then turned on the TV. Using the remote to surf the channels, he paid scant attention to what was on the screen until he saw Lillian Leigh's eighteen-year-old face on the screen. It took him a second to realize he was watching a scene from *Tahiti Temptress*. It would have to be the scene where Lillian, wearing nothing but a skimpy sarong, did a seductive dance for the hapless male lead.

Torturing himself by picturing Lily in an even skimpier sarong, wiggling her hips and batting her lashes at him, Sam watched the entire movie.

It ended with the hero coming to his senses and rejecting the sultry temptress in favor of his childhood sweetheart. The last frame showed Lillian, having learned that sex and deception never win—at least not back when the Hays Code was in effect—knocking on the door of a cloister prepared to exchange her sarong for a nun's habit.

Sam hit the power button and silenced the television set. He looked at the connecting door. Why had he insisted on adjoining rooms? Chad and Desiree weren't going to find them. Not tonight. He didn't need to be next door to Lily.

He ought to be in the same room with her. In the same bed—

With a groan, Sam stripped off his clothes and hit the shower. He did not turn on the hot water. As he slowly turned blue beneath the icy shower, he tried one more time to figure out why Lily was so appealing. If he could figure that out, he'd be able to find an antidote.

Cold water wasn't doing it. He got out of the shower and dried off. He had just entered the bedroom when a light tapping noise sounded.

Sam opened the hall door. No one was there.

The knock came again, louder this time.

The connecting door. That was where the tapping noise came from. Red was knocking on his door. Sam pulled on his pants and opened the door. Not all the way, not enough to let anyone in, but the crack was wide enough that he could see Lily standing on the other side wearing nothing but a silky something that resembled a man's shirt.

"What?" he asked in a strangled voice.

"Let me in. I have to tell you something." Lily pushed on the door.

"Tell me from your side of the door."

Blowing a lock of red hair out of her eyes, Red

blurted, "I don't think we should travel together any longer."

Sam opened the door wide. "Why the hell not? You can't do this on your own, Red."

"I know. But I don't think you're the right man for the job. No, that's not what I mean. I know you're the right man for the job—it's just that you're not the right man for me. Dexter is. I think."

Sam grabbed her hand and pulled her into the room. "Sit," he said, pushing her into the uphol-stered chair next to the bed. He sat on the edge of the bed. "Now. Slow down and tell me what you're talking about."

"I can't be with you, Sam."

"Because . . . ?"

"Because. I'm afraid I might do something stupid if we're together for three or four more days."

"Something stupid? Like . . . ?"

"I don't see the need to go into that. I just think it would be better if we traveled separately from now on. You could rent a car, and we could keep in touch by phone. You can rent a car that comes with a phone, you know."

"Lily. I am very sorry I kissed you. I can see where my actions this afternoon might make you uncomfortable."

"I'm not uncomfortable with you. I'm afraid—"

Sam groaned. "Oh, God. I knew it. I terrorized you. I should never have kissed you. Red, I am re-ally sorry about that. I don't know why I did it. It has something to do with your grandmother."

"Lillian? You kissed me because of Lillian?" Lily narrowed her eyes. "Did you watch *Tahiti Temptress* tonight?"

"Yeah. Just from the sexy dance part."

"How many times have you seen Lillian's movies?"

"I don't know. Lots."

Abruptly, Lily got out of the chair and began pacing. "You weren't kissing me this afternoon. You were kissing her." She stopped in front of him, a horrified look on her face. "Good grief. You've got a crush on my grandmother."

"Don't be ridiculous. She's old enough to be my—"

"I'm not talking about Lillian Redmond. You've got the hots for Lillian Leigh. Here I thought it was me that made you lose control. I should have known better. I'm not the type to drive men wild. I'm glad I found out before I fell in love with—" Lily put her hand over her mouth. "Oops. I wasn't going to say anything about that. I know your feelings on the subject of quickie romance."

"You are not going to fall in love with me."

"I most certainly am not. I could never love a man who yearned for my grandmother. Ick."

"I do not yearn for Lillian. I admit I might have had a few dreams about her when I was fifteen. But I knew who I was kissing this afternoon, Red. That was you. Nobody else but you."

"Oh. You're sure about that?"

Sam nodded. "But that's no reason for you to think you're about to fall in love with me. Real love doesn't work that way. Trust me. I know. I've been through this before, remember?"

"I know. You said your first wife fell in love with you at first sight. But, Sam, whatever I'm feeling now, it was not first sight. I didn't like you at first sight. At least, not after you opened your mouth and started snapping orders. I liked you better after you saved me from Chad, but I didn't love you then. But then you kissed me, and it started me thinking. And what I think is, I shouldn't take a chance on hanging around with you any longer."

"What is it? What did I do that makes you think

you're in danger of falling in love with me? I need to know, Lily. If I could figure out what's going on, I could do something about it."

"Do something about what?"

"Keeping women from coming on to me."

Lily sank onto the foot of the bed next to him. "I forgot about that. Women fall in love with you all the time."

"Not love. It isn't love. Love happens between people who have known each other for a long, long time. Like you and Dexter. None of those other women had known me for longer than a few weeks."

"How many women are we talking about here?"

"Not many. Five. One client. The other women worked at Hunter and Sons—a research assistant, one receptionist, two secretaries."

"All the women you work with fall in love—*think* they fall in love with you?"

"Not all. I never said all. And only the single ones. So far, I haven't had to fire a married woman."

"You fire them?" Red sounded outraged. "You make them fall in love with you, and you *fire* them?"

"Pay attention, Red. It isn't love. I don't do anything—not anything I'm aware of. I do not encourage them in any way whatsoever. But once they . . . start thinking they want to be with me, I have to do something. Women who think they're in love do not work. They sit around mooning and sighing and making nuisances of themselves." Sam got up. Sitting next to Lily on a bed was making him think evil thoughts. He began pacing. "Besides, I don't do the actual firing. Phil does."

"You make your brother do the dirty work?"

"He's better at it than I am."

"Does Phil have the same problem you do? Is it a family thing?"

"No. Phil is what you might call a ladies' man. But he has to do the chasing."

"Whereas you don't do anything at all, and women fall at your feet."

"Yeah. Don't look at me like that. It's not like I enjoy it."

"Stand still for a minute, will you?"

Sam stopped his restless pacing. "What for?"

"I want to look at you. I'm trying to see the attraction. I know I did it before, but it's hard to get the full picture when you're seated behind the wheel of a car." Lily looked him over from head to toe, then stood up and walked around him. Twice. "Hmm. Outstanding body. Especially without your shirt on."

"Red. I never take my shirt off at work."

She stopped in front of him and stared at his face. "You didn't grab any of those other women and kiss them, did you?"

"Absolutely not. I told you, Red. I am not a grabber. Usually. What I did to you this afternoon was completely out of character."

"Hmmm. That's interesting. This whole conversation has been an eye-opener. And a real turnoff. Knowing that you're so irresistible to all those other women makes you a lot less attractive to me. Now that we've had this talk, I'm almost sure what I'm feeling is some combination of gratitude and lust. Not love, or anything close to it. It will be perfectly all right for us to travel together. Whatever it is you've got going for you, I am now immune."

"Glad to hear it."

"Good night, Sam."

"Good night, Red." Sam closed the door and set the dead bolt. He had never met a woman like Lily Redmond. Women whose thoughts were easily readable from their eyes and their body language, yeah. But never a woman who made it a practice of telling him exactly what she was thinking.

And she was thinking she was immune to him.

Tuesday morning at the Marriott Courtyard, a ringing telephone woke Lillian. She opened one eye. It wasn't the hotel room phone. It must be Archie's cell phone. Next to her on the big bed, Archie was snoring softly. It sounded like a big cat's purr. Smiling, Lillian slipped out of bed and found his cell phone in his coat pocket. "Hello," she whispered.

"Mrs. Redmond?"

"Yes. Who is this?"

There was a long pause. "Philip Hunter. Uh. Is my father available?"

"Archie is here, but he's sleeping. I hate to wake him. We had a long day yesterday." And a long and energetic night. Lillian smiled at the memory.

"Oh." Philip cleared his throat. "Well. I have some information I wanted to pass on to him. But I wouldn't want to interrupt—that is, I know he needs his rest, but —"

"Is it something you can tell me?" Poor boy. She'd managed to shock him. Well, she'd shocked herself, too. Who would have thought she'd turn into a wanton hussy at her time of life? "And don't worry, Philip dear. You're not interrupting anything at the moment. Does the information concern me and my investigation?"

"Well. Yeah. It does. I guess it would be all right to tell you."

"I promise I'll give your father the message as soon as he wakes up. What is it?"

"Sam called me late last night. He and Lily are in Houston. He checked with the nursing home as soon as they got there. The receptionist told him that Max Segal had four visitors last night."

"*Four* visitors?"

"Yeah. Two of them were you and Archie, right?"

"Yes. But Mr. Segal wasn't much help, I'm afraid. He has Alzheimer's."

"Ah, gee. That's too bad. Well, anyway, according to Sam, another couple got there after you left. Sam thinks it's the same two who hassled Lily in Baton Rouge."

"Someone hassled Lily?" Lillian's voice rose in alarm.

"She's all right. This couple—Chad and Desiree—cornered Lily in the ladies' room and tried to make her tell them where you are. She didn't tell them, and Sam rescued her."

"Lily had to be rescued? In a ladies' room? Oh, my. I'm going to wake Archie up. He needs to hear this. Archie?" Lillian poked him in the ribs.

"I'm awake," grunted Archie. He sat up, stretched and yawned. Then he gave her grin that had her pulse rate racing. "Good morning, lady. Who's on the phone?"

"Philip. Do you want to talk to him?"

"Yeah." Archie took the phone from Lillian. He gave her a smacking kiss on the mouth before putting the phone to his ear. Being waked up by Lillian made the whole world seem like a better place. "Phil?"

"Yeah. Did you just kiss Lillian Leigh?"

"Yes, I did." Archie heard the smug satisfaction in his own voice and grinned. "And not for the first time. What's up?"

"Got lucky, did you?"

"Very. Son. I know you find my situation fascinating, but get over it. Why did you call?"

Philip repeated what he had told Lillian. "Any

ideas of who else could be interested in your girl-friend—in Lillian?"

"Not at the moment. Sam's sure it's a man and a woman?"

"Yeah. And he's got their first names—Desiree and Chad. So far, I haven't been able to find out who they are, much less who they might be working for."

"Well, stay on it."

"Something else. I'm pretty sure Fazio Grimaldi and Joe Bones are the pair in the Mercedes. You haven't seen them again, have you?"

"No. I think we lost them for good."

"One more thing, and then I'll let you get back to . . . whatever you were doing. Sam said Desiree and Chad have a copy of Lillian's address book. Since they showed up at the nursing home, he thinks they must have a list of the people connected with the Winthrop murder, too. So you may cross paths with them, sooner or later."

"How did they get Lillian's address book?"

"They grabbed Lily and took it from her. Sam got her away from them before they did any real harm. But things may escalate the closer you get to Hollywood. Sure you don't want to forget about Winthrop and come home?"

"Very sure. I haven't had this much fun in years." Archie winked at Lillian. She winked back and gave him a sultry smile. "And if that's why Sam and Lily are coming after us, you can tell them to turn around and go home. Lillian and I can take care of ourselves."

"And each other," Phil muttered. "Aren't you too old for this sort of thing?"

"Not by a long shot. You'll think differently when you're my age—then you'll be glad you've got my genes. I'll talk to you later." Archie ended the call.

"What was that about my address book?" asked Lillian.

"Chad and Desiree—the couple that hassled Lily at the mall. They got it from your granddaughter."

"Phil said Sam had rescued Lily from them. Who are they?"

"Don't know. Phil's working on it. Don't worry about Lily. Sam will take good care of her from now on."

"That's wonderful. Now that I know she's safe, I can tell you something. Lily needed rescuing, and I don't mean from the likes of Desiree and Chad. She needed to be rescued from a boring life. As I did. Thank you for last night, Archie. I haven't felt this good in years."

"You're welcome. And you have my eternal gratitude. I haven't made illicit love in a cheesy motel room in decades. Does wonders for a man's self-esteem." Archie tugged her closer, fitting her next to him with her head on his shoulder. His bare shoulder.

Archie didn't have a stitch on, and neither did she. Lillian smiled. "You know what? Being old has its advantages."

"Besides senior citizen discounts?" he asked, stroking her bare arm.

"Yes. If we were young, we wouldn't have ended up in bed so soon. We would have wasted days wondering if we were doing the right thing, obsessing over whether we were suited to each other, worrying about what would happen the next morning. I'm glad we're old enough not to have time for that kind of nonsense."

"You've got a point," he said absently.

"What are you thinking about?"

Archie kissed the tip of her nose. "That other couple. I just remembered something. When we left the nursing home last night, a van was pulling in. A van with Illinois plates."

"You think that Chad and Desiree were in that van?"

"I don't know. Besides Gus, who in Illinois would be interested in Eric's murder?"

"Couldn't Gus have sent them, too?"

"I doubt it. Fazio Grimaldi and Joe Bones should be enough muscle for Gus." Archie kissed her on her temple. "I figured the biggest danger you would face would be from whoever killed Winthrop."

"Archie, I think I've been assuming that the murderer would be dead by now, or too old to cause any trouble. I guess I was wrong. I've really stirred up a hornet's nest, haven't I?"

"Do you want to give up?"

"No, I most certainly do not. I started this, and I'm going to finish it."

"That's my girl." Archie gave her a possessive squeeze.

"I'm glad you're with me, Archie. And that Sam is looking out for Lily. I don't like all these people chasing after me and Lily."

"Neither do I, especially not the two jokers in the deck. Chad and Desiree. I did manage to get the license number, even though I'm getting old."

"Not so very old," said Lillian, snuggling closer.

"Maybe not," Archie said. "My son had the gall to ask me if I wasn't too old for this."

"Smart aleck."

"Exactly. Now where were we? Oh, yes." Archie pulled her on top of him.

"I don't think this is where we were. I distinctly remember being on the bottom."

"I thought you might like a change."

Lillian sat up, bracing herself with her hands on his chest. "Perhaps I would." She slid her hands down, pausing at his belly button to see what waited for her. "Oh, my. Look at you. That didn't take long."

"Having the Tahiti Temptress straddling me is better than a prescription for Viagra."

"Really? Well, then. Remember the scene where I seduced the poor, innocent fisherman on the deck of the fishing boat? Just to make the hero jealous?"

"It's one of my favorites," Archie gasped.

"Of course, back in those days we could only hint at what was going on . . ."

"Hence the cut to the waves pounding against the rocky shore."

"Exactly. But what I imagined was happening was something like this."

Later, nibbling Danish and sipping coffee while still in bed, Lillian said, "This couple—Chad and Desiree—they followed us to Max, using my address book. They've probably figured out that we'll be visiting David next. David Epstein directed me in *Tahiti Temptress* and *Siren of Singapore*—he's living in New Mexico now. I'm thinking we should skip him and go on to Sedona."

"Who's in Sedona?"

"Cathy's assistant—Robert Kaminski. He was at the studio that night. His name isn't in my address book—Cathy gave it to me."

Archie thought for a minute or two. "I like it, Lillian. We can call Epstein, see if he has any useful information. And warn him about Chad and Desiree. The more I think about them, the more I'm convinced they must be working for Gus, too. He's the only one, besides the murderer, who has a reason to keep you quiet."

"I don't see why anyone but the murderer would want to do that. Gus is *not* the murderer.

That is one thing I am sure about. If anything, my investigation will clear him once and for all."

"Is that why you're doing this? To clear Gus's name?"

"That's one reason."

"The other being to see justice done."

"Yes. But my motives aren't all that noble. The truth is, the main reason I want to find whoever murdered Eric Winthrop is for me. I want to clear *my* name. I don't want to go to my grave with people still thinking I lied to protect a killer."

"People like your son and daughter-in-law?"

"And Lily, and my other grandchildren. I have another selfish reason, too. I wanted to have one more adventure before . . ."

"Oh, I think you've already accomplished that, don't you?"

"Yes. And illicit sex in a cheesy motel is even better than I remembered. Probably because this time, I'm with the right man."

That earned her a bear hug and another kiss. "I've got a plan."

"To find the killer?"

"No. To have us one really fine adventure. Let's slow down—"

"Slow is good. Fast is okay, too."

"Woman, get your mind off my body for a minute or two."

"Oh. Sorry. You were saying we should slow down."

"And take our time getting to Hollywood. There are places between here and there that I've always wanted to see—the Alamo. Mexico."

"Oh, Archie. That's a wonderful idea. Have you ever been to the Grand Canyon? I don't think it's very far from Sedona."

"We'll do it. We'll hit every tourist spot between

here and there. Heck, we'll even stop and read the historical markers if you want. We'll take our own sweet time."

"That sounds like a wonderful plan. Slowing down, taking side trips—we'll confuse and confound all those silly people chasing after us. You're wonderful, Archie." She beamed at him.

"Thank you, madam. And along the way, we'll compare our Winthrop murder files. I'll bet you a silver dollar that we'll figure out who the killer is before we ever get to California."

"That's a bet. But where will we find a silver dollar?"

"There must be one or two left in Las Vegas, don't you think?"

Lillian's eyes lit up. "Las Vegas? That's another place I've always wanted to go."

Sam's first thought on waking Tuesday morning at the Holiday Inn was that Lily thought she was immune to him.

That had to be a good thing.

He might want her for some inexplicable reason, but he did not need her. When his marriage ended, Sam had made a solemn vow never to do that again. He was not interested in another committed relationship. He had been uncommitted for seven years, and he intended to stay that way. Lily Redmond, with her red hair and her big, brown eyes and her C.D.-in-lieu-of-engagement ring was not the kind of woman a man took on a brief sexual odyssey.

Hell. At almost twenty-five, she barely qualified as a woman. Sam's lips puckered up of their own volition, reminding him that Lily sure could kiss like a woman.

With a groan, Sam got out of bed and headed

for the bathroom. Maybe one more cold shower would drown his lascivious thoughts about Red once and for all.

The shower gave him goose bumps, but didn't rein in his libido. Sam was downright crabby when he met Lily for the free breakfast in the hotel lobby.

"Good morning," Lily said. She was chipper. "Did you sleep well? I did. I feel much more like myself this morning."

"Who did you feel like yesterday? Little Red Riding Hood?"

"Well. You certainly sound like a grumpy old wolf this morning." She winked at him. "And I did find you in my grandmother's bed. My what a big mouth you have, Mr. Wolf."

Sam showed her his teeth. "Better watch out, Red. I eat little girls like you for breakfast." Maybe he could scare her into keeping her distance.

She shoved a donut in his mouth. "Eat that instead. I called the nursing home. Visiting hours are at nine. But I was thinking—do we really need to go there? We know we missed catching up with Lillian and Archie. The longer we hang around here, the farther behind we're going to get. Whatever Mr. Segal knows, he's already told them."

Sam swallowed the donut. "I want to see if we can find out who his other visitors were."

"We know that, too. Chad and Desiree."

"Chad and Desiree what? We can ask Mr. Segal to tell us their last names."

"Oh. Good idea. I hadn't thought about that."

"No reason why you should. I'm the professional. It will be much easier for Phil to find out who they work for if I can give him their full names."

* * *

Lily and Sam arrived at the nursing home promptly at nine o'clock. Sam drove around the parking lot before pulling into one of many vacant slots.

"What are you looking for? Your father's SUV?"

"No. I'm sure he and Lillian are on the road west. I was checking for cars with Illinois plates." Sam pulled into a vacant slot. "I didn't see one."

When they approached the desk, the receptionist said, "Max Segal? My goodness, but he's popular. You're the third group of visitors he's had lately. Your names, please? And I'll need to see a picture I.D."

"Who were the other visitors? Are they around?" asked Sam, pulling out his driver's license and handing it to the receptionist.

"Sam Hunter. Nice name," said the receptionist, studying Sam's license and making notes on a message pad. "Mr. Segal's other visitors came last night, the last couple right before visiting hours were over."

"Oh, darn. We missed them," said Lily. "I don't suppose they said anything about where they were going next?" She handed the receptionist her license.

The woman jotted Lily's name on a visitors' log, barely glancing at her I.D. "Not to me. I wasn't on duty last night. I just saw their names on Mr. Segal's visitors' list."

"Names? Maybe it wasn't Lillian and Archie," said Lily, grabbing Sam's arm. "Maybe it was his family."

"Who were yesterday's visitors?" Sam asked the receptionist, trying to read the list upside down.

"I'm so sorry, Mr. Hunter." The woman batted her lashes at Sam. "I really, really wish I could help you, but that's confidential information."

"Don't worry about it," said Sam. "I understand."

"Oh, I'm so glad. I was afraid you'd hold it against me."

Lily snorted.

Sam glared at her, then grinned at the receptionist. "Now why would I do that? You're only following rules. I'm a big believer in rules."

With a shuddering sigh, the receptionist pointed to a double doorway. "The visitors' lounge is through there. Please wait, and someone will bring Mr. Segal to you."

"We can ask Mr. Segal who visited him yesterday," said Lily. "Maybe they told him—"

"Oh, dear. I'm afraid he won't remember anything they told him," said the receptionist. "Mr. Segal is an Alzheimer's patient, you see."

While Lily and Sam waited for Max Segal, Lily couldn't resist pointing out, "Those were goo-goo eyes."

"What?"

"The way the receptionist was looking at you when you asked who Max's other visitors were. I thought she was going to climb over the counter and grab you." In a quavering falsetto, Lily said, "I'm really, really sorry I can't do your bidding, my darling lover man."

"That's not what she said."

"It's what she meant. I'm merely expressing her subtext out loud."

An orderly wheeled an elderly man into the room.

"Mr. Segal?" asked Lily. "How are you?"

He beamed at her. "Fine. Feeling fine. I love redheads. Redheads have the best skin tone for the camera, did you know that?"

"No, I didn't."

"Treat your skin with care. Moisturize and stay out of the sun."

"I do. I will. Mr. Segal, do you remember Lillian Leigh?"

"Who, dear? Redheads have the best skin, did you know that? Freckles can be hidden." He squinted at Lily. "You don't have many, only a few on your nose."

"Thirteen. About Lillian—she's my grand-mother, by the way—do you remember her?"

"She had red hair, too," said Sam.

Max's brow wrinkled, and his eyes filled with tears. "Lillian? I don't remember."

"He's becoming agitated," said the attendant.

"I'm sorry, Mr. Segal. I didn't mean to upset you. Thank you very much for your advice."

"Advice?"

"About staying out of the sun."

"Red hair, fair skin. The sun's not your friend."

Lily and Sam paid their respects to Mr. Segal, then started back to the receptionist's desk. "Ask her to show you the ladies' room," Sam hissed. "I'm going to check out the visitors' log."

"I think it would work better if you asked her the way to the men's room. She'll follow you any-where."

Lily was right about that. The receptionist prac-tically crawled over the counter in her rush to help Sam. Curling her lip at the demonstration of Sam's power over the female sex, Lily hurried behind the counter and found Max's chart. The visitors' log was on top. She flipped it open, found the two names following Lillian and Archie's and committed them to memory. She was standing innocently by the exit door when Sam and the receptionist returned.

Sam's cheeks were flushed, and the receptionist had that cat-who-just-ate-the-cream look.

Once they were outside, Lily asked, "What happened? Did she follow you into the men's room? Did you need help with your zipper or something?"

A muscle in Sam's jaw worked. "I don't want to talk about it. Did you get the names?"

"Desiree Anderson and Charles Boyd."

"Good job, Red. That will give Phil something to work with."

"Assuming they used their real names. What if they didn't?"

"They probably did—unless they had phoney I.D.'s. We had to show the receptionist our driver's licenses, remember?"

"Yes, but that could have been a ploy—she wrote your address on a message pad. She didn't do that for anyone else."

"What's that look about?"

"What look? I'm sure I don't know what you're talking about."

"That disgusted look. I can't help it, Red. You think I like being some kind of babe magnet?"

"Yes. I do. Why wouldn't you? But if I'm disgusted, it's not with you. It's me. I can't believe I almost—"

"Almost what?"

"Never mind. I didn't, and I'm not going to. I feel much more myself today. I knew I'd feel better after a good night's sleep. Now, be quiet. I'm going to call Dexter."

Lily hit the speed button for Dexter's number at work. He answered on the first ring. "Hi. It's me."

"Lily. About time. I expected you to call me last night, and when you didn't, I got worried. I would have called you; but it was late by the time I decided you weren't going to call me, and I didn't want to disturb Lillian."

"I'm sorry. But we've been so busy, I didn't have a chance to call until now."

"How is Lillian? Has she calmed down yet?"

"Fine. Calm, cool and collected."

"Good. How are you, honey?"

"Fine. I'm fine. But busy, like I said. Lillian wants to see everything, do everything there is to do. She's got every minute of the day scheduled with some activity or another. She's waiting for me even as we speak."

"I won't keep you long. But don't hang up yet. I've missed hearing your voice."

"That's sweet. I may not be able to call you every day, Dexter."

"I'll call you. What's your number at the hotel?"

"You've got my cell number. Why do you want the hotel number?"

"Just in case there's some kind of emergency."

"What kind of emergency? There won't be an emergency. Why don't you let me call you? If you call, you may interrupt an important discussion. This trip isn't all fun and games, you know. With Lillian zipping around from place to place every minute of the day, it's going to be hard enough finding quiet time to talk to her."

"Oh, right. I hadn't thought of that. I wouldn't want to interfere with your mission. How is that going, by the way?"

"I've only just started. I've got to hang up now, Dexter. I think I hear Lillian calling for me."

"Oh. Well, give her my best. I miss you, Lily. I love you."

"I miss you, too. Good-bye, Dexter." Lily ended the call and stuffed the cell phone in her purse.

She hadn't told Dexter she loved him. Why not?

Eight

Knowing he should leave it alone, Sam couldn't resist commenting on Lily's conversation with her fiancé. "That was interesting."

"What?"

"You just told your fiancé a string of lies—I counted at least five—and you didn't blush once. That doesn't bode well for your future." Unless her future included forgetting about Dexter and having a fling. With him. In the light of day, Sam couldn't believe he'd backed off from sharing a room with Red. Was he nuts, or what?

But Lily was engaged to another man—not any man, but a man she'd grown up with. Dexter had given Lily her first kiss. He'd taken her to her high school prom. Sam didn't believe for a second that Lily would give that kind of history up for a quick roll in the hay. Not without regretting it later.

Sam didn't want to take a chance on hurting the woman seated next to him. Red was special.

Lillian stared at him, her mouth open. "Fancy that," she murmured. "I did, didn't I? I lied to Dexter. And I didn't have a bit of trouble doing it." She felt her cheeks. "I didn't even blush, did I?"

"Nope. Not only that, you didn't tell him you love him." Engaged or not, Lily couldn't be in love with Dexter the dork. Maybe it wouldn't be such a bad thing to show her that she could do better.

And then what? Offer himself as a substitute bridegroom? That was not going to happen. One impulsive marriage was enough for him.

Lily slid down in the seat, until her tail bone was on the very edge. "No. As a matter of fact, I noticed that before you brought it up."

"So? What's going on? Having second thoughts?"

"No. Maybe. Yes. I am having second thoughts. Sam, Dexter gave me a C.D. when he knew I wanted an engagement ring."

"So he's not romantic. You must have known that about him."

"I guess I did. It never seemed important until now. Until I met you and started thinking about . . . you know."

"Sex?"

"Yes. That doesn't seem like the right thing for an engaged woman to do—fantasize about sex with another man. If I really love Dexter, that is."

"You know what? I think you want to have sex with another man—any other man who happens to be convenient—to punish Dexter for that C.D."

"That's an awful thing to say. I don't want to punish Dexter. And I don't want to have sex with any other man. I want to have sex with you."

"I thought you were immune."

"I lied about that, too. I've never told so many lies in my whole life. What do you think that means?"

"That you're away from home and family for the first time. On your own. With a man."

"With you. Why can't we have an affair? Last night, I tried to talk myself—and you—out of it, but in the light of day, that seems like a really good idea."

"Red. Think about it. You're an old-fashioned girl. OFGs don't have sex with other men on the eve of their wedding day. Not without a helluva provocation. I can see where a C.D. might be that provoking, but—"

"Today is not the eve. We haven't set a date yet, so there can't be an eve. OFG? Where'd you get that? I'm not old-fashioned. I'm thoroughly modern. Up to date. Maybe even a little ahead of the curve. You're the one who's stuck in ancient history."

"I know I'm going to regret asking, but how do you figure that?"

"Before I was born—before you were born—in the sixties there was a sexual revolution. People, men and women, revolted against the double standard, against suppressing sexuality. The rebellion was in favor of—"

"Free love. I heard about that, Red. But nothing is free. Not sex. Not love. Especially not love. There's always a price to pay."

"My goodness, but you're just full of dire warnings and doom and gloom. Lighten up, Hunter. All I've offered you is a good time."

"Which I turned down. Think about this, Lily. This trip is going to end soon. A few more days, and you'll be back with Dexter."

"Whoopee. You know what, Sam? I am having more than second thoughts about Dexter. Third and fourth thoughts, too. I really wanted an engagement ring. And I wanted one years ago. I also wanted to have sex with Dexter before we got engaged. Dexter ignored what I wanted. What if he never changes? What if he never gives me what I want, when I want it?"

"We already decided he's not a romantic." Sam was beginning to think Dexter was not only a dork but an idiot. He had a woman like Red in love with him, agreeing to spend the rest of her life with him, and he wouldn't give her what she wanted? When she wanted it?

"Dexter is practical. My father was impressed with the C.D. Dexter gave me. He said Dexter got a very favorable interest rate."

"Hold on. Your father was there when Dexter handed over the C.D.?"

Lily nodded. "So was my mother. And Dexter's mother and father. Dexter proposed after Sunday dinner at my parents' house."

"Wait. One. Minute. Let me get this straight. Dexter asked you to marry him in front of your parents? And his?"

Lily nodded.

"God. He is an idiot." Sam adjusted his opinion of the man. Downward. No reason to feel sorry for a manipulator like Dexter. Lily definitely could do a lot better. Not that he was putting himself in competition for Lily's hand in marriage, but he didn't have to worry about taking advantage of a nice guy. Dexter was not now and never had been in that category. "But you must have known that about him."

"That he's an idiot?"

"That he's not romantic. He must have other good qualities. Something made you say yes when he proposed."

"I suppose so. He's a hard worker. He will be a good provider. Dexter is trustworthy. Faithful. Practical. Dull."

"See. I knew you couldn't love a complete loser."

"You think dull is a good thing?"

"Dull isn't necessarily a bad thing," Sam hedged.

"Lillian thinks dull is a definite drawback. She thinks Dexter is not the right man for me. Mostly because he's not very exciting."

"Dexter must get excited about something."

"Well, yes. He gets animated when he talks about things like prime rates and Alan Greenspan."

Sam gave up. The man had no redeeming qualities. "You know what, Red? Lillian is right about Dexter. He *is* dull. And not only that, he's devious."

"Devious? Dexter?"

"Exactly. Devious Dexter."

"How did you reach that conclusion?"

"He proposed to you in front of an audience. It would have been very difficult for you to say no, wouldn't it?"

"No."

"Red."

"All right. Yes. It would have been hard to say no. My parents have been expecting us to get married practically since the day I was born. His, too, for that matter."

"And old Dex made you wait until you're twenty-four years old before he got around to popping the question? What was that about?"

"He wanted to wait until—"

"Until?"

"—he was sure I wouldn't do something crazy like Lillian did."

"Are you talking about the time Lillian left her home to pursue an honorable career? Dexter thinks that was crazy?"

"He's not the only one. Everyone thinks that was crazy."

"Do you?"

"I did. Now I'm not so sure."

"Are you sure you want to spend the rest of your life with him?"

"No. I am not sure. I don't want to talk about Dexter and me anymore. Tell me about your divorce."

"What do you want to know?"

"How long ago?"

"Years. Five, to be exact."

"Children?"

"None. Thank God."

"You don't like children?"

"I like children fine. I'm thankful that I don't have children with her. That would have kept her in my life."

"My goodness. What did she do to you?"

"Lied, cheated and stole."

"What did she lie about? How did she cheat you? What did she steal?"

"Red."

"You don't want to talk about it."

"Right."

"That's okay. I wasn't really interested. I was only trying to find another topic of conversation, something for us to talk about besides Dexter. Talking about Dexter was making me feel guilty." Her brow furrowed, Lily said, "We haven't discussed Mr. Segal."

"Not much to say. Poor guy. I wonder why he's in Texas. Think he's got family there?"

"I hope so. He must have, don't you think? He had to have some reason to leave California after he retired."

"I hope Dad never has to go through that. But if he does, Phil and I will be close by."

"I was thinking the same thing about Lillian. Do you suppose they worry about things like that? Losing themselves?" Lily asked.

"I don't know. I know Dad's reflexes aren't as fast as they used to be, and he complains about

various aches and pains from time to time.
Physical aches and pains. He doesn't seem to have
a memory problem."

"I wonder if that's why Lillian decided to write
about her life—because she's worried about forgetting her past."

"She may be doing it for you. I know, after my
mother died, there were things I wanted to ask
her, memories that I shared only with her."

"I feel awful."

"Why? Because Mr. Segal has Alzheimer's?"

"No. Well, yes, of course. But I was thinking of
the way we—me and my family—have been treat-
ing Lillian. As if she needed a keeper. Imagine
being told to go on a vacation with your granddaughter, to a children's theme park. No wonder
she ran away."

"Your parents meant well. Didn't they?"

"They said it was for her own good. That she was
lonely and needed to get away. Mother thinks
Lillian still misses Granddad. Daddy said she was
spending too much time brooding about the past.
I've come to the conclusion that they were both
wrong." Lily kept to herself the disloyal thought
that her parents had been motivated as much by
their fear of tabloids as their concern for Lillian.

"Your grandmother doesn't miss her husband?"

"They weren't wrong about that. But she doesn't
brood, and she isn't lonely. Lillian has tons of family and friends. She's active in her church, the garden club, and she volunteers at the library."

"Lillian did agree to go to Disney World with
you, didn't she?"

"Yes, but she never intended to go with me. And
she didn't trust me enough to be able to tell me
where she did intend to go. I let her down. We all
did. I feel really, really awful."

"Oh, geeze. You're not going to cry, are you?"

"What is it with you and crying?" Lily asked, sniffling.

The cell phone burbled, relieving him of the necessity of answering that question.

Lily answered the phone, then handed it to Sam. "It's your brother."

"Good. I can give him those names." Sam took the phone. "Hey, Phil, I've got news—"

"I've got bigger news. Dad is having an affair. I think. I'm almost sure."

"What?" Sam shot a quick look at Lily. She was staring out the window, but by the tense way she was holding herself, he could tell she was listening to every word. "I don't believe it."

"Believe it. I called him this morning, and she answered the phone."

"That doesn't mean anything. Lily answered this phone, and we're not—"

"I should hope not. You're in a moving vehicle. Lillian and Archie, on the other hand, were in bed together at the time I called him."

"How did you reach that conclusion?"

"Dad was asleep. I could hear him snoring. Mrs. Redmond—Lillian had to wake him up."

"Still circumstantial. Maybe they had adjoining rooms or a suite, and she'd just come in to wake him up or something." Sam noticed that Lily had stopped looking out the passenger window. Now she was staring straight at him, her eyes wide. He gave her a weak smile.

"Sam. Dad kissed her when she woke him up. A big, smacking kiss. And she giggled."

"Good God."

"Yeah. That was my initial reaction, too. But after thinking about it for a while and reflecting on something he said, I decided it's okay. Better than okay. This is a good thing, Sam."

"How do you figure that? What did Dad say?"

"That when we're his age, we'll be glad we have his genes. Besides, you know Dad's been lonely ever since Mother died. He deserves to have a little fun."

"I'm still not convinced. Dad could have been pulling your leg." Sam managed to pull a curtain on the image of Archie and Lillian together. "Back to the problem at hand—I've got information for you, too."

"Don't tell me you and Lily shared a room. Am I the only Hunter male not getting any?"

"No. We didn't, and I'm not." He almost added that it was driving him nuts, but Lily was still hanging on to his every word. "I do have information for you. Names. Desiree is Desiree Anderson, and Chad is Charles Boyd. See what you can find out."

"This should be a piece of cake. I have a license number to go with those names. Dad gave it to me this morning."

"How did he manage that?"

"He saw a beige GMC van pull into the nursing home as he was leaving. It had Illinois plates, so he memorized the number. You know Dad and his memory game."

"Yeah. That had to be Chad and Desiree—a beige GMC van, huh? That's good to know. Call me as soon as you find out who sent the odd couple after us."

"Will do." Phil hung up.

Sam gave the telephone back to Lily. She stuffed it in her purse. "Well? Are you going to tell me what he said?"

"I don't know if you can handle it."

Lily gasped. "Oh, no! Something's happened to Lillian. What? Tell me she's—"

"Hush. She's fine. Dad's fine. They're both fine."

He paused, trying to come up with a delicate way to give her the news. "But . . . they shared a room last night."

Lily gave him a blank stare. "The motel was full?"

"No. I don't know. Phil thinks they shared a bed, too."

"Don't be ridiculous. My grandmother would never—why did he think that?"

"Maybe because he called Dad early this morning and Lillian answered the phone. She said Archie was asleep, but he woke up and talked to Phil."

"That doesn't prove anything."

Sam stuck out his hand. "That's what I said, but Phil is convinced. Give me the phone. I'm calling Dad. He damn well better answer this time."

"You can't dial and drive at the same time." Lily rummaged in her purse and pulled out the phone. "What's his number."

"312-555-3426."

As soon as she'd dialed, he held out his hand again. Lily slapped the phone in his hand. "If Lillian is there, I want to talk to her."

A woman answered on the first ring. "Yes, who is it?"

"Mrs. Redmond?"

"Is that you, Sam?"

"Yes, ma'am." He cleared his throat. "Uh. How are you?"

"Wonderful. Absolutely wonderful. And you? Have you recovered from that awful trick I played on you?"

"Yeah. Yes, ma'am. I'm okay. Uh. You didn't happen to tell my father . . . ?"

"About the handcuffs? I'm afraid so. By the way, Phil told me that you rescued Lily. Thank you for that. She needs rescuing. Has she told you about Dexter?"

"Yes, ma'am."

"Try to do something about that, will you? Do you want to talk to Archie?"

Do something about Dexter? What did she have in mind? Sam quickly decided it was better that he not know. "Uh, yeah. Put him on. Please."

"Hello, Sam. Isn't it a beautiful day?"

"Dad. Where are you?"

"You don't need to know that."

"Yes, I do, Dad. I need to talk to you face-to-face."

"Why?"

"I want to see if you're all right."

"Trust me, son. I'm better than all right. I'm sitting on top of the world this morning."

Sam heard a feminine giggle. "Are you going to see David Epstein next?"

"I'm going to have brunch with a beautiful lady next—provided she puts some clothes on first."

"Good God." It was true. His father was having sex with Lillian Redmond.

"After brunch, we may decide to do a little sightseeing. Or we may crawl back in bed. As for Epstein, we may or may not pay him a visit. We have a couple of other stops to make along the way, but we're not in a rush. Why don't you toddle on back to Chicago? Phil needs help."

"He does not need help—Phil likes being in charge. And I can't go back to Chicago, not as long as Lily insists on chasing after her grandmother."

"You can't talk her out of that? Tell her to go home and wait for Lillian there?"

"Don't you think I've tried that?"

"Stubborn, heh? Takes after her grandmother, I see."

Sam heard a throaty feminine laugh. "Yeah. I can't leave Lily alone." Sam winced. "I mean, I can't let her go."

Lily giggled. Her giggle sounded just like Lillian's. Sam said, "I can't let her go by herself, that is. She needs my help. So do you, Dad. We need to work together on this."

"We can work together. That doesn't mean we all have to be in the same place at the same time, now does it? Sam, you take care of Lily. Lillian is very fond of her granddaughter. She wouldn't want anything bad to happen to her."

"It won't. Not while I'm around."

"Good. Now, if you two insist on coming after us, why don't we meet at the Beverly Hills Hotel? Lillian and I plan to stay there when we get to California."

"Why don't we meet you now? You are still in Houston, aren't you?"

"Son. Last night Lillian and I had hot, monkey sex. We plan to repeat the experience frequently. This may come as a shock to you, but the last thing we need is an audience, especially a disapproving audience."

Sam couldn't say anything for a full minute, too busy dealing with the fact that his father was having an affair with the movie star of his dreams. "It's not that I don't approve—I don't want you to get hurt."

"Who do you think is going to hurt me? Lillian?"

"Maybe. But I was referring to all the people chasing after her and you. Dad, there's a murderer in the mix somewhere."

"I know that. And Lillian and I are going to expose him. Or her. In our own good time. In the meantime, if you're not going back to work, consider this a vacation. We are. And, for the last time, we don't want you and her granddaughter tagging along."

"Dad—"

Archie hung up, but not before Sam heard that laugh again.

"Good God. Those two belong together."

"What? What did he say?"

"Are you sure you want to know? It may shock you."

"Sam. Tell me."

"He said that he and Lillian had hot, monkey sex last night, that they plan to do it again and again. They don't want us within a hundred miles of them."

Lily gasped. "Hot, monkey sex? With my grandmother? What kind of sex fiend is your father?"

"My father is a decent man. Your grandmother, on the other hand, is a well-known siren and temptress. If there is a sex fiend in that hotel room, it's Lillian Leigh Redmond."

"My grandmother is not a siren—she played one in the movies, that's all. I want to talk to her. I want to hear from her own lips that she's carrying on with your father. Call him back."

Sam tossed her the phone. "You call—just hit redial. He won't answer. He refused to tell me where they are—said they didn't want an audience for their affair. Want to go home now?"

"I most certainly do not want to go home." Lily punched the redial button and put the phone to her ear. "I don't believe my grandmother is having an affair. Ladies her age don't have affairs." She held the phone away from her ear and stared at it. "This thing has rung ten times. They aren't going to answer."

"I didn't think they would. I'm surprised they picked up the first time—Dad must have thought Phil was calling back with the information on the license number Dad gave him. Now they're too busy making whoopee. What are you going to do when you're Lillian's age. Crochet doilies?"

"Of course not. No one has doilies anymore. Do you even know what a doily is?"

"Yeah. Those little lacy things that some people still put on end tables and the arms of chairs. My mother crocheted."

Lily gave him a sympathetic look. "Oh, Sam. Are you upset because your dad is fooling around with my grandmother? Because he's being untrue to your mother?"

"My mother has been dead for five years. I don't think Dad is betraying her. I was a little surprised to hear that he's getting laid, that's all. What's with all the euphemisms—carrying on, fooling around— can't you say the words 'having sex'?"

"Yes, I can. And I wish you would, too. 'Getting laid' is crude. And you said 'making whoopee.' "

"So I did. It's hard to say the word sex in the same sentence with a parent."

"I can do it. I am appalled that my grandmother and your father are having sex."

"Appalled?"

"Aren't you?"

"Surprised. Maybe even shocked. But not appalled. 'Appalled' implies disapproval. I don't disapprove. Do you? Why?"

"Because it means Lillian's wild streak has surfaced again. It's . . . not ladylike."

"Good sex trumps good manners every time. Or is Dexter polite even in bed?"

"How would I know?"

Sam took his eyes off the road and stared at Lily. Her cheeks were flame red. "What are you saying? That you and Dexter haven't . . . carried on? Fooled around? Made whoopee?"

"We've fooled around. Some. But not . . . that."

"Why the hell not?"

"Not because of me. Dexter . . ."

"He's gay, isn't he?"

"No, he's not. Not if half of what Mary Alice McAllister said is true. And she delighted in giving me all the gory details. I think Dexter was afraid to go too far with me, at least before we were engaged."

"What's he scared of?"

"Getting me pregnant and being forced to marry me. I'm sure his parents have told him about my parents."

"Your parents had to get married?"

"Yes. They really love each other, so it worked out. But it was something of a scandal at the time. But I'm sure my father, or Dexter's father, or both of them have impressed upon him the danger of—"

"Fooling around."

"Yes. My mother sat me down and explained about the consequences of unprotected hanky-panky when I was fourteen. And she gave me a book on every kind of birth control available. Not that I ever had occasion to use the information."

Sam worked on disarming that bombshell. It exploded anyway. "So. What you're telling me is that you're a v-virgin."

"Don't you dare tease me about that. It's not my fault. I've tried—"

"Seducing Dexter?"

"Yes."

"And he was able to resist you?" Dexter was a dork, and an idiot and a fool. And a stronger man than he was. If Red started any hanky with him, he wouldn't be able to call a halt at panky.

"Yes. Don't forget, my father is his boss. If we had . . . done it, and Daddy ever found out . . . well."

"Shotgun wedding?"

"Something like that. At least your father and my grandmother don't have to worry about that."

"No. I'm beginning to see some advantages to getting old. Lillian and Archie sure sounded like they were having a good time—I could hear her giggling in the background. I guess we shouldn't worry about them."

"I'm not worried. Not exactly. And it's not that I'm a prude or anything. I just never thought of my grandmother and sex. Until I found you in her bed."

"You thought I was fooling around with your grandmother?"

"It seemed like the obvious explanation. But then I saw the handcuffs, and I was pretty sure you weren't. Having sex. But I was shocked then. And now."

"Phil was shocked, too. So was I, for that matter. It takes some getting used to."

Lily was silent for a while. Sam wished he knew if her mind was filled with the same images distracting him "Ohmigosh. If we're shocked, I can just imagine how Daddy and Mom are going to feel— they'll be mortified if this comes out. When it comes out. It's bound to come out. Lillian and Archie probably aren't being the least bit discreet."

"So what? No one's going to get upset over two seniors having a fling. Once they get used to the idea."

"Oh, you don't know my mother and father— they will be a lot more than upset. Dexter will be, too. He may—"

"What about Dexter? Think he'll break off the engagement?"

"No. Dexter is a gentleman. He keeps his word. He promised to marry me, and he will. But he's going to have a few second thoughts. What if I am a late bloomer like Lillian thinks? I'm years older than she was when her wildness came out—the wildness that made Lillian run off to Hollywood—but I could have that same wild streak. As a matter of fact, after yesterday, I'm almost sure that I do."

"Are you feeling wild, Red? Is that why you kissed me yesterday?"

Lily's head whipped around, sending her red hair flying. She glowered at him. "I did not kiss you, Mr. Hunter. You kissed me. Not that I'm complaining. I wish you'd done more than kiss me."

"Red, you've got to stop saying things like that."

"Things like what? Like I want to have sex with you? Right now."

"Yeah. Things like that. If you're not careful, some guy's going to take you up on that offer."

"But not you?"

"Not me."

"Well. I don't think that's fair. You started it. You got me all hot and bothered and ready for anything, and then you stopped. Why?"

"You know exactly why, Little Miss Innocent. You're innocent. A fact I was unaware of at the time, you may recall. I've never met a twenty-four-year-old virgin before. You ought to wear a sign."

"That's nothing I should have to apologize for. I told you . . . it's not my fault."

"It's lucky I came to my senses and called a halt before things went too far." Sam had to do some quick backpeddling. He'd almost convinced himself that he and Red could try for some of the hot, monkey sex.

But he couldn't do it. Not with a virgin.

"You didn't come to your senses. You're not making any sense at all. I do not see what difference the extent of my experience has to do with this."

"You have zero experience."

"Well. How am I going to get any experience if you won't cooperate?"

"Dexter."

"He won't help. Don't you think I've tried? Who wants to get married to someone they've never experienced? Not me."

"Red. Shut up. Or at least change the subject."

"Oh, all right. Did Archie say where they were?"

"Somewhere in Texas. I'm pretty sure they are still right here in Houston."

"We're *sooo* close. Why didn't he tell you exactly where they are?"

"They don't want us catching up with them. Dad said it would put a damper on their affair to have us giving them disapproving stares."

"It's not that I disapprove. If Lillian is having a good time, it's about time. She hasn't giggled since I can't remember when. But what if Archie has his fling and abandons her?"

"Archie would never hurt a woman."

"No? How many of his former lovers have you interviewed?"

"He doesn't have any former lovers. Archie did not cheat on my mother."

"How about before he got married? How many hearts did he break?"

"None."

"Women don't fall in love with him at first sight? You didn't inherit your fatal charm from him?"

Sam decided a change of subject was in order. "Get out the map. I want to chart a route to Cloudcroft, New Mexico."

"Avoiding the question, are we?"

"Yeah."

Lily got the map of the western United States out of the glove compartment and opened it. "Good grief. According to the mileage chart it's almost 800 miles from Houston to El Paso. We'll never make it there today."

Sam groaned. "Another night on the road?"

"Unless we want to drive straight through."

"Not a good idea. We need to be sharp. In case we meet up with Desiree and Chad again. Or Fazio and Joe Bones. I wonder what they're doing now?"

"Maybe they've given up and gone back to wherever they came from."

"Yeah." Sam didn't believe that for a minute, but if that thought gave Lily peace of mind, he wouldn't point out the flaw in her reasoning.

Someone wanted Lillian Redmond to keep quiet. If not Gus Accardo, then whoever had murdered Eric Winthrop. In his experience murderers, especially the ones who thought they'd gotten away with it, didn't give up that easily.

Nine

Tuesday afternoon Lillian and Archie strolled hand in hand along the banks of the San Antonio River. Lillian wore her favorite summer dress, a gauzy cotton in a deep shade of turquoise. The six silver and turquoise bracelets Archie had bought her at a shop in the River Walk jangled pleasantly as they swung their hands back and forth. Archie had dressed up, too. He wore a dark gray suit and a crisp white shirt. He had requested her permission—graciously given—to leave off the tie in deference to the sultry San Antonio weather.

When they arrived at the restaurant recommended by the concierge, they were seated at a window table with a view of the river. Archie ordered margaritas for them both, then picked up the dinner menu. "The Alamo was quite impressive."

Lillian nodded, watching the flat-bottomed tourist boats glide by on the narrow, winding river. "It seems strange to have that historic building in the middle of a lot of skyscrapers. It's a good thing Texans didn't tear it down to make room for another tall building."

"Oh, I don't think there was ever any danger of

that," said Archie. "Are you up for sharing an order of beef fajitas? The menu says one order serves two people."

"I'd rather have chicken."

Returning with their drinks, the waiter heard Lillian and assured them that they could have the fajitas half beef and half chicken. As soon as the order was given and they were alone again, Lillian asked, "Shall we discuss what I learned from David?" She had placed a call to her old director before leaving Houston that morning.

"Why not?" Archie looked at her. "Did you know before today that Eric Winthrop was about to dump Madeline?"

"No. If anything, I would have thought it would be the other way around—I heard Madeline complain about Eric's wandering eye once or twice. She was getting fed up with his infidelities."

"But Epstein seemed to think that Eric was getting serious about another woman. None of his casting-couch indiscretions were serious, were they?"

"Not that I know of. If Eric was seriously involved with a woman other than Madeline, I don't think it could have been someone at the studio. We would have heard about that. But if it was a civilian—someone not in the business—how will we ever find out who it was?"

"Madeline may know. If she was the jealous type, she might have hired someone to follow Eric."

"A private detective, you mean?"

"It's possible. Before Sam and Phil started pushing the security end of the business, a fair number of Hunter and Sons' clients were people checking up on their spouses or significant others."

Lillian took a sip of her margarita. "That's a sad commentary on the state of romance."

"Oh, romance is alive and well. You just have to

find the right person to be romantic with." Archie treated her to an exaggerated leer.

Lillian arched a brow and in her sultriest voice purred, "Aren't you the lucky one? You found me."

Archie reached across the table and took one of her hands in his. "I certainly did. And it only took me four decades to do it."

"Oh, Archie. You had romance in your life before now. So did I. What about your Mary? My Alan? We didn't waste those years on the wrong people."

"No. Of course we didn't. I loved Mary. And you loved your husband." Archie grinned. "But I've never believed there was only one woman for me."

Lillian laughed. "Just like a man. You wanted a harem."

"That's not what I meant. Although, now that you brought it up . . ."

"Not a chance. I'm not sharing you with anyone else."

"Oh. Jealous?"

"Of course. And, for the record, I expect you to be the same way."

"No problem there. I'm not an advocate of sharing, either."

The waiter returned with their fajitas, a stack of flour tortillas and bowls of guacamole, sour cream and pico de gallo. Conversation halted while they built their fajitas.

Once she had gotten her chicken, green pepper and onion wrapped in a tortilla and topped with guacamole, Lillian said, "I believe we were discussing Eric and his mysterious lover."

Archie had just taken a healthy bite of his fajita. Once he'd chewed and swallowed, he replied, "You have no idea who it was?"

"No. Everyone knew about Winthrop and what

happened on the sofa in his office from time to time. And we all knew about his two ex-wives. He complained about them often enough. David said Eric only mentioned this other woman one time. And he swore he didn't tell anyone about her, not even the police."

"Did he say why?"

"I asked. David said since he had no idea who Eric had been talking about, he didn't see how the information could have helped find his killer. After all, no one saw a woman enter or leave Eric's office that night."

"As far as we know. I believe I mentioned that I was a cop for a few years before I joined my father in the family business. A common problem in police investigations is people not revealing all they know because they decide it's not important. What they don't realize is that some detail they left out might be the one that leads the police to a solution."

Flashing him a smile, Lillian said, "Then we do have a chance of solving this mystery. Other people besides David may give us details they didn't give the police."

"It's already happened twice. Cathy told you that her assistant stayed late that night. I don't remember seeing his name on the list of people interviewed. David told you about Eric's infatuation with a mystery woman. With every additional fact, we have more questions to ask of the others."

"We can ask Madeline if she knew about this other woman. Of course, if she did, she may not tell us. That would give her a motive."

"Her motive couldn't have been jealousy," said Archie. "Madeline must have known about Winthrop's predilection for starlets before they got engaged."

"Yes, but David made this woman seem more

important, somehow. The one time Eric spoke about her, David said he sounded almost in awe of her. Eric Winthrop was not a man who was easily awed."

"Too bad your old director didn't have any idea who the woman was." Archie began constructing another fajita. "If I had listened to my hunch and stayed around that night—"

"Archie Goodwin Hunter! Don't you dare blame yourself for Eric's death."

Archie topped his fajita with a healthy spoonful of pico de gallo. "I don't blame myself for his death. I didn't pull the trigger. But if I'd hung around the studio that night, I might have seen the killer."

"Yes. And you might have gotten yourself killed, too. Besides, if things had happened that way, you and I wouldn't be sitting here tonight, now would we?"

Archie gave her a big grin. "No, we wouldn't. Who knows what else might have happened differently? You might have stayed in Hollywood and become a bigger star than you were."

"Well, thank heavens that didn't happen. I had my adventure. To tell you the truth, the tinsel in tinsel town had begun to tarnish even before Eric's murder. That, and becoming the overnight darling of the sleazier tabloids, ended my desire for the limelight. When Alan came to get me, I was more than ready to go home." Lillian took her last bite of fajita, chewed, swallowed and asked, "Why did you think Eric had an appointment that night?"

"He told me to take off, go home. It was late, after eight, and we had both been at the studio since early that morning. Even so, I usually stayed until he left the office. That night he didn't want me around."

"And that had never happened before? Not even when he had a date with one of the starlets?"

"No. He liked to have an audience for his dates."

"He let you watch?"

Archie laughed. "No. And we never heard anything, either—his office was soundproofed. But Winthrop always made a show of closing and locking the office door—after giving me and whoever else was in the outer office a lecherous wink. And he always told us not to disturb him for at least an hour."

"Humph. Fifteen minutes is what I always heard. The man had no stamina."

"Who told you that?"

"Several of his victims. They tried to warn the new girls. Some of us heeded the warning. Others didn't. A few of them believed they could sleep their way to stardom."

"I suppose he could have been waiting for one of them that night, but I always thought it was a man. Maybe because he never attempted to be discreet about his affairs. But maybe it was the woman—the one Winthrop told Epstein about. For some reason, he didn't want anyone to know who she was."

"You think she may be the one who killed him?"

"A triangle always has the potential of ending in violence. Maybe Eric decided to stick with Madeline, and this other woman killed him because she was jealous."

"Who could she be? And how will we ever find her? We don't have much to go on."

"We'll look through our files when we get back to the room. Make a list of names, figure out which one of them could have been having an affair with Eric."

"What if her name isn't there?"

"It will be on the log of people in the studio that night."

"Only if she came in through the main gate. There were other ways into the studio—the truck entrance at the back, the side entrance at the office building."

"Both of those were locked, according to the police reports. I personally checked the door into the office building before I left that night."

"What if Eric unlocked it after you left?" Lillian asked.

"If Eric unlocked the door and let someone in, and she left by the same door, it would have locked behind her. There would be no record of her entering or leaving."

"The wardrobe department was on the same floor as the exit door. Maybe Cathy's assistant saw her."

"If he did, he didn't tell the police."

"Cathy didn't think the police ever interviewed him."

"That's possible. The cops were so intent on pinning the murder on Gus Accardo, they could have gotten sloppy."

"I remember all too well how focused on Gus they were. They interviewed me for hours."

"You stood up to the third degree."

"It wasn't too difficult—I was telling the truth—and they never pulled out the rubber hoses. What does third degree mean, exactly? What are the first and second degrees?"

"Good question," said Archie with a chuckle. "I don't know."

Tuesday evening somewhere west of San Antonio, Lily rolled her head from side to side, then unbuckled the seat belt and arched her back. She leaned forward and touched her forehead to her knees, then raised her arms and reached for the ceiling of the car.

"What are you doing?" asked Sam.

It was the first time he'd spoken in hours. He'd clammed up shortly after she'd slipped and told him she was . . . inexperienced. What was it with men and virgins? Sam had reacted in horror, as if she had some kind of disease.

"Stretching. I'm stiff." She glanced at the clock on the dashboard. "It's six o'clock. We've been in this car for eight solid hours."

"We've stopped a few times. Don't tell me you have to pee again."

"No. But my neck is stiff, and my tail bone aches. I could use a massage. How are you as a masseur?"

"You'll never know."

"Sam, I think it's time to find a motel. Aren't you tired of being in this car?"

"Nope. Fresh as a daisy, that's me. It's only six o'clock—plenty of daylight left."

"That doesn't mean we have to keep driving. I bet we're miles and miles ahead of Lillian and Archie. They're taking a nice, leisurely approach to this trip. That's smart of them. Their way means they'll have more nights together. I think we should slow down, too."

Sam stepped on the accelerator. "It's too early to stop for the night."

"Can't we at least stop and eat? Please. I'm starving."

She heard a shuddering sigh. Sam said, "All right. We're only a few miles out of Sonora. There should be a choice of restaurants there."

Once they reached the west Texas town, Sam followed signs to a steak house. He parked, helped Lily out of the car and, his hand on her elbow, es-

corted her into the restaurant. The hostess led
them to a booth in a secluded corner of the restaurant, told them their server would be Betty and
handed them menus.

Sam opened his menu and said, "This may be
our last stop for a while. I'm thinking about driving straight through."

Lily stopped her perusal of the menu. "All the
way to California? I don't think that's a good idea,
Sam. I read somewhere that fatigue is a bigger
cause of accidents than driving drunk."

"I said I was thinking about it. I was also thinking about flying. We probably couldn't get a com-
mercial flight any sooner than El Paso, but we
might be able to rent a private plane in Fort
Stockton."

"My. You certainly are in a hurry all of a sudden."

"It's not sudden. I need to end this—the sooner,
the better."

"Scared?"

"What would I be afraid of?"

"Me. I think you're afraid of me. You won't be
able to resist me forever."

"You have nothing to do with it. I have professional reasons for wanting to get this over with. I
can interview a few people in Los Angeles before
they arrive. And I'll be able to get duplicate copies
of the old police files—Dad took the only set we
had. I'd like to be able to figure out who killed
Eric Winthrop before Dad and Lillian get there."

"Really? You think you could do that?"

"Maybe. I don't think Dad and Lillian are going
to find out anything new on the way to California.
Everyone they're stopping to talk to on the way
was interviewed by the police at the time. The police reports have got to be a better record of what

they knew back then than their current memories."

"I suppose so. Unless they were lying. A person might remember the truth better than whatever lie they told forty-five years ago."

"Hmmm. You may have a point. Plus, the reason for lying may have disappeared with the passing years."

"Lillian told me once that Eric Winthrop was a notorious womanizer. Any number of women may have wanted to kill him. Madeline Morrow, for one."

"She's in Palm Springs. Jealous husbands and boyfriends are on the list of possibles, too. And Eric's brother."

"Thomas Winthrop? I never knew he was a suspect."

"He had an alibi, if I remember right—I think he was with Madeline that night."

"I wonder why?"

"Some kind of business meeting, I think. But Thomas did inherit the studio."

"That's a pretty good motive. Did Archie ever say who he thought was the killer?"

"No. He did say that if Lillian hadn't spent the night with Accardo, Gus would have been the odds-on favorite to be charged with the murder."

Lily picked up her menu and opened it. "Lillian didn't lie about spending the night with Mr. Accardo."

"I didn't say she did."

"A lot of people think she lied. I think my parents may be among them."

"Why would they doubt her word?"

"They would rather have her be a liar than a scarlet woman."

"Your parents are—"

"—idiots," Lily finished for him.

"I was going to stay priggish."

"That, too. Lillian says that they're obsessed with propriety. I'm beginning to understand what she meant."

"How come? I mean your father is her son."

"Part of it is the bankers-must-be-above-reproach thing. And part of it is because of their scandal."

"The having to get married scandal?"

"Yes. Ever since then, they've never taken one step off the straight and narrow path to . . . wherever that path leads. Now that I think about it, all my life everyone I care about has been waiting for me to stray off that path. In other words, for me to do something scandalous."

"Everyone?"

"My parents. Granddad, when he was alive. Dexter. Dexter's parents."

"Lillian?"

"Her, too, but she at least wanted me to do something . . . maybe not scandalous, but different."

"Different?"

"My grandmother wanted me to do at least one thing that no one would expect me to do. One thing that I wanted to do."

"Yeah? Well, you've done that, haven't you? No one expected you to take off after Lillian on your own."

"That doesn't count. I didn't want to do that. I had to do it." Lily looked Sam in the eye. "There is something I want to do, though. Something that no one in my family would expect me to do. Except Lillian. Maybe."

"What?"

"I want to have sex. With you. As soon as possible."

Sam dropped his fork onto the plate. "Back to that again? Give it rest, Lily."

"Not because I've fallen in love with you. You don't have to worry about that. But this may be the only chance I'll ever have to—"

"—cheat on Dexter?"

"I wouldn't put it that way."

"How would you put it?"

"I need to do this. For me and for Dexter. The fact that I'm so attracted to you must mean something. If I have sex with another man, and I don't feel guilty after, then maybe I'm not ready for marriage."

"You want to use me?"

"Well. Yes. I know. It's selfish of me, but this is my very first chance to test my feelings for Dexter against my feelings for another man."

"You think if you can have guiltless sex with me, that will mean you're not in love with Dexter?"

"Yes."

"Forget about it, Red. I'm not into deflowering virgins."

"Oh! That's an awful thing to say." She sniffled.

"Oh, God. Are you snuffling again?"

"I don't know," she sniffed. "Is it anything like sniffling?"

"No. You sniffle when you've got a cold. Or allergies. Snuffling is that awful noise women make when they cry."

"You've made a lot of women cry, haven't you?"

"Not on purpose. I'm not into hurting women, physically or emotionally. What if we made love and you decided it was love? I'm not going to marry again."

"I'm not going to fall in love with you. I only want to make love with you. No strings, no expectations. One night of passion—maybe two or three—"

"Stop. We're not having a night of passion. I am not going to have sex with you, Red."

"Why not? What's wrong with me?"

"I told you. You're a twenty-five-year-old virgin. That makes you an endangered species."

"I'm twenty-four. It makes me ready."

"You're engaged. If you've waited this long, you ought to wait for your wedding night."

"I don't see why. Dexter didn't wait. I bet you didn't, either. Were you a virgin on your wedding night?"

"That's none of your business."

"That means you weren't. Suppose I hadn't told you about my . . . lack of experience—would you have gone to bed with me?"

"No."

"Oh, yes, you would. The top of your ear is turning red. I've been very honest with you, Sam. I would appreciate it if you would tell me the truth. Why won't you make love with me?"

"Because I choose who—with whom I have sex. I decide who, when, where and how. Me. Not you. And I make it a rule not to have sex with young, impressionable women engaged to other men, men they've known all their lives."

"Oh, yeah? I bet that's a brand new rule you just made up this minute. Don't forget, Sam, you are the one who started this. If you hadn't grabbed me and kissed me, I never would have gotten the idea that I wanted you to be my first lover."

"Don't lay a guilt trip on me. You tantalized me into kissing you. You knew exactly what you were doing."

"Oh, for heaven's sake. You just said I was inexperienced. Now you tell me that I knew exactly how to entice you into kissing me?"

"It's that combination—innocent but enticing.

You know how to entice, Red. Just like Lillian did in *Siren of Singapore*. It must be genetic."

"You really think I'm enticing?"

"Yes."

"Well, then—"

"That's it. Shut up."

Lily opened her mouth, then closed it. Maybe she had revealed too much, too soon. But once she'd started saying exactly what was on her mind, she couldn't seem to stop. She didn't want to stop. All those years of saying, yes, Mama, yes, Daddy, whatever you say, Dexter, she hadn't realized how much fun it was to let loose.

Lillian knew. She'd always known. Lillian had tried and tried to prod Lily into speaking up, speaking out, speaking her mind.

She should have listened to her grandmother and started sooner. Much sooner. Then, when Dexter had given her that C.D., she could have told him what to do with it. A giggle escaped.

"Are you laughing at me?" asked Sam.

"No. At me."

"Why?"

"Because if I don't laugh, I'll cry. And I know you wouldn't like that."

"Why do you feel like crying?"

"Because I'm a twenty-four-year-old virgin, and you don't want me."

"I never said I didn't want you."

"Do you?"

"Oh, yeah."

"I knew it. I just knew it. Here comes the waitress with our food. We can ask her to direct us to the nearest motel."

Sam turned an interesting shade of purple. "We're not asking the waitress for directions to a motel, a hotel or a bed and breakfast. I'm not having sex with you, Red. Not because I don't want you, but because it wouldn't be the right thing to do."

The waitress served them their food. Of course, the woman flirted with Sam.

As soon as she gave up and moved away from the table, Lily asked, "What's wrong about it? Two consenting adults. Who would we hurt?"

"Each other, Red. We would hurt each other."

"No . . ." She'd been about to quip "no pain, no gain," but thought better of it. Sam seemed awfully determined to resist her. Because he didn't want to hurt her. That was so sweet of him, to put her well-being above his own desires.

Lily moved her food around on her plate.

The first man she met who made her want to do wild and crazy things, and he had to be *honorable*. He refused to participate in a night of passion with a virgin who happened to be engaged to another man. If she'd had an engagement ring, Lily would have taken it off and thrown it at him.

Sam looked at her, then back at his plate. "Something wrong with your meal?"

"No. Nothing. Something's wrong with me."

"Red. There is nothing wrong with you."

"All right. Not with me. My technique. I don't know how to seduce a man."

"Oh, baby. You know exactly how to do that."

"I don't think so. You didn't have any trouble turning me down. Maybe you could tell me what I did wrong? Too much talk? I bet that was it. I shouldn't have told you what I wanted. I should have . . . what? Waited until we were alone and—"

"You did just fine. There's nothing wrong with your technique. It was honest, straightforward. Just like you."

"Well, then? Why aren't we in bed together right now? Is it some kind of guy rule? A don't-mess-around-with-another-man's-woman thing? Especially if the other man hasn't fooled around with her yet?"

"Yeah. You got it. That's the rule."

"I should have known. You're very big on rules."

"That's me. Straight-arrow Sam."

"I'll bet that's why women find you so attractive. You're safe."

"Safe? I thought I was dangerous."

"You *look* dangerous. Your profession sounds dangerous. But you're safe. It's only taken me, what? A day and a half to figure out that you're an honorable man. The kind of man who won't take advantage of a woman, who won't poach on another man's territory."

"And that makes me safe?"

"Yes, it does. You stopped me before I got hurt—you said we might hurt each other, remember? And you fired all those other women who wanted you to have sex with them. Word about that must have gotten around. You're a safe bet to fantasize about because you will never make a woman's sexy dreams about you come true. Am I making sense?"

"No." Sam didn't feel honorable. He felt like a heel. And a coward. And a fool. He *was* a fool. A smart, sexy, gorgeous woman wanted him to make love to her, and he had turned her down. To add insult to injury, she now thought of him as safe, just when he'd gotten used to the idea of being a dangerous man. "Do you want dessert?"

"Yes. A Sam sundae. You, with hot fudge sauce."

"Good God. Waitress! Check, please."

Sam threw money at the waitress and hauled Lily out of the restaurant and into the Honda. "Do not say one word, Lily Redmond. Not one word."

Lily pressed her lips together and made a zipping motion with her fingers.

"You're a very attractive and appealing woman, Red. But I am not going to be your experiment or your dessert or your lover. Do I make myself clear?"

She nodded.

Then her chin trembled. Her brown eyes grew misty.

"Oh, no. Don't try that. It won't work. I am immune to tears. Heart-of-stone Hunter, that's me."

"May I speak?" Her voice quavered.

"Do you have to?"

She nodded again.

"All right. But no more sex talk."

"I am not going to c-cry. You hurt my feelings, but I know you didn't do that on purpose. But when a person offers a person something important, and the person treats the offer like something disgusting, then——"

"How can you say that? When have I ever said or done anything that made you think I was disgusted with you?"

"You sneered when you said you weren't into deflowering virgins. You did, Sam. You acted as if being inexperienced was worse than being a serial killer. I know you said no sex talk. I'm not talking about sex. I'm talking about respect and kindness and compassion. None of which you demonstrated with that remark."

"I'm sorry."

"I know you didn't mean it that way."

"No, I didn't. But I should not have sneered. That was thoughtless. It's just that you're so damn——"

"Yes? So damn . . . ?"

"Much fun. So damn much fun."

"Oh. I thought you were going to say so damn sexy. Or smart. Or beautiful."

"You're all those things, too. But an adventure——

the kind of adventure you're talking about should be fun. Losing your innocence would be painful. Not enjoyable. Not fun."

"Not necessarily. It doesn't always hurt. And even if it does, it's only for a little while and then—"

"Stop. How do you know all this?"

"I've been a bridesmaid five times, Sam. Every one of the brides has told me and our other girl-friends about her first time in exquisite detail. Oh, and only one of those first times coincided with a wedding night. That one and one other deflower-ing involved the groom. What do you think women talk about at bridal showers anyway?"

"You just told me more than I ever wanted to know."

"Sam. This is the twenty-first century not the Victorian age. Virginity isn't important."

"Oh, no? Then why haven't you lost yours along the way to the ripe old age of almost twenty-five?"

"Because I'm discriminating. You're the first man I've met who met my very high standards."

"What about Dexter?"

"I'm not talking about fiancé standards. I'm talking sex here."

"Stop. I don't want to hear any more."

"Coward."

"Damn right."

"In all your vast experience, you have never made love to a virgin?"

"Never."

"That's why you're afraid. The unknown is al-ways scary."

"Yeah. So why aren't you afraid?"

"Knowledge is power. I know all about first times. I could talk you through it."

Sam choked. "Talk me through it?"

Lily couldn't tell if he was shocked or outraged. "I'm sure you wouldn't need much help. You must have heard stuff from other men about their first times. Haven't you?"

"No."

"Men don't talk about this kind of thing?"

"No."

"That's odd. Women talk about sex all the time."

"Men talk about sex."

"But not about their first time?"

"Not in detail."

"Details are what make it interesting. For instance, Betsy Baxter said—look, there's a Motel 6. Aren't you ready to stop?"

"I'm not stopping. Not until we get to California. Maybe not then. I may keep on driving to Hawaii."

"I really am making you nervous, aren't I?"

"You are playing with fire. You're going to get burned if you don't shut up."

"Now. See. All I did was talk about sex, and you're aroused. Betsy told me that sex talk was a subtle form of foreplay."

"Subtle? You call this subtle?"

"Not the right word?"

"There are no words. Shut up."

Ten

Sam drove for hours. Just when Lily thought he really was going to keep going forever, Sam pulled into a motel on the outskirts of Fort Stockton, Texas. He got them rooms on different floors. Then he escorted Lily to the elevator and her room, handed over her suitcase and closed the door in her face.

Lily turned her back and leaned against the door. Time was slipping away, and she hadn't begun to reach her goal. But how could she? Did she really want Sam to compromise his principles?

Darn tooting.

The trouble was, she didn't know how. Kissing him back with all the enthusiasm she could muster hadn't worked. Telling him exactly what she wanted hadn't worked. The man thought he was being noble—putting her well-being above his own desires. Sam Hunter was stubborn.

But oh, so sexy.

Thinking about Sam's broad shoulders and in-fomercial muscles made her toes curl and her knees quiver. Watching his eyes change from sea green to almost black, seeing that one unruly lock of hair fall onto his forehead gave her the shivers. Remembering how he'd burst into the ladies room to rescue her added a big glop of icing on the cake of Sam's appeal.

If she didn't have him, and soon, she would dry up and wither away.

Dry up and wither away? Because of sex? Or lack thereof? Surely not. She hadn't dried up because Dexter had avoided consummating their relationship—even during adolescence when hormones and curiosity had made her eager to try anything.

Why now? Why Sam?

A tiny voice way in the back of her head whispered, *You're in love.*

Lily slid down the motel room door until her bottom hit the floor. She sat there, arms wrapped around her bent knees, staring into space. Love? She couldn't be in love with Sam Spade Hunter. *Why not?* asked the tiny voice.

Why not, indeed? Sam was brave, smart and funny. She'd already mentioned sexy, but Lily added it to the list again.

But there was Dexter. She was supposed to be in love with him. Was she? Everyone, including her, expected her to be in love with Dexter. All her life, or at least for as long as love and marriage had appeared on her personal radar, Lily had known she and Dexter were going to marry some day.

A person was supposed to love the person she married.

She was engaged to marry Dexter. Had she told herself she was in love with him because she knew that was what he expected, what their parents wanted, what everyone she knew had thought of as inevitable?

Everyone, that is, but Lillian.

A person could not love two men at the same time.

If she loved Dexter, she could not love Sam. And if she loved Sam, she could not love Dexter. Sam? Dexter? Dexter? Sam?

Sam. Definitely Sam.

Lily got that hollow-in-the-middle feeling. A not-so-tiny voice, a voice which sounded suspiciously like Lillian's voice, said, *I told you so!*

And she had. Lillian had told her over and over to be true to herself, to say what she thought, to do what she wanted to do, to fall in love with the right man, not the man her parents had chosen for her when she was a baby.

That was why her grandmother had handcuffed Sam to her bed. Lillian had wanted her to see a man who would make her think about what she really wanted. Well. She had thought. She knew what she wanted. Now she even knew why she wanted Sam so desperately. She loved him.

Golly. Now what?

She couldn't tell Sam. He wouldn't believe her. Or if he did believe she had fallen in love with him, more or less at first sight, he would remember his ex-wife—the woman he had met on Tuesday and married on Sunday—and run like hell.

Sam would never fall in love with another stranger—he claimed he would get serious only about someone he had known for at least six years. That was his way of saying he would never fall in love and marry again, period.

Nope. Sam would never believe she had met him on Monday and fallen in love with him by Tuesday. Not in real, forever kind of love.

He might believe she had fallen in lust with him, however. How long did lust take? Not long. One look at Sam sprawled on Lillian's bed had done it for her. And something of the sort had happened to him, too. Sam was the one who had dragged her out of the car and kissed her the first day they'd met.

She could build on that. Lust could and often did mature into love. The next step was obvious—she would have to seduce Sam. But how? He had avoided kissing her again. He had refused her offer of no-strings sex. Just as well—that offer was off the table. Any sex they had now would have strings—but she wouldn't tell him that. He was smart. He could figure it out for himself. After he had fallen in love with her. But seduction would come first.

Lily sighed. She wished her grandmother would talk to her. She needed help, and Lillian Leigh Redmond would know exactly how to seduce Sam.

"I am not a temptress, but I played one in the movies." Lily could remember Lillian saying that, using her super sultry voice, when her grandfather had teased her about being a femme fatale. It was a well-known fact that femme fatales always got their man. Not for forever, of course.

She didn't want forever.

All right, she *did* want forever.

And she hoped a successful seduction would lead to love, followed by marriage and children. Lily wished for a lifetime with Sam. But she would take what she could get. If that turned out to be only a tiny bit of Sam's time—one or two days, a week at the most—she would settle for that. For all she knew, what she thought was love could turn out to be nothing more than infatuation. After she had her way with Sam, he might not seem so . . . Sam.

He had said she could get hurt. That didn't scare her. She had managed to avoid any serious heartache for almost twenty-five years. It was time for her to venture out of her safe little cocoon, past time for her to take a chance and risk getting hurt. Lillian had lost her first love and her career before she'd turned nineteen. That hadn't kept her from having a loving and lasting marriage with another man.

Sam was worth the risk of a broken heart.

Lillian must have known that when she'd hand-cuffed Sam to her bed. And Lillian knew all about seduction, in real life and in the movies. She had seduced a notorious mobster when she was only eighteen. Lily regretted that she had never asked Lillian how she'd done that. But she had seen Lillian's movies.

Tahiti Temptress and *Siren of Singapore* were better known, but her personal favorite was *The Belle of Baton Rouge*. In that one, Lillian had been cast as a sexy southern seductress who came between the hero and his New York fiancée with the usual disastrous result. The hero betrayed his fiancée; the fiancée cried a bucket or two of tears before she came to her senses, forgave the hero and won him back. At the end Lillian, defeated by true love, slunk away into the bayou and was eaten by an alligator.

But before Lillian had gotten her comeuppance, she had seduced the hero at his engagement party. How had she done it? Lily let the scenes from the movie play in her mind.

Lillian had arrived at the engagement party late, dressed for seduction in a slinky black gown. The hero was on the terrace alone, smoking a cigarette. He had just had an argument with his fiancée. All sweet and sympathetic concern, Lillian asked what was bothering him. He told Lillian about the fight and asked her advice.

Lillian took him by the hand and led him to a bench in a dark corner of the terrace. While the hero expounded on the reasons for the argument, Lillian had kept her eyes on his mouth. She stared at his mouth, and she put her hand on his thigh and stroked it. Lillian had kept it up until the hero gradually became aware of her sultry looks and sensual touches. First he stuttered; then he gave her a few tortured looks. Finally, with an audible groan, he pulled her into his arms and kissed her passionately.

A crescendo of music, and the screen had faded to black.

Everyone knew what that meant.

All right. Time to review. She had to get Sam talking about something, then stare at his mouth. Touch him. Stare and stroke. She could do that.

But not when she was on the second floor in room 2230 and Sam was in room 3109 on the third floor. Lily picked up the phone and called the front desk. A short time and a generous tip later, and Lily was in room 3111. There was no connecting door between her room and Sam's, but the two rooms had outside balconies separated by nothing more than a wrought-iron railing.

She'd gotten close to Sam, but not close enough. The next step would be getting into his room. She couldn't hope for as dramatic an entrance as Lillian had made in the movie—for one thing, she hadn't packed a spectacularly sexy dress. Since she'd thought she was going to Disney World with her grandmother, she hadn't packed anything the least bit slinky.

Lily opened her suitcase and examined the contents.

She had shorts, jeans, capris, various blouses and tees, all in cotton. One sundress, another dress suitable for wearing to church, and a couple of unisex—make that sexless—nightshirts to sleep in. Lily briefly considered going to Sam's room in the buff, but decided she wasn't that brave. The balconies overlooked the motel swimming pool, and there were several people still lounging about around the pool.

Lily continued unpacking her suitcase. At the very bottom she found a cropped-top tee in soft cotton. The tee was hot pink, and she had never worn it in public. She wasn't sure why she'd packed it. Rummaging around in the pile of clothes on the bed, she found the bikinis with the hot pink hearts scattered on a white background.

Frowning, Lily looked at the two items of clothing she held clutched in her hand. She couldn't go to Sam's room wearing nothing but a tee shirt and her underpants. That wouldn't be at all subtle. And Lillian had been subtle, slowly letting the man she wanted figure out that she wanted him.

Sam had stared at her bare legs the first time he'd seen her, and he'd remembered that Lillian had worn shorts and a tight sweater in *Tahiti Temptress.* Lily found the shorts and added them to the cropped tee and her panties. She ignored the bras scattered on the bed.

At the last minute, she tossed the bikinis into the suitcase. The shorts and tee shirt would do nicely, she decided. Too bad about the hot pink color, but maybe her bare legs and midriff would be enough to keep Sam from noticing that the tee clashed with her hair.

Lily took a leisurely bath, using a liberal amount of the gardenia-scented bath salts she had packed. She dried off, donned her shorts, tee shirt and strappy sandals. Lily wiped the steam off the bathroom mirror. The hot bath had made her hair curl just enough. Lily used her fingers to tease the curls into a sexy tangle. She didn't need blusher—her lascivious thoughts were enough to make her cheeks an attractive shade of pink. A touch of gloss to put a shine on her mouth, and she was ready.

Lily took a deep breath.

She walked across the room to the sliding glass doors. Easing the door open, she stepped onto the balcony. There was a light in Sam's room. Heart pounding, Lily stepped across the railing onto his balcony.

He had closed the curtains.

She tried the door. It was locked.

Lily knocked on the door.

Sam opened the curtain. He had taken off his shirt. Lily's mouth went dry, and she wasted several seconds ogling his chest before she remembered she was supposed to be staring at his mouth.

Sam took one look—a long one—and opened the door. Only a crack, not wide enough for her to enter.

"How did you get here?" he asked. "Climb up a drain pipe?"

Lily shook her head and stared at his mouth. She thought he was staring back, but with her gaze focused on his mouth, she couldn't tell exactly where he was looking. She had the impression his stare was aimed lower, at her braless breasts, or her bare midriff.

Sam spoke. "You had them change your room, didn't you?"

She nodded, and kept staring. She couldn't stroke, because the glass door was between them. Improvising, Lily put her hands on the glass and stared harder. She felt like her eyes were bugging out. While Sam's eyes were still glued to her torso, she blinked rapidly.

Sam's gaze shifted to her eyes a second after she resumed staring at his mouth. "Why don't you say something? Is something wrong? Did you hear from Lillian?"

He opened the door wider. Wide enough that Lily managed to squeeze inside his room.

"Hello, Sam." Her voice was husky. "How are you?"

"Fine. How are you?" Sam's tone was wary.

Lily stared at his mouth. She sighed. "Not so fine."

"You don't feel well? Are you sick?" He sounded more suspicious than concerned.

"No. I don't think so. I feel . . . strange, though."

"Strange? Where?"

"Here." She put a hand on her bare abdomen. "And here." She put her other hand on her heart—which happened to be under her left breast.

Sam's hand came up.

Lily held her breath. He was going to put his hand on hers. His long fingers would graze her breast.

His hand dropped to his side, and he took a step back. "Should I call a doctor? Take you to an emergency room?"

Lily shook her head and took two steps closer to Sam. He took three steps back. Staring at his mouth wasn't working, and she couldn't get close enough to stroke. "I know what's wrong with me."

"You do? What?"

"I've got the fever. You've got the cure." She launched herself at him.

Sam caught her, his hands going to her waist. Her naked waist. His touch on her bare skin had her moaning. "Oh, Sam." Her hands slid up his naked chest and wrapped around his neck. Lily stood on tiptoe and pulled his mouth close to hers.

Before their lips touched, she felt his grip on her waist tighten. He pushed her away.

"Sam? Don't you want me? I want you."

"Go. Away. Now." His voice was hoarse.

"I. Don't. Want. To." She threw herself at him again.

Sam feinted to the right and moved left. Her momentum carried her forward, and Lily ended up facedown on the bed. She rolled over, raised herself on her elbows and grinned at him. "Well. This is exactly where I wanted to be." Lily sat up and patted the bed. "Why don't you join me?"

Sam stared at Lily. There was a lot of Lily to stare at. Her long legs were bare, one bent at the knee, the other straight. When she'd twisted around, her tee shirt had twisted, too, tightening and molding to her full, firm breasts. Sam's palms began to itch. He had to touch. Now. Or he would go up in flames.

He moved a step closer to the bed.

"Sam?" Lily sighed his name. She held out her arms.

Sam fell on her. His mouth found hers at the same time his hands found her breasts. His senses overloaded, and Sam couldn't think. But he could feel. And that was enough. More than enough. His hands had minds of their own again, and they were moving all over Lily from her wild red hair to her silky shoulders, back to her breasts. Her tee shirt inched higher as she writhed beneath him. He shoved it up, and his hands felt soft, bare flesh.

Lily's hands were matching his caress for caress. She stroked his shoulders, his back, slid her hands under the waistband of his jeans and clutched at his buttocks.

"Sam?" Lily said his name against his mouth. "You're squishing me." She sounded breathless.

Sam rolled off her onto his back. Before he had caught his breath, Lily crawled on top of him. She straddled him and pulled off her tee. Sam's hands reached for her bare breasts. His fingers teased her nipples into tight pearls. Lily wiggled, gasped, sighed. She leaned forward, found his mouth with her lips and kissed him.

His hands moved from her breasts to her smooth, silky back. Sam stroked the indentation of her spine from her nape to the waistband of her shorts. He found the button and unbuttoned it, then unzipped the zipper. Sam rolled again, onto his side. Lily fell next to him, facing him, their lips still joined.

His hand reached inside her shorts. "Lily Redmond. You're not wearing panties."

"I didn't think I'd need them," she gasped.

"You were right about that." Sam shoved the shorts past her knees. She kicked free of them. "Don't move," he said.

Sam stood up, unzipped his jeans and shoved them and his briefs off. He took a breath and stood looking down at Lily.

Her gaze was on his groin. Sam grinned. She looked . . . impressed? Blinking, Sam cleared the sensual mist clouding his vision. He looked closer. No. Not impressed.

Lily's brown eyes were opened wide. A small furrow creased her brow. She looked worried. More than worried.

She looked scared. Terrified, in fact.

Damn. Sam mentally hit his forehead with the palm of his itchy hand. "You're a virgin." He bent over, picked up his briefs and put them on. Lily's tee shirt and shorts were next to the bed. He picked them up and dropped them on her naked body.

"Sam! What are you doing?" She sat up. The clothes slithered onto the bed.

He pulled his jeans on and walked to the door. "Seeing you to your room. Put your shirt on. Let's go."

"No. Why?"

He didn't turn around. He couldn't look at her. "Lily. You're a virgin. An engaged virgin. You don't want to do something you'll regret."

"I won't regret it. I swear I won't, Sam. You don't understand. I don't love Dexter. I love you."

Sam faced her. "No, you don't. Love doesn't happen like this. After a day, two days. Trust me, Lily. Whatever you think you're feeling, it isn't love."

She took a deep breath. Her bare breasts jiggled. "Okay. I don't love you. I'll trust your judgment on that. But I want you. A lot. A whole lot. I want you to be my first lover."

Sam strode to the bed. He picked up her tee shirt and pulled it over her head. She refused to put her arms through the arm holes, but at least her breasts were covered. Sam got her long legs into the shorts and pulled them up to her waist. He didn't bother with the zipper.

Tossing her over his left shoulder, Sam headed for the balcony door.

Lily tried wiggling free, and he gave her bottom a pop. "Ouch! Don't do this. Please. I'm begging you. Please, Sam. Don't throw me out."

As they went through the sliding glass doors, she grabbed the door jamb and held on. Sam backed into the room until she was forced to let go. He draped her around his neck and held her legs with one hand, her hands with the other. "Sam! Put me down. I want you to make love to me. Please!"

"No." He got her through the door and lifted her over the railing. Sam deposited her on her balcony and beat a hasty and inglorious retreat to his own room.

As he slid the glass door closed, Lily yelled at him. "Sam, come back here! This minute! If you don't, I'll jump off this balcony. I mean it."

"Be sure you aim for the deep end of the pool. And jump feet first." Sam closed the door and let the curtain fall into place.

Alone in his room, Sam sat down—it was either sit or fall down. His knees had almost buckled when he'd carried Lily from the room. Not because she was heavy, she wasn't.

Because he wanted to believe her.

He wanted Lily to love him.

But he knew love had nothing to do with what Lily was feeling. She wanted an adventure, and she'd decided he was it. If she thought about it, she'd realize that adventures were short term, not lifetime events.

Sam locked the balcony door. He didn't trust Lily not to try again, and he didn't trust himself to resist her twice. No two ways about it—he had to come up with a way to throw cold water on Red's hot ideas before they both got burned.

Lily spent the remainder of the night staring at the digital clock next to her bed. She watched it click away the minutes and hours until six o'clock. Then she got out of bed, took a shower and dressed in jeans and a pale green blouse. Lily sat on the end of the bed—there was a mirror opposite—and used cosmetics to conceal the shadows under her eyes.

While she brushed her hair, a tear escaped and slid down her cheek. She dashed it away. Tears wouldn't sway Sam. He hated weeping women. He hated her. She'd *begged* him to make love to her, and he'd rejected her. He'd tossed her out of his bed, and he'd thrown her out of his room. To top it all off, he'd told her to take a flying leap into the swimming pool.

The only thing he hadn't done was laugh at her.

To her face. He'd probably snickered himself to sleep last night.

There was a knock at her door.

Lily tossed her hairbrush into the suitcase and closed it. She opened the door. Sam stood there looking grim but rested. He didn't have dark circles or bags under his eyes. His green eyes were clear as glass. Sam had slept. While she had tossed and turned and stared at the clock, Sam Spade Hunter had *slept*.

"Good morning, Red." His voice was quiet, cautious.

"What's good about it?" she snarled. She handed him her suitcase and headed for the elevator. "Let's get out of here."

Juggling the two suitcases, Sam caught up with her just as the elevator doors opened. "Breakfast?"

"Not hungry."

"I am. And I need coffee. Lily. I'm sorry—"

The elevator doors opened on the first floor. Lily exited. Sam followed. "The restaurant is to the left. You may not be hungry, but I am. I'll check out, load the car and meet you there."

Lily walked to the restaurant and sat down at the first empty table for two. She had to get over being angry. Even if anger did mask other, more painful emotions. She couldn't snap and snarl at Sam all the way to California. And she couldn't take time to deal with those other feelings. Not now. Later. When she was home again, and Lillian was home and safe, she would think about what she'd done and why she'd done it.

But not this morning. What was there to think about, anyway? Sam had made his position clear. He wanted her, but not enough to betray his principles. Sam would not have a quicky affair with an engaged woman. No, that wasn't it. Sam would not have sex with an engaged virgin. That was what had stopped him. Not her engagement. Her maidenhead.

Lily ground her teeth together. She should never have told him. But she had, and Sam would never forget it.

And he wouldn't forget that she'd said she loved him, either. Even if he didn't believe her. He thought she was too . . . young or too stupid or too inexperienced to know that what she felt was *love*.

Sam would never fall in love with her. They wouldn't be together long enough. Sam would not believe that love was the emotion pulling them close, not until they'd been together for at least six years.

They weren't going to be together for six days.

There was absolutely no reason for her to hang around with Sam Hunter. She would continue on to Cloudcroft and points west by herself and wait for Lillian at the Beverly Hills Hotel. Why hadn't she left last night? She had her set of keys to her car. But she'd been too hurt, too humiliated, to think straight during the long night.

She would do it. Today, at the first opportunity, she would ditch Sam.

The decision made, Lily felt better. In control of her own destiny. She might not be a successful seductress, but at least she'd tried. Lillian would be proud of her.

Lily discovered she was ravenous. When Sam joined her, she had a plate of eggs, bacon, grits and hash browns on the table in front of her, and she was buttering her second biscuit.

He gave his order to the waiter. "I'll have the same," he said, pointing to the stack of food in front of her. "Plus a side order of pancakes." When the waiter left, he said, "I thought you weren't hungry."

"I changed my mind." She took a big bite of the biscuit and glared at him.

"You're mad at me."

Swallowing, Lily managed a smile. "No, I'm not. What makes you think that?"

"You have every right to be mad. I should never have . . . let things go as far as they did."

"No. You should have let them go a lot farther."
She picked up a slice of bacon with her fingers and
began nibbling. Between small bites, she said, "But
you didn't, and that's that. I won't bother you
again."

"Lily—"

The waiter brought Sam's food.

"And I won't embarrass you with protestations
of love again. Much as I hate to admit it, I've decided you were right. I don't love you. I couldn't
be in love with someone like you."

"Someone like—what's that supposed to
mean?"

"A once-burned-twice-shy coward."

"You think I'm a coward."

"About love, yes. You're afraid."

"I'm not scared. I'm smart. I learn from my past
mistakes."

"Uh huh." Lily kept shoveling food in her
mouth. Eggs, bacon, grits and hash browns. She
ate every bite.

Sam was pushing his food around on his plate.

Lily pointed to the pancakes. "Are you going to
eat those?"

"You want them?"

"Uh huh."

He shoved the plate to her side of the table.
"Lily. We need to talk."

Lily poured syrup on the pancakes. "No, we
don't. Eat your breakfast."

"I'm not hungry. Red, I never meant to hurt
you."

"I'm not hurt." She took one last bite of pan-
cake, then pushed away from the table. "I'm full as
a tick. Are you finished?"

"Yeah. I'm finished all right." He tossed some
bills on the table and helped Lily out of her chair.

"I'll drive," she said, when they reached her car.

"Fine." Sam opened the driver's side door for her, then walked around the car and climbed into the passenger seat.

Lily started the car. "Which way? Back to I-10?"

"No. Follow the signs to Pecos." Sam checked the Texas map. "That's State Highway 285."

Lily found the turnoff and noted that the mileage sign said Pecos was fifty-two miles away. She kept her eye on the odometer, and when they'd gone twenty miles, she started watching for a gas station. She finally saw one, with a convenience store attached, and pulled off the highway into the station.

"What are you stopping for? We don't need gas. I filled the tank before we left Sonora."

"I need to pee."

"Oh. All right."

Lily got out of the car and headed for the ladies' room.

When she returned, Sam was already behind the wheel. "I'll drive for a while," he said.

She climbed into the passenger seat and put on the seat belt. Before Sam started the engine, she said, "Oh, Sam. I forgot. Would you get me a bottle of water?"

"If you drink water, we'll just have to stop again."

"Are we in a hurry?"

"Yeah. We are."

"I'm thirsty. And staying hydrated is very important in the desert."

Sam unhooked his seat belt and got out of the car. "Fine. I'll get you water."

As soon as he went into the convenience store, Lily climbed into the driver's seat. Sam had taken the keys, but she'd anticipated that. She put her key into the ignition and started the car. She pulled out of the gas station the same time Sam came out of the store.

Lily got one look at his astonished expression before he disappeared from view.

Sam stared openmouthed as Lily drove away in the Honda. His heart rate speeded up, and breathing got hard. It took Sam a few seconds to realize what that meant. Panic. He was having a panic attack because Lily had run away. Away from him and straight toward trouble.

Taking a deep breath, Sam switched the bottle of water to his left hand and reached in his pocket for the cell phone. He called Phil.

For once, his brother answered on the first ring.

"Lily's gone," said Sam. "We've got to get word to Dad."

"What do you mean, gone?" Phil asked.

"G. O. N. E. Not here."

"You lost Lily?"

"More like she lost me. On purpose. I've got to get her back, Phil. Before the other people chasing her realize she's on her own. Oh, God. What if Chad is waiting for her somewhere?" Sam's stomach knotted. He could feel beads of sweat popping out on his forehead.

"Hey! Calm down, bro. What happened?"

"We stopped at a gas station. She said she had to use the facilities. Then she asked me to get her a bottle of water. When I got out of the car, she drove off."

"Why would she do that? What did you do to her? Oh."

"Not a damn thing. What did that 'oh' mean?"

"There's only one reason Lily would run from

you. Damn it, Sam. I knew this was going to happen sooner or later."

"What? What happened?"

"A nice girl fell in love with you. And you didn't believe her because of Elly. Listen, Sam, just because—"

"Shut up. Lily did not fall in love with me. I—" Sam almost said he'd fallen in love with her. That couldn't be true. He'd learned a long time ago that love didn't happen in a day or two. "I did hurt her feelings, though. Not intentionally. But I did."

"Why'd you go and do something like that? Dad's going to be upset if you let something happen to Lillian's favorite granddaughter."

Sam ground his teeth together. "I know that. Don't you think I know that? I'm pretty sure I know where she's going—to Cloudcroft, New Mexico, to see David Epstein. Chad and Desiree may be there already. Waiting for Lillian to show up. Or waiting for Lily. Chad hurt her the last time—"

"He what? You didn't tell me that. What did he do?"

"He pinched her—in a sensitive place. And he bit her ear. The guy's a psycho. No telling what he might try if he has more time with her—"

"Hold on. I've got something for you. I found out that Desiree works for the Santori for Governor campaign."

"Santori? Senator Santori? Gus Accardo's nephew?"

"The one and only. I can't figure out why Santori would want to shut Lillian up. He can't be helping Gus. There's never been any love lost between those two branches of the family."

"Maybe Santori doesn't want his uncle arrested for murder—bad publicity for a tough-on-crime candidate. What kind of work do they do for Santori's campaign?"

"I'm not sure. I called Santori's office, but after confirming that she works for the campaign, they clammed up. I'm talking to the opposition's campaign manager later today. He may know more about her. And Chad Boyd. No one at Santori headquarters would admit knowing him. I have a feeling they may be Santori's dirty tricks squad."

Sam's stomach twisted into a tighter knot. "I think you're right. And I don't want them playing their tricks on Lily."

"How can I help? What do you want me to do?"

"I need a car. Can you call an agency and have them bring me one? I'm at . . . Where am I?" Sam asked the attendant.

Chris—his name was embroidered on his shirt pocket—said, "About thirty miles northwest of Fort Stockton, twenty from Pecos. You needing to get somewhere fast?"

"Yeah. Have you got a car you'd loan me?"

"Nope. But I know a fella with a helicopter. Would that do?"

"Phil, hold on. I may not need a car after all. I'll call you back."

"You better. I want to know what—"

Sam ended the call. "Tell me about this helicopter."

"Like I said, fella up in Pecos has one. Two, actually. Herds cattle with them."

"A helicopter is perfect. I'll be able to get to Cloudcroft before her. Come on, Chris, let's go."

"Hey. I can't leave the station."

"Do you have the guy's number? I'll call him."

The station attendant didn't know the number. Sam had to waste more minutes calling information and getting the number for a helicopter service.

It took more time to convince the pilot to drive
to the gas station to pick him up—plenty of time
for Sam to think about Lily and what he was going
to do to her once he had her safe with him again.

She would pay for this. When he caught up with
Lily, he would give her exactly what she wanted.
Him.

Eleven

A few minutes after eight o'clock Wednesday night, Lily passed the Cloudcroft city limits sign. She pulled into a strip mall's empty parking lot, intending to call and warn Mr. Epstein before she arrived on his doorstep. Her cell phone was not in her purse. An image of Sam putting the phone in his pocket popped into her brain. Sam had her phone.

Looking around, Lily spotted a pay phone outside a cleaners. She got out of the car, walked to the phone and dialed Epstein's number. When he answered, she explained who she was. Mr. Epstein's voice sounded strained, as if he were tired, but he agreed to see her and gave her directions to his house.

Lily turned off the state highway and onto the narrow dirt road Mr. Epstein had told her how to recognize. A narrow, winding dirt road. Around one curve, her headlights picked out a beige van blocking the road. Lily hit the brakes. She put the car in reverse, but before she could back away from the danger, Chad opened her car door.

He had a gun.

Why had she ever gone off by herself? No matter how embarrassed and hurt she'd been by Sam's rejection, she should never have let her emotions overrule her common sense. Sam would know how to deal with a man with a gun. She didn't. Over the pounding of her heart, Lily tried to think of a way out.

Chad didn't wait for her to come up with a plan. "Hello, Cupcake. Did you miss me?" He reached across her, brushing his forearm against her breasts, and jerked the keys from the ignition. Then he unhooked the seat belt and pulled her out of the car.

"Help!" Lily yelled. "Mr. Epstein!"

"Not gonna hear you, babe. His cabin's another couple of miles up the road. And you're alone. That's a bonus. We thought we'd have to deal with your boyfriend. No one can help you now." He motioned with the gun. "Get in the van. Now."

Desiree opened the van's rear door, and Chad shoved Lily inside. She landed on her knees, but it didn't hurt as much as it might have—she landed on a large pillow. There were two of them in the back of the van, spread out like a mattress.

"Cozy, huh?" Chad put a knee in the small of her back, forcing her into a prone position. He leaned down and whispered in her ear. "We're going to have a lot of fun tonight, Cupcake."

Desiree climbed into the driver's seat and turned to look at Chad. "Move her car. We can't just leave it in the middle of the road. Pull the car off the road—hide it in those trees over there."

"Why hide it? Who's gonna care about an abandoned car?"

"The police. Epstein's probably calling them even as we speak—why did you have to pull a gun on him? Why do you even have a gun? Santori said low profile. No violence."

"I didn't use the gun. And if I hadn't pulled it, he would have told Cupcake not to pay him a visit."

"I know he's calling the police. If he hasn't all ready, he will when she doesn't show up at his cabin. We've got to get out of here." Desiree sounded almost hysterical.

For some reason, the other woman's hysteria calmed her down. Lily lay still and absorbed what she'd heard. *Santori.* That was a name she hadn't heard before, the name of the person who gave Chad and Desiree orders. She had to remember that. If she ever got away from them, she needed to tell Sam. . . . Lily's heartbeat speeded up again. What if she never saw Sam again? What if she never saw anyone again?

Lily closed her eyes and took a couple of deep breaths. That was not the way to think. Desiree had said this Santori person did not want violence. Shooting someone was violent. Chad wouldn't shoot her.

Feeling better about her chances of survival, Lily resumed her analysis of Desiree's remarks. Chad and Desiree had known that Mr. Epstein was expecting her. They had been with him when he took her call. Chad had threatened him with a gun—no wonder his voice had sounded strained. But he must be all right if Desiree expected him to call the police. Lily said a quick prayer that he would do just that.

"All right. Don't get in a panic. Let me tie her up first." Chad stuffed the pistol in the waistband of his jeans and reached for a coil of rope. "Bought this just for you, Cupcake. Clothesline, made out of cotton. Be gentler to your skin than scratchy old hemp. Wouldn't want to leave nasty old rope burn marks on you, now would we?"

In a matter of seconds, Chad had her hands tied

behind her and her ankles bound together. "Be right back, babe. Don't go anywhere." He giggled.

Lily managed to flop over onto her back and sit up. She scooted so that her back was to the side of the van. "What are you going to do with me?"

Desiree twisted around and looked at her. "Nothing. I'm not going to do anything to you. All I ever wanted was to talk to your grandmother."

"Why? Who sent you to talk to her?" Lily thought it prudent to pretend she hadn't heard the name Santori.

"Never you mind. You better tell Chad what he wants to know, and fast. If you do, I think I can talk him into letting you go."

"Let me go now, before he comes back."

"I can't do that. He's got a gun. I may be able to control Chad for a while, as long as you tell him where your grandmother is. But the longer you keep quiet, the longer he'll get to play with you. I don't think you'll like the games he plays."

"What do you want to know?" asked Lily. It was an effort not to whimper. The thought of Chad and his games made her feel as if spiders were crawling all over her.

"For starters, who was the man you were traveling with?"

"Sam Hunter. He's a private detective. I hired him to help me find my grandmother."

Chad returned to the van in time to hear Lily's response.

"A private dick, huh?" He climbed into the van and shut the door. Chad squatted in front of Lily and asked, "So. What did you do with him?"

"I fired him. He wasn't getting the job done. I don't know where my grandmother is. If that's what you want from me, you're out of luck."

Chad giggled. "Nuh huh, Cupcake. You're the one who's out of luck."

"Chad. If she doesn't know, she doesn't know. Why don't we let her go? We can find Lillian without her. We've got her address book. I can figure out where she's going next."

"Yeah, right," sneered Chad. "Like you figured out she'd come here to visit Epstein?"

"So Lillian skipped him. We know she has to go to Hollywood. We'll catch up with her there."

"We'll catch up with her all right, and we'll let her know we have her granddaughter. As long as we have Cupcake, we can make the old lady do whatever we want her to do. Drive, Desiree. And keep your eyes on the road. You don't need to know what's going on back here."

Desiree started the van.

Chad jerked on Lily's ankles, pulling her flat on her back on the pillows. "Soft pillows, huh? I got them just for you."

Lily tried to get her knees up, but before she could manage it, Chad fell on top of her.

Lily screamed again.

Chad laughed, his wet mouth next to her ear. "You're gonna make yourself hoarse if you keep that up. And we wouldn't want you to lose your voice. 'Cause you're gonna talk, babe. Sooner or later, you're gonna tell us everything we want to know." He reared up and straddled her, one knee on either side of her hips. "Later's okay by me, by the way. I've had a lot of time thinking up things I want to do to you."

Lily shook her head. "It won't do you any good. I don't know where Lillian is."

"Too bad. Guess you'll just have to take whatever I give you then." Chad unbuttoned the top button on Lily's blouse.

Lily squeezed her eyes shut. She couldn't stand seeing Chad looming over her, that sick smirk on his face. She felt his knuckles brush her bare skin as each button came undone.

When Chad reached the last button, Lily opened her eyes. Chad shoved the blouse open. "Hey, Desiree. Cupcake likes fancy underwear." He traced the lacy edge of her bra with his finger. His touch made Lily's skin crawl. "Lacy, you know? Pink. I thought redheads weren't supposed to wear pink."

Lily forced herself to lie still. Her instincts told her that struggling would only inflame Chad. Between clenched teeth, she said, "This isn't going to do you any good. I do not know where Lillian is. Why do you think I was going to talk to Mr. Epstein? I thought she might have visited him."

"She hasn't been here," Chad offered, palming her breasts. "But she called."

"How do you know that?" Lily gasped, trying not to squirm.

"Epstein's an old guy—must be at least eighty. He answered all our questions right away. We were talking to him when you called and asked for directions."

Desiree said, "Epstein talked, but he didn't know much. Your grandmother didn't tell him where she was calling from, or where she was going next."

"Yeah, and we're sure he told us everything he knew. He was scared. Plenty scared. Too scared to lie to us."

"I'm not lying. I haven't talked to Lillian since Sunday night. Why do you think I hired a private detective?"

"Well, now. Let's see. Maybe to protect you from me?" Chad stopped kneading her breasts and squeezed. Hard.

Lily felt her eyes fill with tears. She blinked rapidly. No way would she let Chad see her cry. "I do not know where my grandmother is. Or where she is going next. I swear I'm telling you the truth. Do you think I want your hands on me?"

"Now, Cupcake, keep that up and you're going to hurt my feelings." Chad unbuttoned her jeans and slid the zipper down. "Well, now, isn't that pretty. You're panties are the same color as your bra." He ran his fingers along the waist band of her bikinis.

"I can't tell you what I don't know," Lily said. To her dismay, her voice quavered. She didn't want Chad to know how scared she was.

Desiree spoke up. "If your grandmother is visiting everyone she knew in Hollywood, this should have been her next stop. Why wasn't it? Why did she settle for a phone call?"

"I don't know. I told you. I haven't talked to Lillian since she left Fair Hope. I want to find her as much as you do, but I don't know where she is, or where she plans to go next."

"I almost believe you," said Chad. "It doesn't really matter if you don't know or if you don't tell. Like Desiree said, we'll find Lillian. She won't be so anxious to stir up that old murder once she knows we've got you."

"Why do you care about something that happened forty-five years ago? Are you working for the murderer?"

"You don't get to ask questions, Cupcake. That's my job. Is your hair naturally red?" He began tugging her jeans off. "I'm about to find out."

"Chad!" yelled Desiree.

Chad jerked his head up. "Fuck. What do you want now?"

"Someone is following us," said Desiree, her voice shrill. "There's a dark sedan behind us. Must have come from Epstein's place—there weren't any turnoffs after the place we ambushed her."

"So what? The road continued past his place—there must be other cabins farther along. Just because they're on this road doesn't mean they're following us. This is the only way out of here." Chad got off of Lily and looked out the rear window. "Damn. They're close. I hate fucking tailgaters."

"I can't pull over and let them pass. The road's too narrow." Desiree sounded almost hysterical.

Chad continued to squat at the rear door, his attention on the car behind.

Lily took deep breaths. A dark sedan. Could it be the dark blue Mercedes Sam had seen in Fair Hope? The Mercedes that Phil and Sam thought contained two of Gus Accardo's thugs? Would that be a good thing, or a bad thing? It only took Lily a second to decide anything would be better than Chad, even going from the frying pan to the proverbial fire.

Chad yelled at Desiree. "Speed up. I don't like them being so close."

Desiree stepped on the accelerator.

"Faster."

"I can't go faster. Not on this road. Too many curves."

"Shit. I should be driving."

"I told you to drive. But no. You wanted to play your sick games with her."

"She'll wait. Won't you, baby?" Chad reached down and squeezed her ankle.

Lily kicked out at him and screamed. "Help!"

"Oh, God, oh God, oh God. This is bad, real bad," Desiree said. "Look how close they are."

"They can't hear her yell," said Chad. He grabbed Lily's ankle and twisted. Lily screamed again. "You're gonna pay for that, Cupcake. Later."

"I think we're almost back to the highway."

"About time. First chance you get, let them pass."

"Don't worry—"

There was a sickening crash as the other car slammed into the rear of the van. Chad fell back on his butt, and Lily slid off the pillows, bumping her head on the back of Desiree's seat.

Desiree reacted instinctively, slamming on the brakes. The van went into a spin, then came to an abrupt halt against a fir tree. The air bag deployed.

Chad hit his head on the roof of the van. The pillows protected Lily. Before she knew what was happening, the back of the van opened, and a man looked in. He was a dark shadow, silhouetted in the headlights of the car that had rammed the van. "Help," Lily said, her voice breathless. "These people are kidnaping me."

"You Lillian Redmond's granddaughter?"

"Yes. Who are you?"

Before the man could answer, Chad recovered from the blow to his head. Lily saw him reach for his waistband, but the gun wasn't there. She saw it in the corner of the van, where it must have fallen when the van was rear-ended.

"Look out," she screamed. "He's got a gun." She pointed to the corner with her feet.

The man picked up the gun and shoved it in his jacket pocket. Then he reached inside his coat and pulled out a bigger gun. He pointed it at Chad. "Well, well, well. If it ain't Mick. What are you doing here?"

"Taking care of business," Chad said, rubbing his head. "Or trying to. Leave the girl here, Joe. I need her to fulfill a contract."

"Yeah. I've heard about you and your needs. Who're you working for? What about the blonde? Doesn't she satisfy your needs?"

"That iceberg? No way. But you always liked blondes, didn't you? Take her, if you want."

"Chad?" Desiree had fought free of the air bag. She sounded scared and angry at the same time.

Lily was only scared. Lying on her back, her blouse open, her jeans unzipped, she felt naked and vulnerable. Even though no one was looking at her.

"Thanks, but no thanks. You better do something about that nose bleed, honey," said the man with the gun. He jerked his head in Lily's direction. "I'm taking this one with me. Any objections?"

"Yeah," said Chad. "Plenty. But I got nothing to back them up. I'll see you around." He made it sound like a threat.

"Good. Now. I've got a message for you two. Tell your boss to lay off Lillian and her friends. Otherwise, Mr. Accardo will be seriously angry. Got it?"

"Oh, God. Oh, God. I'm bleeding," said Desiree. "My nose won't stop bleeding."

Chad, or Mick, just grinned.

The man restored his gun to his shoulder holster, reached in and grabbed Lily by her legs. He pulled her out of the van and slung her over his shoulder. The man seemed to stagger a little under her weight, but he made it to the waiting car. He opened the back door of the sedan—it was a dark blue Mercedes—and tossed her in the backseat.

He climbed in the front seat, closed the door and told the driver, "Drive, Faz."

The driver obeyed, and the powerful sedan sped down the dirt road, leaving a cloud of dust in its wake.

When they reached the highway, the man who had pulled her from the van turned around and looked at her. "You okay?"

"Yes, thank you." From the glow of dashboard lights, she could see both men were well past middle-age. The driver was bald except for a fringe of white hair. The man who had taken her away from Chad and Desiree had a full head of hair, but it was grizzled and gray. "Could you untie me, please?"

"Sure thing. I'm Joe Bones, by the way. That mug in the driver's seat is Fazio Grimaldi. Gus sent us along to keep an eye on your grandmother. Gus has a soft spot in his heart for her, you know?"

As he talked, Joe Bones reached in his pocket and pulled out a knife. Lily swallowed a giggle. She would have thought a real, live gangster would carry something a little more lethal than a Swiss Army knife. Lily began to relax.

Leaning over the seat, Joe opened a blade and sliced through the rope around her wrists. She immediately pulled her blouse closed and began buttoning it. As soon as she was done, he handed her the knife. She sliced through the rope around her ankles, then returned the knife to its owner.

"Hey, Faz. You ever meet up with a guy named Mick O'Reilly? Stocky. Young. Used to do odd jobs for that Russian gang."

"Yeah. I've heard of him. Why?"

"He was in the van. From what I seen, he was about to do the girl."

Faz looked in the rearview mirror. "You okay, honey?"

Lily nodded. "Yes. I think so."

"Do you know who those two work for?" asked Joe.

Lily quickly zipped up her jeans. Joe and Fazio didn't seem all that threatening, but she decided against telling them she'd heard Desiree mention the name Santori. "No. I know who they are— Desiree Anderson and Chad Boyd. At least, those are the names they're using. They're from Illinois. But I don't know who they work for."

Fazio snorted. "Chad Boyd. Sounds like a prep

school name. Mick's not from Chicago—he's from New Jersey."

"The Russians wouldn't have any reason to go after Lillian Leigh. Mick must be working for someone else," said Joe. "Don't you worry about those two anymore, little lady. If they're smart, they'll turn that van around and head back to wherever they came from."

"Where did you come from?" asked Lily. "How did you know I was in the van?"

"We visited Mr. Epstein," said Joe. "We got there a little before those two arrived. We stayed in the bedroom while Mr. Epstein talked to them—told him we'd come out if they tried to get rough. They wanted to know if he'd heard from Lillian Redmond. He told them, yeah. A phone call earlier today. But that was all he told them. They didn't push it, not after he stopped to take the call from you."

"Yeah. They left pretty quick after that," said Fazio. "The guy said something about being happy to see his cupcake again."

"We didn't like the way he said that. And Epstein told us they pulled a gun on him. We decided to follow the van and see what happened. But we couldn't follow too close—not on that twisty little road. Sorry about that. He didn't have time to . . . do anything?" asked Joe.

"No. They came after me because they thought they could make me tell them where my grandmother is. I can't. I don't know where she is." They seemed so sympathetic, Lily almost asked them about Santori, but decided against it. She knew who they worked for, and Gus Accardo's reputation was enough to make her cautious.

"We don't know, either," said Fazio. "But the boss told us not to worry about it. We know she's on her way to California. If we don't run into her before, we'll for sure hook up with her there. Hey, Joe. Think we should go back and have a little talk with those two? Maybe shoot out their tires? They roughed up—what's your name, honey? Lily?"

Lily nodded. "I was named after my grandmother."

Joe shook his head. "Nah. After hitting that tree, those two are going to be out of commission for a while. Did you see the steam coming from under the hood? I think they busted up their radiator. And the blonde got wacked pretty good by the air bag—she had a bloody nose. Besides, dollars to doughnuts Epstein has called the local cops."

"Yeah, you're right. Let the law take care of those two. We need to get out of here before the police show up."

"Wait!" Lily cried. "You don't have to take me with you. My car. They hid my car in the woods. If you'll let me out, I can walk back and get it."

Joe stared at her, his brow wrinkled in concentration. "Nah. I don't think so. Mick might be waiting for you. You're better off with us. Faz?"

"Yeah, we'd better check with Mr. Accardo before we do anything else. Sorry, Miss Lily. We can't take a chance on going back now. Not with the cops most likely on the way."

"I can't leave my car. My purse is in it. My suitcase, too. I don't have any money. Or any clothes."

Joe Bones reached over the seat and gave her an awkward pat on her knee. "Don't worry about it. I'll call the boss right now and ask him what to do." He took a cell phone from his jacket pocket and dialed a number.

"Mr. Accardo? Joe Bones, here. Yeah. We talked to Epstein. He hasn't seen Miss Leigh. He had a phone call from her today, but she didn't tell him where she was."

There was a pause.

"Yeah. Will do. There's something else you should know. We've got her granddaughter. A couple of lowlifes grabbed her—a woman and Mick O'Reilly. We grabbed her back." Joe took the phone away from his ear. "Mr. Accardo wants to know if you're okay."

Lily nodded. "Fine. I'm fine."

Joe repeated her answer into the phone. "Yeah. Looks just like her. They had her in their van, all trussed up like a Christmas goose. The van is out of commission—they ran into a tree." There was a pause. "No. She don't have any idea who they're working for. Do you?" He addressed the last question to Lily.

"None," said Lily. "All I know is that they've been after me ever since I left Fair Hope. They had my car bugged, but Sam got rid of that."

"Sam?"

"Sam Hunter. He and I traveled together for a little while."

Fazio asked, "That wouldn't be old Archie Hunter's son, would it?"

"Yes. Do you know him?"

Fazio shrugged. "Might have seen him around a time or two. Joe, you better tell the boss."

Joe passed the word about Sam. Something Gus said made Joe chuckle. "So. What should we do with her? We need to get down the road, before the local cops show up at the scene of the accident."

Another pause, and Joe said, "Got it. Will do." He handed the phone back to Fazio. "The boss wants us to drop her off in the next town. Says he don't want us taking a rap for snatching Lillian's granddaughter." He turned and looked at Lily. "He also told me to take good care of you—on account he owes your grandmother. Big time."

"I would never accuse you of kidnaping, Mr. Bones. You saved me from those two."

"Yeah. Well. We always do what the boss says. Don't worry about being broke. We'll loan you a couple hundred dollars when we drop you off."

"You're not going to leave me on the side of the road, are you? What if the van is okay and Chad and Desiree come after me? I think I would rather stay with you, if you don't mind."

"We won't leave you on the road. Next town we come to we'll drop you off at a motel, or a restaurant. Someplace where there are people around. You'll be okay."

"Yeah," said Fazio. "We gotta do that. We have a few errands to take care of on our way to L.A. We'd like to take you along, but it would be better if you weren't seen with us. Cops have a way of judging people by who they hang out with."

"That's the truth, Miss Lily," said Joe. "Someone in the know gets a look at you with us, and next thing you know you're on the cover of one of them grocery store rags."

Fazio said, "And they'll call you a mobster's moll or some such silly name. We don't want that, do we?"

Lily found the idea of being a gangster's moll somewhat intriguing. But she didn't want to get Fazio and Joe Bones in trouble with Gus. "No. I guess you're right. Although, you've been perfect gentlemen. Thank you. You're very kind. I never thanked you for saving me." Impulsively, Lily leaned over the front seat and gave Joe Bones a kiss on his cheek.

"Now, now. Don't get all mushy on me."

As they drove through the night, Faz and Joe whispered to each other occasionally. Lily closed her eyes, but she couldn't sleep. Her brain refused to shut down. Why had she thought running away was a good idea? She should have swallowed her pride and stayed with Sam. Lillian would be ashamed of her, and with good reason. She could not take care of herself. Emotionally or physically. She'd fallen in love with a man who was not about to return the feeling. She'd gotten grabbed twice by a slime ball with aliases.

And now she was in a sedan with two of Gus Accardo's henchmen. They seemed nice enough, and hopefully they were telling the truth about letting her go soon.

But then what would she do? No money. No clothes.

No Sam.

The pilot circled the cabin. "That ought to be the place."

"Can you land?" asked Sam.

"Not by the cabin—too many trees. Closest I can get you is that turnaround on the highway. That'll get you within a mile of the cabin. Hey—look at that van. It's off the road against that tree. Must have been some kind of accident."

Sam recognized Chad and Desiree's beige van. And a few yards behind it, he thought he caught a glimpse of silver. His heart stopped. "Land. Now."

The pilot landed, and Sam took off at a run down the dirt road. He paused at the van, but no one was in it. The rear door was standing open. Sam looked inside, but it was empty. There was some blood on the air bag—that could have happened when the bag deployed. A woman's purse was on the floor in front of the passenger seat. Two large pillows were in the rear of the van, along with an impressive amount of electronic surveillance equipment.

"Lily!" he yelled. Silence.

Sam returned to the van and gave it a quick but thorough search. He found nothing identifying the occupants until he opened the purse. There was a driver's license for Desiree Anderson, and another card identifying her as an employee of the Santori for Governor campaign. Sam replaced the items and closed the purse, tossing it back where he'd found it.

He walked slowly around the van. The rear wheels were still on the dirt road. The ground behind the van was churned up. Tire tracks and footprints mixed together. At the driver's side, Sam found a clear set of foot prints where the driver had jumped from the van. Small prints. Desiree's.

Too bad. He'd hoped the blood belonged to Chad. Broken branches showed where someone had entered the woods.

Sam followed the trail, finally coming to a spot where the ground was clear. Two sets of footprints, one the same as the driver's, the other much larger. A man's prints. Chad. Only two people had walked away from the van.

Where was Lily?

He continued down the road. Around a curve in the road, he saw Lily's Honda. "Lily!" he yelled again.

No one answered. Sam reached the car and opened the door. Lily's straw purse was on the front seat, and the keys were hanging halfway out of the ignition. Sam got in, fired up the engine and headed for Epstein's cabin. Maybe Lily was there. He hadn't driven far when a figure staggered onto the road in front off him. Sam slammed on the brakes.

"Help!" said the woman. It was Desiree. Her nose was bleeding, and she appeared dazed.

"Where's Lily?" asked Sam, getting out of the car and grabbing the woman.

"You! How did you get here? She said she fired you."

"Where is she?" Sam shook her.

"Hey. Not so rough. I'll tell you. I'll tell you everything. This is not how it was supposed to be. We only wanted to talk to Mrs. Redmond. Just talk. Then Chad showed up with all his fancy-dancy equipment. He has a gun. No violence. I am opposed to violence and—"

"Where is Lily Redmond?"

"Those men took her. They rammed the van, and then they took her."

"What men? What did they look like?"

"I don't know. It was dark. My face was buried in the air bag."

"What kind of car were they driving?"

"Some kind of sedan. Dark. I only got a glimpse of it in the rearview mirror before they rammed the van. The man who took Lily knew Chad, but he called him something else."

"What?"

"I don't know. Mike. Micky. Mick. That's it. He called him Mick. Who the hell is Mick? This never should have gotten so complicated. I need a doctor. My head hurts, and my nose won't stop bleeding."

"I'll see that you get medical attention. First, we're going to see Mr. Epstein. I want to make sure he's all right."

"We didn't hurt him. Chad pulled a gun on him—a *gun*. What was he thinking? I didn't know he had a gun."

Sam shoved her in the car and slammed the door.

When he made it into driver's seat, he told her,

"Don't bleed on Lily's upholstery." Sam found the box of tissues Lily kept in the car behind the passenger seat and gave it to Desiree. "Here. Tilt your head back and use the tissues.

"What happened to Chad?"

"I don't know. After the crash he told me to find everything with identification on it and get out of the van. I did, except I couldn't find my purse. He went into the woods, but I couldn't keep up with him. My nose won't stop bleeding. I need a doctor. Take me to a hospital."

"I'll take you to Epstein's cabin. You can call 911 from there. Then I'm going after Lily."

Epstein opened the door before Sam's knuckles hit the wood. "What happened to her? Who are you?"

"Sam Hunter. Archie Hunter's son. I'm looking for Lily—Lily Redmond is Lillian Redmond's granddaughter."

"That's not her," Epstein said, pointing to Desiree. "She was here earlier. She had a man with her. He was a mean one—pointed a gun at me and asked me where Lillian was. Told them I hadn't seen or heard from her for forty-five years. That she called me today, but didn't say where she was. Those other characters were listening, too, and—"

"What other characters?"

"Two men. Said they worked for Gus Accardo. They wanted to know about Lillian, too, but they were polite about it. They were all here when Lily called. They all left right after I hung up. Lily never got here."

"I need a doctor," whined Desiree, holding the wad of bloody tissues to her nose.

"What happened to her? Did you pop her on the nose?"

"No. There was an accident. She got hit in the

face by an air bag. And I found Lily's car. That's it in your driveway."

"It wasn't an accident," said Desiree. "They rear-ended the van on purpose."

"What happened to her boyfriend?"

"I don't know," said Sam. "He wasn't around when I got there. But he may be headed back this way."

"He's got a gun," said Epstein. "I called the sheriff as soon as they all cleared out. He'll be along soon."

"Good. I'll hand her over to the law. Then I've got to go after Lily."

"You think Gus's men took her?"

"It looks that way." Sam heard the sound of a car.

Epstein moved toward the front window. "The sheriff is here." He opened the door and admitted a man in uniform wearing a deputy sheriff's badge.

"There's a wrecked GMC van down the road a piece. Is that why you called?"

"Among other reasons."

Between them, Sam and David Epstein explained what had happened.

"You would classify this Boyd guy as armed and dangerous?" asked the deputy.

"Yeah," Sam said, his voice grim.

The Otero County deputy repeated Sam's description of Joe Bones and Fazio and the make and license number of their car into his radio.

As soon as he was done, Sam scribbled Lily's cell phone number on a Hunter & Sons card and handed it to the deputy. "I'm going now. I need to find Lily before Chad does."

Desiree stirred. "Am I going to get medical attention any time soon?"

"The ambulance is on the way," said the deputy. To Sam, he said, "Wait up, Hunter. I think you ought to stay put and help us sort this mess out."

"I've told you all I can. If you or your bosses have questions, call me. Unless you're placing me under arrest, I'm going. I've got to find Lily."

"She's important to you?" asked the deputy.

Sam nodded, unable to speak because of the lump that had formed in his throat. Nothing was more important to him than Lily. He had to find her and tell her how sorry he was that he'd forced her to run away from him.

The deputy gave him a sympathetic look. "You're not under arrest. Go. But keep us informed."

"You do the same. I want to hear immediately if anyone catches sight of that Mercedes."

"Will do," said the deputy.

Sam shook hands with the deputy and with David Epstein. "Thanks for your help."

"When you catch up with Lillian, tell her to come for a visit," said Epstein. "We'll have a lot to talk about."

"I'll do that." Sam hurried out the door. He wanted to get well away before the deputy sheriff or his superiors changed their minds about letting him go.

Once he was in Lily's car, racing down the dirt road faster than the speed limit, Sam realized he did not know which way to go. He eased up on the accelerator. Chasing Lily at full speed wouldn't do any good if he charged off in the wrong direction.

Even after he slowed the car, at first Sam couldn't hear himself think over the beat of his heart pounding find-Lily-find-Lily-find-Lily. He was back at the junction where the road to Epstein's house met the paved highway before he managed to calm down enough to think.

Which way would Fazio and Joe Bones go?

Sam made himself review what he knew. They had lost track of Lillian while still in Louisiana. There had been no sight of them at the nursing home, but they must have gone through Houston. Gus's men had been waiting at Cloudcroft, and he had to assume that was because they expected Lillian to show up there. She hadn't, but her granddaughter had.

Accardo's men did not usually rescue damsels in distress. They had snatched Lily for a reason. Accardo must intend to exchange Lily for Lillian's silence. Lillian had eluded her pursuers so far, but everyone knew she would end up in California sooner or later.

Sam pointed the car west.

Twelve

Late Wednesday night, Lillian walked out of the bathroom at the Fort Stockton Inn in time to hear Archie end a phone call. He looked worried. When he met her gaze, his worried look intensified. "What's wrong?" she asked, suddenly afraid.

Archie said, "That was Sam. It's Lily. She's been kidnaped."

Lillian felt her heart jump into her throat. "How?" she managed.

"Chad and Desiree were lying in wait close to Epstein's cabin. They grabbed Lily before she got there. But they didn't have her for long. Gus's men caused the van to crash, and they took Lily away."

Sinking onto the bed, Lillian went numb. "A crash?"

"Lily is all right. The van hit a tree, but Sam said the damage to the vehicle was minor. Desiree got a bloody nose when the air bag deployed, but other than that—"

Blindly, Lillian fumbled for the telephone on the table next to the bed. "I'm calling Gus. "If he hurts my Lily . . ."

"Do you have his number?"

Lillian dropped her hand into her lap. "No. Do you?"

"Not with me. Phil can get it for you. I'll call him." Archie picked up the phone. Once Phil was on the line, Archie listened for a few minutes, interrupting with questions. Lillian heard him ask, "Santori? Sam said Desiree was working for Tony Santori?"

Lillian wrinkled her brow. Who in the hell was Tony Santori, and why would he send people after her? As soon as Archie hung up the phone, she asked the question out loud.

"Anthony Santori is Gus Accardo's nephew. He's a state senator, and he's running for governor of Illinois."

"I don't understand, Archie. From what Sam said, some of Gus's men saved her from his nephew's gang of two. Why would Gus's nephew be working at cross purposes with him?"

"I'm not sure, although there is no love lost between the two branches of the family. Renata Santori hasn't spoken to brother Gus in decades. Maybe Santori thinks a revival of the story of Eric's murder would interfere with his campaign. What do they call it? Getting off message?"

"Yes. I would think that kidnaping an innocent young girl would get him off message, too. Archie, I don't like it that Chad is out there. That man is dangerous." Lillian felt a sudden spurt of anger. Lily should not have been alone. "I thought Sam was looking after Lily. Where was he when Lily was taken?"

"Lily left Sam somewhere between here and Pecos this afternoon. They had some kind of misunderstanding."

Lillian stalked across the room. When she was nose to nose with Archie, she poked him in the chest with her forefinger. "What do you mean, she left him? What kind of misunderstanding? What did he do to her?"

Archie grabbed her hand. "Sam did not do anything to your granddaughter. Lily tricked him out of the car at a gas station, and then drove off."

"She wouldn't do that. Lily may be young, but she's not stupid."

"I don't know about her age or IQ, but your granddaughter brought this on herself. She left Sam. He didn't abandon her."

Lillian shook her head. "She wouldn't run away from him for no reason. Maybe he made unwanted advances."

Archie leaned down so that he was nose to nose with Lillian. Through clenched teeth, he insisted, "My son doesn't make unwanted advances. I taught him better than that."

"Sam should have kept her from running off on her own. That's his job, isn't it? To guard bodies? He should not have let Lily out of his sight."

"Sam is a professional. If she got away, it has to be because he had no reason to think she'd do something so reckless. He did all he could do to try and catch up with her before she got herself in trouble. Sam rented a helicopter to take him to Cloudcroft, for crying out loud. Do you have any idea how much that cost?"

Lillian gave Archie an I-don't-care look. "He didn't do enough."

"Your granddaughter got herself into this quest of yours, not Sam. Hell, they never would have met if you hadn't left Sam handcuffed to your bed."

Guilt over her part in involving Lily with the likes of Chad and Desiree—not to mention Gus Accardo's minions—was almost enough to make Lillian stop blaming Sam. Almost, but not quite.

"Lily is a smart girl. She wouldn't have gone off on her own if Sam hadn't done something."

"I raised my sons to treat women with respect. He wouldn't have done anything to her. More likely, she came on to him, and he repelled her advances."

"My granddaughter is a lady. She doesn't make advances to strange men." Lillian tried to suppress her memories of the number of times she had urged Lily to do just that, but failed. This was her fault, not Sam's, but now that she had started the blame game, she couldn't seem to stop. "Your son must have forgotten your lessons. If he ever learned them in the first place."

"Are you calling me a liar?" Archie yelled.

Lillian shook her head. Tears filled her eyes.

Pulling her into his arms, Archie tucked her head on his shoulder. "Don't cry, Lillian. I know you're worried about Lily, but Sam will find her."

"Do you really think so?" Lillian asked, blinking the tears away.

"I do. They must have had some kind of argument. Once Sam catches up with her, everything will be all right. He said he would call as soon as he finds her." Archie sat down in the overstuffed chair next to the bed, taking Lillian with him.

Lillian curled up in his lap. "What would they have to argue about?"

"We managed to have a little spat just now."

"Yes, we did. I'm sorry. It's just that I'm worried about her. And about what I'm doing. If anyone's to blame for what happened to Lily, it's I. I'm the one who decided to find out who killed Eric. Maybe I should forget all about it and go home. As soon I know that Lily is all right."

"Do you want to quit?"

"No. I want to call Gus. Where is that number Phil gave you?"

"On the pad next to the phone. It's his office number. His home number is unlisted. There may not be anyone there this late."

Lillian got up and went to the phone. She dialed the number Archie had scribbled on the pad. A man answered on the first ring.

"Hello. Connect me with Mr. Accardo, please."

"Mr. Accardo is not available. May I take a message?"

"You certainly may. This is Lillian Leigh Redmond. Tell Mr. Accardo if I don't hear from him within the next fifteen minutes, he'll regret it to his dying day." Lillian rattled off the hotel number. "Room 221."

As soon as she hung up the telephone, Archie said, "My, you sounded fierce."

"I feel fierce." Lillian felt her face crumple. Tears welled in her eyes.

Archie opened his arms, and she walked into them. "Oh, Archie. If anything happens to Lily, I'll never forgive myself."

"Nothing's going to happen to her. Gus has no reason to harm Lily."

Fourteen minutes later, the telephone rang. Lillian grabbed the receiver. "Gus?"

"Yeah," said a gravelly voice. "Been a long time between calls. How're you doing, Lil?"

"Right this minute? Not well. What have you done with my granddaughter?"

"Not a thing. She's okay. My men had to rescue her from a couple of jokers who snatched her. My guys happened to be in the neighborhood because I sent them along to keep an eye on you, Lil. You're making some people nervous. You know I would never hurt you or yours, don't you?"

Lillian breathed a sigh of relief. "I didn't think so. Are you sure Lily is all right? Where is she?"

"Still with Joe and Fazio. I talked to them a few minutes ago. They'll take good care of her."

"I hope so. Who are those other people? The ones who grabbed Lily in the first place? Are they working for you, Gus?"

Gus snorted. "No way. Don't worry about them. I'll take care of those two."

"The woman has been arrested."

"Yeah, I figured that might happen. But Mick is still on the loose."

"Mick? Who's that? I thought Chad and Desiree were the ones who had my granddaughter."

"Chad Boyd has a couple of aliases. Mick O'Reilly is one of them."

"Aliases? A man with aliases is after my granddaughter?"

"He's after you, Lillian. Be careful."

"Who is he? Why is he after me?"

"Don't worry about him. I'll take care of Mick. About your granddaughter—Joe and Fazio are going to drop her off as soon as they get far enough away from the action at Epstein's cabin. She'll be okay."

"Thank you, Gus. And thank your men for saving her."

"I'll do that. Good talking to you, Lil. Maybe I'll see you in a few days." He ended the call.

"Well. I feel better. Lily is with Gus's men, but they're going to let her go soon. But, Archie— she'll be all alone. She can't call me because she doesn't know where we are."

"She'll call Sam. He has her cell phone. It was in his pocket. He had her car and her purse, too."

"Her purse? She has no money? What will she do?"

"She'll call Sam," Archie repeated. "Sam will take care of everything. What was that about aliases?"

"That Chad person has an alias—Mick O'Reilly. Archie, Gus said Chad or Mick or whatever his name is is after me. But he wouldn't tell me why, or who he's working for. He just said he'd take care of it."

Archie took Lillian by the shoulders. "Lillian, I believe events are conspiring to put an end to our leisurely journey. We need to solve this case quickly, before someone does get hurt."

"I agree. Let's go to Sedona right away. We can see the Grand Canyon later." As soon as the words were out of her mouth, Lillian realized she was assuming she and Archie would be together after the mystery was solved. It was just as likely that her travels with Archie would end in California. "If you want to continue, that is."

"Oh, I want to see the Grand Canyon with you and nobody else but you. And that's not all. I want to see Paris, London, Rome and Athens with you by my side."

"That will take months," said Lillian, feeling misty-eyed again.

"Years."

"I'm an old lady."

"And I'm an old codger. But we have years and years to be together."

Lillian sniffed. "Don't you dare say anything about our sunset years."

"I wouldn't dream of it."

"I have a temper."

"I noticed. I think I can live with that. The real question is, can you live with me?"

"You want me to move in with you?"

"I want you to marry me. Will you?" When Lillian could only stare at him with her mouth open, he added, "Please?"

"Marriage? At our age?"

"What's age got to do with it? We have years and years left. I love you, Lillian. Say yes."

Lillian said, "Yes."

Lily said no when the desk clerk at the small hotel in Las Cruces asked her if she had luggage. "Not at the moment."

"Airline lose it?"

She nodded. "Something like that."

"Credit card?"

"I don't have one. I lost my purse, too. But I have cash." She reached in her pocket and pulled out the wad of bills Joe Bones had given her.

The clerk made her pay in advance, but she got a room key. Once she was in the room, Lily washed her face and looked longingly at the bed.

She had to let someone know where she was, but who? She couldn't call Lillian because she didn't know where she was. Calling home wouldn't accomplish anything except upsetting her parents. Same reasoning applied to Dexter. Lily wanted to call Sam.

She didn't know where he was, either.

Lily picked up the telephone and called information. She got the number of Hunter and Sons from Chicago information and called Phil. He sounded sleepy when he answered the phone. "Did I wake you? What a silly question. Of course I did. It's the middle of the night."

"Lily? Hey. Are you all right? Everyone's been calling me all night, asking about you."

"Everyone?"

"Archie called. I talked to your grandmother, too. They're still in Fort Stockton, but they're leaving tomorrow morning—I guess that would be this morning, now. Oh, and Gus Accardo called. He wants us to let him know what's going on. Archie said to cooperate, since Gus's men saved you from Chad and Desiree. They still haven't found Chad, by the way. How are you, kid?"

"Fine. Did Sam call about me?" she asked in a small voice.

"Only every fifteen minutes. He's driving me nuts. Where are you?"

"At the Buenas Noches hotel in Las Cruces. I don't have any clothes, or a car, or my cell phone. And I think the night clerk thought I was a hooker." Lily sniffled. "He made me pay for the room in advance."

"Sam has your car. And your phone. Do you want to call him, or should I? What's the number where you are?"

"You call him. I don't think he wants to talk to me." Lily gave him the number at the hotel and her room number.

"Okay. Got it. Now. You stay put. Sam will be there soon."

"I'm not going anywhere, except to bed."

"Okay, I'll call Sam and give him the good news right away. You're wrong about him, you know. I'm sure he wants to talk to you. Get some rest, sweety."

"I will. Thanks, Phil." Lily hung up the telephone. Phil might think Sam wanted to talk to her, but she knew better. If anything, he probably wanted to yell at her. Sam had to be furious—she'd left him at a gas station in the middle of nowhere.

How had he managed to get to Cloudcroft so fast? He must have gotten there if he had her car. She almost called Phil again, but decided on a shower and bed instead. It had been a very long day.

* * *

Ten miles outside of Las Cruces, Lily's cell phone rang. Sam answered it. "Lily?"

"No. But she's all right, and I know where she is." Phil gave Sam the name of Lily's hotel, and her room and telephone numbers.

"She thinks you're mad at her," Phil said.

Sam's hold on the cell phone tightened. "I am mad. But not at her. At me. I didn't protect her."

"Hey! Don't beat yourself up. She didn't cooperate. A client that doesn't cooperate gets—"

"—hurt. Lily isn't a client."

There was a pause. "No? What is she, then?"

Sam didn't answer. He repeated the name of the hotel and the telephone number, then hung up.

Knowing Lily was safe should have made him feel better, but Sam couldn't shake the icy fear that had grabbed him when he had seen Lily drive away from him. The thought that he had almost lost her kept playing over and over in his head.

If he had made love to her as she'd wanted, she wouldn't have run away from him. At the very least, he could have handled rejecting her with more consideration for her feelings. Throwing her out of his room had not been smart, on several levels. If he ever got within grabbing distance of her again, Sam vowed to grab. Grab and hold on.

Maybe forever.

Nah. He couldn't do that to Red. He couldn't just grab her and make love to her without giving her a chance to say no. He might have decided that he, Sam Spade Hunter, was going to be her first lover, but Lily might have changed her mind about him.

Tough. He'd change it back.

Sam groaned. He'd never known what a selfish bastard he could be. But then he'd never wanted any woman the way he wanted Red.

Sam found the hotel, parked and took the luggage out of the trunk. He didn't stop at the desk—the night clerk appeared to be asleep—but headed up the stairs, taking them two at a time. When he got to Lily's room, he set the two suitcases on the floor and took a deep breath.

Do not grab, do not grab, do not grab. He repeated the order to himself like a mantra. He had to give Lily a chance to say no.

Sam made a fist and knocked on the door.

"Who is it?" a sleepy voice asked.

"Who do you think it is? Open the door."

"Just a minute."

Sam heard the click of the security chain being opened, the dead bolt unlocked, the turn of the knob. Finally, the door opened. Lily stood in the doorway wrapped in a blanket. Her hair was a mess, and her face was scrubbed clean. She looked grumpy and beautiful. "You don't have to shout," she said crossly.

Sam grabbed her.

He told himself to let her go, but his arms were doing that mind-of-their-own thing again. Lily wasn't struggling, but with her arms pinned by the blanket, he figured her ability to push free was limited. Hugging her to him, he said, "Are you all right? Did they hurt you?" He ran his hands over the blanket. "Why are you wearing a blanket?"

"Because I didn't have any clothes. Except the ones I was wearing, and they're dirty."

"I brought your clothes." Sam let Lily go long enough to bring the suitcases in the room and shut the door.

Then he grabbed her again.

"Oh, Sam. I'm so glad you're here." Lily let go of the blanket and threw her arms around his neck. The blanket slithered to the floor.

"You're naked," said Sam, his voice hoarse. He'd grabbed when he'd promised himself he wouldn't do that. Now his hands were stuck to Lily's bare back, refusing to let her go.

"I'm sorry," said Lily, burying her face in his chest.

"Don't be sorry," said Sam, his voice hoarse. She was naked, and he was doomed. "It's good that you're naked. Saves time. I need to be naked, too. If you would let go of me for just a minute—"

"You're going to take your clothes off?" Lily raised her head and stared at him, her big brown eyes wide with . . . anticipation? Or apprehension.

"Yeah. I am." Gritting his teeth, Sam overruled his selfish bastard self and made himself ask, "Any objections?"

Beaming a hundred watt smile at him, Lily said, "Why would I object? You're going to make love to me."

"That's the plan." And Lily liked the plan. Relieved, Sam began unbuttoning his shirt with one hand, keeping one arm around Lily's waist. "You could help."

"Oh. Right." Lily took a step back and un-snapped his jeans. She slid the zipper down and shoved the jeans past his hips.

"Oh!" Lily stared at the bulge in his briefs.

Sam winced. Nothing like terrorizing a woman. He should have turned out the lights before getting naked. "Lily—"

Her gaze moved slowly from his groin to his eyes. "You came prepared," she said. Her face turned pink.

"Yeah. But we don't have to do this. If you're not sure—"

She moved against him, rubbing her belly on his erection. "Don't be silly," she said, her voice breathless. "I've been sure ever since I saw you in Grandmother's bed. You were the one who had doubts. What changed your mind?"

"The way I felt when you drove away from me." Sam shuddered, whether from the memory or because of the way his body was reacting to Lily's caresses, he didn't know. "Don't ever do that again."

Lily pushed his shirt off his shoulders. "I won't. I promise. How did you feel when I left you? Exactly?"

"Pissed. Scared. Alone. Hollow." Sam toed off his loafers while Lily sent his briefs to his ankles. Stepping out of his jeans and underwear, Sam said, "I don't ever want to feel that way again."

"I'm sorry."

"Stop apologizing, Red. I'm the one who should be saying that. I let you down. I promised to keep you safe, and I didn't."

"That wasn't your fault. I never should have run away from you. That was stupid."

"Yeah. It was. But I was stupid, too. I should never have tossed you out of my room."

"You were being noble. I'm glad you got over that." Lily put her hand in his. "You're naked. I'm naked. What happens now?"

Sam squeezed her hand and led her to the bed. Lily lay down, and Sam stretched out beside her. "Now we talk."

"Talk? *Talk!* I don't want to talk." Lily propped herself up on her elbows.

"You have to. You promised to talk me through this. You're going to have to help me out here, Red. I've never done this before."

She sucked in a breath. "You have so. You were married."

Sam leaned over and kissed her on the nose.

"I've had sex before. Just never with someone who hadn't. Had sex. Ever."

"Oh. That." She tossed her head, sending her red curls flying. "It's no big deal."

"It is to me. I want to do this right. You want that, too, don't you?"

She drew her brows together in an adorable frown. "Well. Yes. I've heard about the wrong way. It didn't sound like much fun."

"See? I knew it. You've heard all those first time stories from your girlfriends. I haven't. You know more about this than I do. That's exactly why we need to talk. Tell me what you've heard. About the wrong way. And the right way."

Lily didn't answer right away, too busy gazing at Sam. She paid special attention to that part of Sam she hadn't seen before. He looked . . . formidable.

"Lily?"

"What?" She dragged her eyes away from Sam's erection and met his gaze. The heat in his eyes had her pulse racing and her skin tingling. That zingy feeling was back, magnified. "Oh. I remember. You asked about first times. Men don't talk about stuff like that?"

"I would like to hear the woman's viewpoint."

Turning on her side, Lily propped her head on her hand. "Okay. Let me think. The wrong way seemed to involve going too fast. 'Slam bam, thank you ma'am' was a recurring phrase. It was not uttered in complimentary tones."

Sam crossed his arms behind his head and nodded. "Go slow. Got it. I can do that. What else?"

"Ummm. Let me think. There were some complaints about the place—cars with bucket seats and no backseat were not favored. But we don't have to worry about that." She patted the mattress. "Okay. About foreplay. Apparently, some men don't spend enough time above the waist before moving on."

"Not enough kissing, you mean?"

"Kissing is above the neck. I think the problem was below the neck and above the waist."

"Ah! That erogenous zone. Check."

"No grunting. Grunting noises are not romantic."

"What kind of noises are romantic?"

"Heavy breathing. Groans. Moans. Talking is all right, too. Oh. Oh. Oh. I just remembered something. Sally Jane Williams said her first time, after they were naked, the man took her hand in his and said, 'Show me what you like.' That gave me the shivers."

"Do you know what you like?"

"Up to a point. From there on we'll have to wing it. Are we going to get started now? Or do you need more instruction?"

"I think I can handle things from here." Sam raised up and leaned over her.

Lily put her hands on his chest. "Wait! One more thing. Don't pounce."

"I never pounce. Almost never. That time at the rest stop was the only time. Now I'm in control. And I'll stay in control. I'm not going to hurt you, Red, not if I can help it. One more thing. Birth control."

"Are we voting? If so, I'm in favor of it."

"Not voting. Thinking ahead. There are condoms in my jeans pocket."

"Really? How did that happen?"

"I got them at the gas station where you left me. While I was waiting for the helicopter guy. I have to leave you for a minute, while I get them." Sam rolled off the bed and walked over to where he'd dropped his jeans.

"Them, not it? Plural, not singular? We're going

to do it more than once?"

"Probably not." Sam tossed several foil packets onto the bedside table, then got back on the bed next to Lily. He rolled onto his side, facing her.

She peeked over his shoulder at the packets. "Why do you say that? Something else I heard at all those bridal showers—there seems to be some kind of competition. Everyone mentioned how many times they'd done it. In a row. On the same night."

"Yeah?"

Sam looked entirely too innocent. "Aha," said Lily. "That's what men talk about. Quantity, not quality."

"That's what men lie about. Red, this will be your first time. You'll be . . . tender. You may be too sore for multiple . . . acts."

"We'll see. Are we ready now?"

"Yes. We are." He leaned closer.

She put a hand between them. "Wait. One more thing. Tell me what you're going to do before you do it. Please. If you don't mind."

"I don't mind. I'm going to kiss you."

"All right. Good. That's nice, starting with the familiar."

"And while I'm kissing you, I'm going to touch you every place I can reach. Feel free to do the same to me."

"I will."

Sam kissed her. His lips were gentle, coaxing. Lily rolled onto her back and let her head fall onto the pillow. She felt boneless, floaty. Zingy.

True to his word, Sam's hands slid over her body, touching her neck, her shoulders, her torso, her hips.

He reached for her hand. "Show me what you like, Red."

Lily took his hand and put it on her breast. Sam

stroked and kneaded. Her back arched. Sounds
came out of her throat. Not grunts or groans, but
something that sounded like purring.

"If you like that, I think you're going to love
this." Sam took his hand away from her breast.
Before she could protest, his mouth touched her.
He sucked, gently at first, then harder. Her nipples
puckered and turned hard as berries. Sam kissed
her hard, then moved his wicked mouth to her
other breast.

Lily's breathing became shallow. She felt hot all
over, but she was shivering. Her hands were on
Sam's head, her fingers threaded into his thick
hair, holding him against her breast.

Her shivers turned into shudders. Sam raised
his head.

"Enough?"

Lily could only nod.

Sam kissed her again. And again. Until she was
breathless and clinging to him. His hand slipped
between her thighs. "You're wet." He slid a finger
inside her.

Lily jumped and pressed her thighs together.

Sam withdrew his finger. "Too soon?" he whispered against her mouth.

She could feel the tension in him, see the way
the muscles in his neck corded with strain. "No,"
she managed. She was finding it hard to breathe.
Maybe it was the lack of oxygen that made her vision clearer, her hearing more acute. She could
hear Sam's lungs struggling with each harsh
breath he took. Lily buried her nose in the curve
of his neck. She never knew that heat had an odor,
musky and male.

Sam's long fingers entered her again. Entered
and withdrew, entered and withdrew. Lily raised
her bottom off the bed, pressing against Sam's

hand. His thumb found her clitoris and rubbed. Lily moaned.

Her moan almost shattered the last of his control. Blindly, Sam reached for one of the foil packets. He tore it open and put the condom on. Leaning over her, Sam cupped her bottom with his hands at the same time he nudged her thighs apart with his knees.

With one powerful thrust, Sam entered her.

Lily yelped.

Sam froze. "Lily? Did I hurt you?"

"Uh. Yeah." Smiling tremulously, she said, "A little."

Feeling like a monster, Sam started to withdraw. Lily clutched at his buttocks. "Sam. Don't. Move." Frowning, she concentrated on adjusting to Sam's invasion of her body. "Okay. Proceed."

He collapsed on top of her. "I don't think I can do this."

Lily made a fist and hit him on the shoulder. "You're inside me. You have to finish what you started."

"I'm hurting you. I don't want to hurt you."

"It doesn't hurt anymore. It took a minute for me to get used to you, that's all."

Sam raised up on his elbows and gave her a searching glance. Lily was frowning, but her brown eyes were clear, not filled with pain. Or disgust.

Lily raised a brow. "Well? There is more, isn't there?"

He grinned at her. "Oh, yeah, Red. There's more." Sam rolled onto his back, taking her with him. "You finish."

Astraddle him, Lily gave him a bemused look. "I'm not sure what to do."

"Whatever feels good."

She considered that. Having Sam inside her felt

. . . not good exactly. Her body felt full, stretched. She took a deep breath. Sam was beneath her, waiting. From his scowl, she guessed patience was not his strong suit.

She wiggled, testing her ability to move. Sam made a noise that sounded suspiciously like a grunt. Lily forgave him. She moved up and down, tentatively at first; then as she grew accustomed to the feel of him, her movements became surer.

Sam's hands came up to clutch at her waist. His eyes were closed, and his face twisted into something that looked like pain. "Sam?" Lily gasped, feeling something coil deep inside her, coil tighter and tighter until she thought she might burst.

Sam lifted her off of him, making her cry out in protest. Then she was on her back, with Sam inside her again, pumping in and out faster and faster until the coil snapped and she climaxed only seconds before Sam shuddered with his own orgasm.

When she could talk again, Lily said, "Wow."

"You can say that again."

"Okay. Wow." She laughed out loud, then gave Sam an enthusiastic hug. "You're fantastic!"

His eyes still closed, he grinned. "Aw, shucks, ma'am. Tweren't nothing."

"Twas, too. Don't be so modest. It was wonderful. Except for that first bit. The ouch part."

"That's a one-time thing," Sam said, opening his eyes. "You won't say ouch again."

"I didn't say ouch this time. I only thought it."

"You screamed."

"I did not. Did I?"

Sam nodded. "You did. That's when I almost passed out. I couldn't stand hurting you."

"Well. I for one am glad you did. No pain, no gain. Besides, it didn't hurt that much." Lily yawned.

"I'm glad to hear it. Go to sleep, Red."

"I'm not a bit sleepy," she said, yawning again. "I feel great. Wide awake." Her eyes fluttered closed. "I wonder . . ."

"What are you thinking?" asked Sam.

Lily slitted her eyes open. "Oh, nothing important." She was wondering why Dexter, who must know how much fun sex was, had managed to keep her out of the game for so many years. Somehow, she knew better than to mention another man to Sam at this particular moment.

"You're not having regrets, are you?"

He actually looked worried. Lily smiled. "Not one. Not ever. I will never regret this."

Sam put his hand on top of hers. "Good."

Lily drifted to sleep, wrapped in Sam's arms. When Lily woke up the room was filled with daylight, her stomach was growling and Sam was on the telephone.

Lily snuggled up to his side and whispered in his ear. "Who are you talking to?"

He put his hand over the mouthpiece. "Archie. He and Lillian are on their way to Albuquerque." Sam removed his hand and spoke into the receiver.

"Yeah, Dad. I agree. This has got to end, the sooner, the better."

Lily felt a sudden chill. It was too soon to be talking about endings. She knew Sam was talking about finding the solution to Eric Winthrop's murder, but when that was done, what would happen to them?

She sat up and wrapped her arms around her knees. She would not think about that. Not yet.

"She's right here." Sam handed her the telephone. "Lillian wants to talk to you."

"Hi, Grandmother. How are you?"

"Lily, darling. Are you all right? I am so sorry I involved you in my silliness."

"I'm not sorry. I never had so much fun." Lily winked at Sam.

"You think being kidnaped was fun?" Lillian sounded shocked.

"Oh, no. Not that. But getting rescued by Mr. Bones and Mr. Grimaldi was exciting. They were very nice to me, Grandmother."

"I should hope so. Archie and I will spend tonight in Albuquerque, then go to see Cathy's assistant in Sedona tomorrow. We'll leave Sedona early Saturday morning, so we should be at the Beverly Hills Hotel by that evening. I can't wait to see you. I have a surprise." Lillian giggled.

"What kind of surprise? Have you figured out who the killer is?"

"No. My surprise is good news, nothing to do with murder. I love you, Lily. Take care of yourself. Remember, Chad is still out there somewhere."

"I love you, too, Grandmother. Bye."

Sam took the telephone from her and replaced it.

Lily looked at Sam. "Something's going on. Lillian giggled. She never giggles. She chuckles. She laughs. But she doesn't giggle."

"What did she say?"

"That they'll be in Los Angeles day after tomorrow. She also said that she has a surprise for me."

"What a coincidence. So do I." Sam rolled on top of Lily.

Thirteen

Lillian put the cell phone in the holder. She closed her eyes and sighed deeply. Then she looked at Archie in the rearview mirror. "You can't imagine how relieved I am that Lily is all right, and that she and Sam are together again. Did they sound to you as if we woke them up?"

"No." Glancing at the clock on the dashboard, Archie said, "It's almost one o'clock. Sam is an early riser."

"Sam was up half the night dealing with Desiree and chasing after Lily. Lily sounded sleepy to me." Lillian arched a brow. "I'll tell you what I think. I think Sam and Lily were in bed together."

"Are you accusing my son of seducing your granddaughter?" Archie asked, his tone belligerent.

"Oh, I certainly hope so."

After a moment of shocked silence, Archie laughed out loud. "Well. If he did, I hope she made him as happy as you made me. Why didn't you tell Lily about our wedding plans? You're not having second thoughts, are you?"

"Not me. But I want to see her face when I tell

her I'm going to be a bride." Lillian laughed. "Just saying 'bride' makes me happy."

Archie grabbed Lillian's left hand and gave it a squeeze. "You don't think she'll object, do you?"

"Not Lily. Now, my son and daughter-in-law are a different story. They probably will object. Not to our getting married—I'm sure Arthur and Polly would want us to make this relationship legal—but to the locale."

"You're sure you want to get married in Las Vegas? I only suggested it because it's quick, and I'm in something of a hurry to be a groom. But I can wait. If your family would feel better about a big wedding with all the trimmings . . . ?"

"I loved your suggestion. I planned my first wedding to please my family, and Alan's. This time I'm doing what I want. And I want to get married in Las Vegas. Not only in Las Vegas, in one of those tacky chapels where an Elvis impersonator performs the ceremony."

"If that's what you want, that's what you'll get."

"You're not having second thoughts, are you?" asked Lillian. "Do you want to wait so we can have a more traditional ceremony?"

Archie snorted. "Not a chance. The sooner, the better as far as I'm concerned. We could go to Las Vegas from Sedona, you know."

"That occurred to me. But I would like for Lily to be there, and Sam, too. And I want to end this search for Eric's killer."

"We may never find out who did it," Archie pointed out.

"I know. I can live with that if I know we've exhausted all the possibilities. I still think Eric's mystery woman is the key to solving this mystery."

"I'm inclined to agree with you. And I've got a feeling that Bobby Kaminski is going to give us another piece of the puzzle."

After spending Thursday night in Albuquerque, Archie and Lillian arrived in Sedona around noon on Friday. Following the directions Bobby had given Lillian, Archie had no trouble locating his house. The small cottage was painted a pale shade of turquoise which made it clearly visible against the backdrop of red rocks rising in the distance.

Bobby Kaminski opened his door and waved them inside.

"Hello, Bobby," said Lillian, holding out both hands. "Good to see you again."

"Nice to see you, too, Lillian," he said, taking her hands. He peered over her shoulder at Archie. "You look familiar, too."

"Archie Hunter. I was a security guard at Winthrop Studios for a couple of years."

"Oh, yes. I remember. You left shortly after Lillian did. Come on in," Bobby said, waving them into the living room. "Have you two been together ever since?"

"Not quite. I went to Chicago, and she returned to Alabama. We've only got together again recently."

"When I decided to stir up trouble. Bobby, I don't know if Cathy told you, but I'm trying to find out who killed Eric Winthrop. She thought you might be able to help me."

"Me? I don't know how I could help. Sit down, won't you? Can I get you anything to drink?"

"No, thanks. What makes you think you can't help?" Lillian asked, sitting on the sofa and arranging her full skirt around her.

Archie remained standing, leaning negligently against the patio door. "Nice view you've got here, Kaminski."

"Yes. I like it." Bobby sat in a leather chair, facing Lillian. "About the murder—I didn't know any of the people involved. Oh, I knew them by sight.

But I never talked to them. The police never even questioned me."

"We know. But Cathy said you worked late the night Eric was murdered. She thought you might have seen someone enter or leave by that side door that led to the parking lot. The door that was opposite the entrance to the wardrobe department?"

"I know the door you're talking about. And I did see someone that night. But it couldn't have been the murderer."

"Why not?"

"I saw her leave. She was going out the door as I prepared to leave myself that night. She was calm as anything. Not a hair out of place."

"Who was she?" asked Lillian, giving Archie an excited glance. This was new information, information no one had mentioned before. "One of the starlets?"

"No. She didn't work at the studio. I'm positive about that. All the starlets had to come to our department for fittings."

"What time was it when you saw this woman leave?" asked Archie.

"I'm not sure. I know I stayed late—I was the last person in the costume department that evening. It must have been after nine o'clock."

"And you don't know who she was?"

Bobby shook his head. "I don't know her name, but I'd seen her before. Once. Mr. Eric took her on a tour of the studio, including the wardrobe department. Mr. Thomas was with them."

"When was that?" asked Lillian.

"A couple of months before Mr. Eric got killed."

Archie said, "And that was the only time you saw her before the night of the murder?"

"Yes. Mr. Thomas may remember who she was."

"I was thinking the very same thing," said

Lillian, standing up. "Thank you, Bobby. You've been a big help."

"Glad I could do something for you. Nice seeing you again. Let me know how things turn out, okay?"

"Sure we will. Can you recommend a hotel?"

Bobby could and did, giving them precise directions to a nearby inn. Once they were in their room, Lillian twirled around. "A mystery woman! Isn't that exciting? Every mystery should have a mysterious woman."

Archie did not appear impressed. "How will we find out who she is? This is the first time in forty-five years that anyone has mentioned someone leaving Eric's office around the time of death."

"Don't you believe Bobby?"

Shrugging, Archie said, "It seems odd that he never mentioned this mystery woman before."

"Not to me. No one ever asked him about it before. I think the woman exists. She may even be the killer."

Now Archie did appear to be impressed. "You sure can jump to conclusions."

"All right. Maybe she isn't the murderer. But if she was there around nine o'clock—"

"Assuming Bobby remembered the time correctly." Archie reminded her.

"—then she may have seen the killer."

"Why didn't she come forward after the murder?"

Lillian stuck out her tongue at Archie. "Stop being so reasonable. I'm trying to wind up this case so we can get on to more important things."

Archie advanced on her, loosening his tie. "Speaking of important things. We have a room and a bed and only one more night before we're surrounded by family. After tonight, we're going to have to be more discreet."

"Why?" asked Lillian, helping Archie remove his tie. She began unbuttoning his shirt. "It takes more than two people to surround something, doesn't it? I don't think Lily and Sam will mind if we flaunt our relationship. They're having one of their own, remember?"

"That's another conclusion you jumped to. We don't know that for sure."

"Well. If they're not, then it proves that old saying. 'No fool like a young fool.'"

"I thought the saying went 'no fool like an old fool.'"

"Does this make you feel foolish?" Lillian kissed the hollow under Archie's chin.

Archie groaned. "No. It makes me feel young."

Lily and Sam spent Friday on the road, arriving in Palm Springs after seven o'clock. Sam called Madeline Morrow, and she agreed to see them the next morning. "Late morning, darling," she'd said in her trademark sultry voice. Sam had set the appointment for eleven o'clock.

"Oh, good," said Lily. "That gives us another long night together."

"Insatiable woman."

"Is that a complaint?"

"Hell, no. Let's find a hotel."

"Restaurant first. If we're going to have another night like last night, I need sustenance."

"All right. Food first. Me, second."

When they were in their room, Lily pushed Sam onto the bed.

"What are you going to do?"

"Something different."

Sam stuck out his bottom lip. "Yeah? One night and you're already tired of the same ol', same ol'? You really know how to hurt a guy."

"I'm not tired. I'm having the best time of my life. Thank you. Just to show you how much I appreciate all you've done for me, I want to do something for you. I've heard men really, really like this." She climbed on the bed, straddled him and unzipped his trousers. "Oh, look. It's very impressive the way you're always ready."

"This only happens with you, Lily."

"Are you sure talking to Madeline Morrow didn't contribute to your . . . condition? She does have that sexy voice."

"Madeline Morrow is seventy years old. I like tasty young women. Besides, Madeline is a blonde."

"So? Don't gentlemen prefer blondes?"

"Not this gentleman. Redheads are my weakness."

Lily finished undressing him. He reached for her, but she danced away. She walked around the bed, looking at him from every angle. "Oh, my. I'm getting dizzy. You have the most tantalizing body."

"Yeah? And all you're going to do is look?"

"Not all." Lily crossed her arms and grabbed the hem of her tee shirt. She pulled it over her head and tossed it onto the floor. Reaching behind her, she unhooked her bra and threw it on top of the television set. She wiggled out of her shorts, kicked off her sandals and got on the bed.

"Your body is nothing to sneeze at, either," Sam said, wiggling his brows and leering at her.

"Why, thank you, sir. I'm glad you approve."

Sam started to sit up, but Lily poked him on the shoulder. "Down. I want you on your back."

His eyes narrowed into slits. "Why? What are you going to do to me?"

"I told you. Something you're going to like." Lily pushed his knees apart and knelt between them. She stroked his penis, using a light touch. "Do you like stroking?"

"Oh. Yeah."

"I tried to stroke you that night I came to your room. I stared at your mouth, just like Lillian did in *Belle of Baton Rouge*, but I couldn't get close enough to stroke. You kept backing away from me." Lily closed her fingers around him, sliding up and down the length of his shaft.

"I was stupid. I won't do that again." Sam sounded hoarse and out of breath.

That gave Lily all the encouragement she needed. "Keep in mind, I haven't done this before. Tell me if I'm doing it wrong."

"Doing what?"

Lily took him in her mouth, swirling her tongue around, licking, sucking gently. She moved her hands over his body, feeling his skin grow hotter and hotter. Sam made guttural noises deep in his throat, not grunts but almost. He wasn't complaining. She must be doing it right.

Her own breathing became shallow, and Lily felt her heart begin to pound in that now familiar rhythm.

"No more," said Sam, rearing up and tossing her onto her back. He rolled on top of her and entered her. One stroke and he climaxed.

Sam collapsed on top of her.

"Well. Did I do that right?"

"Oh, yeah." Sam saw the puzzled look on Lily's face. "What?"

"There's something I've always wondered about . . ."

"Ask me anything."

"Why do they call it a blow job? Blowing doesn't seem to enter into it."

Sam roared with laughter. He laughed so hard

he fell off the bed. On the floor on his back, he laughed some more.

Lily peeked over the edge of the bed. "Well? Why do they?"

"Red, honey. Trust me. I blew."

"Oh. Oh!" Lily turned as red as her name. "I get it. Well. You learn something every day."

"I've got a few more things to teach you. Starting with turnabout's fair play."

"Sam? What are you going to do?"

He showed her.

When she was snuggled against his side, her head nestled under his chin, Lily said, "Oh, Sam. I do love you so."

Sam stiffened. "No. You don't. It's too soon."

Lily didn't hear him. She'd fallen asleep in his arms.

Sam held her close. He loved her. He knew it deep in his bones. This was not another meet on Tuesday, marry on Sunday, separate six months later situation. This was real. No woman had ever annoyed him, scared him, made outrageous love to him like his Red. He wanted to keep her by his side forever.

He couldn't do that.

Lily might think she loved him, but he knew better.

Sam groaned.

Then he counted. Monday, Tuesday, Wednesday, Thursday, Friday. Five days. Only five days since Lily had found him in her grandmother's bed. He'd lost her on Wednesday, found her again, made love to her on Thursday. And Friday.

He ought to be ashamed of himself. He had grabbed. Sam never grabbed. But he'd wanted Lily from the first moment he'd seen her hovering in the door of her grandmother's bedroom. He was

ashamed of himself. He would be even more
ashamed if she hadn't made it clear, almost from
the beginning, that she wanted him, too.

Yeah. Right. That was the honorable thing to
do—blame her for ending up naked in his arms.

He was older, and presumably wiser. He could
have resisted her. Lily made a sleepy noise and
snuggled closer. Maybe not.

Lily had done more than want him—she'd told
him she'd fallen in love with him that first day. No
matter how much he wanted to believe her, Sam
was positive she couldn't be right about that. Lily
was too young, too inexperienced, to know her
heart that well. From the moment they had met,
she'd been inexperienced, and unsure of her feelings for a man she'd known all her life. Dexter
hadn't helped his cause by giving her a certificate
of deposit instead of the engagement ring she'd always wanted.

Lily had been pissed at Dexter, worried about
Lillian and attracted to him. And he'd taken advantage of her.

He was a heel, a rat, a jerk.

Lily deserved better than him. Much better.

And he was going to see that she got what she
deserved.

Even if it killed him.

When Lily awoke Saturday morning, Sam was already up and dressed. "Why are you dressed? Our
appointment with Madeline isn't until eleven
o'clock?"

"I thought we'd get out of the room. Do a little
sight-seeing."

"I'd rather stay in and sight-see you without your
clothes on."

"Not today, Red. I'm going to talk to the concierge

about tours. Meet me in the restaurant as soon as you're ready."

Frowning, Lily sat up and stretched. Something was different. Sam had seemed . . . cold. No, not cold. Distant. As if he were trying to put some space between them.

Sam timed the sight-seeing so that they arrived at the Morrow mansion a few minutes before eleven. A uniformed maid answered the door and escorted them to a large living room. The room boasted a wall of windows, but the curtains were drawn. Lily had the feeling that the dim lighting was designed to flatter Madeline. She certainly didn't look seventy, but her youthful appearance wasn't all due to calculated illumination. Madeline's last husband had been a renowned plastic surgeon.

"Miss Morrow? I'm Lily Redmond, Lillian Redmond's granddaughter."

"Thank God," said Madeline in her smoky voice. "For a minute there, I thought you were she. In which case, Lillian would have bathed in the fountain of youth." She eyed Sam. "And who is this?"

"Sam Hunter, ma'am."

"Please don't call me ma'am. No reason to remind me that I'm old enough to be your . . . Never mind what I'm old enough to be. What can I do for you?" She batted obviously false eyelashes at him.

Lily cleared her throat. "Ms. Morrow, I don't know if you've heard, but Grandmother is—"

"—looking for Eric's killer. After all these years. Yes, I've heard. David called me. He said you had been kidnaped." Madeline looked at Lily for one brief moment before returning her gaze to Sam.

"I was, but—"

"You saved her?" Madeline squeezed Sam's bicep. "Of course you did. You're a big, strong man." She looked at Lily again. Briefly. "I hope you were sufficiently appreciative."

"Oh, I thanked him, all right. But he wasn't the one who saved me." Lily blew a curl out of her eyes. She wanted to snatch Madeline's hand off Sam's arm, but she restrained herself. "What we need to know is if you and Eric were about to break up."

Madeline hooked her arm through Sam's. "Why don't we get comfortable?" She led Sam to a low sofa and sank gracefully onto it, pulling Sam down next to her.

Lily sat on an ottoman in front of the sofa. It was either that, or sit in a chair an acre or so away on the other side of the room. "Did you end your engagement to Eric Winthrop?"

Madeline gave a low laugh. "I know that's what a lot of people thought. Including David. But I hadn't. Nor had Eric indicated he wanted out of our arrangement. On the contrary, that very day, the day he was killed, we had decided on a date for the wedding."

"That's what you told the police," said Sam. "I've read the reports."

"Yes. Of course I told the police the truth. For a brief time, they had me on their list of suspects. My motive was supposed to be jealousy. But I wasn't jealous. I knew about Eric and his . . . penchant for exercising droit du seigneur with the contract females. Those little encounters did not threaten me."

"And the police believed you?" asked Lily.

"I don't know. It really didn't matter if they did or they didn't believe me. I had an alibi. I had a late supper with Thomas that night. Actually, Eric had intended to be there, too, so that we could tell

Thomas the good news. But he never showed up. Because he was d-dead." Madeline's eyes grew misty, and she choked back a sob.

Lily was impressed. Her luminous beauty might have dimmed, but Madeline could still give a believable performance.

Sam fell for it. He gave her a pat on the shoulder. "When did you find out that Eric had been murdered?"

"Thomas went back to the studio that night—to see if anything was the matter. He found Eric's body."

The shameless woman actually rested her head on Sam's shoulder.

Lily asked, "Do you have any reason to believe that one of Eric's lovers might have killed him?"

"None. David told me that Eric had mentioned one of them to him, in a way that David found unusual. Eric didn't usually talk about his fun fucks. He wasn't the kind of man who bragged to other men. Usually. I suppose that's why David remembered him mentioning her. I have no idea who she might have been, or why he talked about her to David."

"Why do you think Eric finally agreed to set a date for your wedding?" Sam asked.

Madeline put a hand on Sam's thigh. "He'd been putting it off because of financial worries. The studio was in trouble for a couple of years— that was why Eric was forced to borrow money from that loan shark."

"Gus Accardo?" Lily got the name out through clenched teeth. Sam was letting that woman fondle him. In front of her.

"Yes. Eric realized almost immediately that having the mob as a silent partner was not a good thing. He had a tiger by the tail, and he was trying to figure out a way of turning loose without getting eaten. In today's jargon, he was stressed. Not in the mood for orange blossoms and honeymoons."

Sam asked, "What changed? Gus was still around."

"But he was on the way out. Eric got an influx of money from selling the studio's film library to television. He got the first installment of the sale price the day he agreed to set a date for our wedding. Eric was going to pay Gus off and wave bye-bye. I always thought Gus killed him because he wanted to hang around. He probably thought Thomas would be easier to control than Eric."

"But Gus didn't kill him," said Lily. "Gus had an alibi, too."

"Yes. Lillian finally allowed herself to be seduced that very night. Convenient, wasn't it? Gus may not have pulled the trigger, but he didn't hang around afterwards. Thomas paid off the loan, and that ended that relationship."

Lily had had enough. She stood up. "Thank you very much, Ms. Morrow."

Sam rose. "Yeah. Thanks. You've been a big help."

"Have I?" She smiled at Sam. "Well, then. You owe me, don't you? I'll have to think of a way for you to repay me."

Madeline remained lounging on the sofa as Lily dragged Sam out of the house. Once they were in the sunshine again, she said, "Well. That was a disgusting display."

"What?"

"Madeline. She had her hands all over you."

"You're not jealous."

"Of course not. Of a woman old enough to be your grandmother?" Lily was seething with jealousy, but she wasn't about to admit it.

"Madeline may be old, but she still looks good," Sam said.

"How could you tell? It was dark."

"Not that dark. And she's still got that voice."

"Anyone who smokes like a chimney can have a voice like that," Lily said. Her voice sounded squeaky. She cleared her throat and tried lowering it an octave or so. "Why did you tell her she'd been a big help? We still don't know who Eric was fooling around with."

"We know that she didn't feel threatened by whoever it was. We didn't know that before. What's wrong with your voice? Are you catching a cold or something?"

"Or something," Lily said in her everyday voice. "So Madeline Morrow is off the suspect list?"

"Madeline Morrow was never on my list. She had an alibi. That was in the police reports."

"She had the nerve to insinuate that Lillian gave Gus a phoney alibi. What if her alibi is the one that's phoney? What if she and Thomas killed Eric? I'll bet that's exactly what happened. Thomas was mad at Eric for getting the studio mixed up with the mob. Madeline knew Eric was about to dump her for another woman. So they killed him. Together. And gave each other an alibi."

"Red. Thomas and Madeline had a late supper at the Brown Derby. At least a hundred people saw them together that night."

"Oh." Lily made a face. "Well. It was a good theory."

"As long as you don't mind ignoring the facts." Sam pulled into a MacDonald's.

"Fast food?" Lily asked.

"Yeah. If we hurry, we'll get to Los Angeles in a couple of hours."

"Are we in a hurry?"

"I am."

Lily smiled smugly and ordered a Quarter-Pounder. She must have misread the signals this morning. Just because Sam had been eager to get out of the hotel room, she'd thought he was already tired of her. But if he wanted to get to Los Angeles several hours before Lillian and Archie . . . well. She knew what that meant. He couldn't wait to be alone with her again.

They arrived at the hotel shortly after four o'clock. While Sam checked them in, Lily wandered around the lobby of the Beverly Hills Hotel looking for celebrities. She didn't see anyone she recognized.

Sam caught up with her and handed her a room key. "Here. Your room is on the ninth floor." He turned to walk away. "I'll see you later."

Lily hurried after him. "Wait a minute. Where are you going?"

"To talk to Thomas Winthrop. While I was at the front desk, I called his office and made an appointment to see him. I've got to hurry—he's only going to be at the studio for another hour."

"I'll go with you."

"No. Wait here for Lillian and Archie. If they get here before I get back, tell Archie my room number is 709."

"Seven . . . I thought you said our room is on the ninth floor."

"Your room is. Mine isn't."

"You got us separate rooms?"

"Yeah. Party's over, Red." With that, Sam walked out the door, hailed a taxi and was gone.

Lily watched the taxi drive away. "The party's over?" Something was most definitely wrong. She had the scary feeling she had just gotten dumped.

"Is anything wrong, miss?" asked a bellhop.

"No. No. I'll just go to my room now." Numb, Lily headed for the elevator. She got off on the ninth floor and found her room. Once inside, she threw herself facedown on the bed. She felt as though she should cry, but tears wouldn't come.

Everything inside her—tears, thoughts, memories, her heart—was frozen solid.

After a while—Lily wasn't sure if minutes or hours had passed—a tiny flame of hope appeared, and the awful frozen knot inside her melted a little.

Maybe she was overreacting. Maybe Sam had gotten them separate rooms because he thought she would be embarrassed to share a room with him when Lillian was around. Or maybe he was embarrassed to share a room with her under his father's nose.

"Party's over" could mean only that they would have to be more discreet from now on.

Lily sat up. That had to be what he'd meant. Sam was a good guy, a hero. A hero wouldn't walk away with nothing but a callous remark.

But. He had never told her he loved her.

She'd told him more than once. Usually her declaration got her another bout of lovemaking.

Maybe he didn't know how to tell her he loved her.

Or maybe, Sam didn't know how to tell her he *didn't* love her. Maybe "the party's over" had been the best he could do.

Lily felt tears welling up in her eyes. She blinked them away. Sam did love her. He had to love her. He couldn't be so tender and gentle and rough and demanding with her if he didn't love her.

Lily called his room number and left a voice mail message asking him to call her as soon as he returned to the hotel. Then she unpacked and waited.

And waited.

And waited.

Sam didn't call.

* * *

When Sam returned from his meeting with Thomas Winthrop, the message light on the telephone was blinking. He listened to the message, but he didn't dial Lily's room. He didn't know what to say to her. "Party's over" had been the best he could come up with.

Or the worst.

He'd never known he was a coward. That seemed like another character flaw he should have been aware of sooner. Years ago, in fact. It was humiliating to discover at his age that he was a selfish bastard and a coward to boot.

Lily deserved an explanation.

But if he got close to her again, he would forget why he had to let her go. If he called her, what could he tell her? That he loved her, but she deserved better? That was true, but she wouldn't buy it.

Red was stubborn.

She would just have to find out for herself that what she felt for him wasn't love. Lust, excitement, maybe even a good portion of "like." But not love.

Sam consoled himself with the thought that Lily would never completely forget him. A woman never forgot her first lover.

Fourteen

Saturday evening a little after seven o'clock, Lily's phone rang. It was Lillian. "We're in a suite. Come on up. And hurry. I can't keep my surprise a secret one more minute." Her grandmother rattled off the suite number, sounding so cheerful that Lily felt guilty for wanting to throw herself in her grandmother's arms and bawl like a baby.

She couldn't do that. Lillian was happier than she'd been since becoming a widow. Maybe later, after the surprise was revealed and things had settled down a little. Maybe then she could ask Lillian's advice.

Lily ran a comb through her hair and added a touch of blusher to hide her paleness, then headed for Lillian's room.

Lillian opened the door to the suite on the first knock. She pulled Lily into the room and gave her a smacking kiss on her cheek. "You look wonderful! As if you'd never been assaulted in a ladies' room, or kidnaped at gunpoint." She lowered her voice. "Not to mention finding Sam in my bed."

Lily lowered her eyelashes, hiding the pain that Lillian's mention of Sam caused. "I guess excitement agrees with me. You look pretty good, your-self. What's the surprise?"

"Come with me." Lillian took Lily's hand and led her into the living room. Archie was uncorking a bottle of champagne. Sam was standing next to him.

Lily didn't want to look at him, either. She stared at the wine bottle instead. "Champagne? What are we celebrating?"

Lillian walked to Archie's side. "Lily, I would like to introduce Archie Goodwin Hunter, my future husband."

Transferring her gaze to Archie, Lily stuck out her hand and said politely, "It's so nice to meet— what did you say?"

"Archie and I are getting married."

"Oh, Grandmother." Lily burst into tears. "I'm so h-happy for you."

Lillian rushed to her side and pulled her into a bear hug. "Oh, baby. Don't cry."

"It's just that I'm so h-happy," Lily wailed. She couldn't see Sam through her tears, but she knew he was cringing. He hated tears.

Tough. He might think she was crying over him—and maybe she was—but a person could weep because she was happy and sad at the same time. With a final sob, Lily got herself under control. Rubbing her cheeks dry, she managed a watery smile. "You must have fallen in love at first sight," she said.

Sam sucked in a breath. Lily didn't think anyone but she noticed.

"Second sight," said Lillian. "We met once before, many years ago."

The champagne cork popped, and Archie quickly filled four glasses. Sam proposed a toast to the engaged couple. Lily downed her champagne in one gulp, causing Lillian to look at her closely. "Are you all right, Lily?"

"Fine. Never better. May I have another glass?"

Sam shook his head, but Archie filled her glass. "Your grandmother hasn't told you everything."

"There's more?" asked Lily, sipping her champagne slowly this time.

"Yep. We're not only getting married, we're getting married as soon as we finish up here. In Las Vegas. We want you and Sam to be our witnesses."

"Las Vegas? How . . . impulsive," Lily said. "And romantic."

"I suppose I'd better confess all," said Lillian. "We're getting married in the Chapel of the King. By an Elvis impersonator."

"No! Really?" Lily giggled. She felt light-headed, whether from the champagne or from the strain of pretending her heart wasn't breaking, she couldn't tell. "That's wonderful. I want to grow up to be just like you, Grandmother." Her lip trembled. Lily quickly took another sip of champagne.

Lillian patted her on the shoulder. "What a sweet thing for you to say."

"What do we have to do to finish up?" asked Sam.

"Solve a murder," Archie said. He and Lillian sat side by side on the sofa. "Let's review what we've learned."

"Our first clue came from David. He thought Eric had gotten serious about someone other than Madeline." Lillian looked at Sam, who was standing at the window. "Did he tell you that when you saw him?"

Sam nodded. "Yeah. But yesterday, Madeline told us that he'd finally agreed to set the date for the wedding."

"On the same day he was murdered," Lily added, determined to be as businesslike as Sam. She took a seat in one of a pair of leather armchairs facing the sofa.

"That's interesting," said Lillian. "But there *was* another woman. Bobby Kaminski told us that he saw a woman come in the side door to the office building as he was leaving. But he didn't know who she was."

"And Bobby could only give a sketchy description of her—said she had dark hair and eyes." Archie looked disgusted. "Oh. He did say he'd seen her once before."

"When was that?" Lily asked.

"A few weeks earlier—Eric escorted her on a tour of the studio," said Lillian. "I told Archie that meant the woman couldn't have been a starlet. Eric only ever acted as tour guide to VIPs. He said Thomas was with the two of them."

"I wish I'd known about the tour when I talked to Thomas Winthrop this afternoon," said Sam. "He thought there was another woman, too. But once Madeline told him she and Eric had agreed on a date to marry, he forgot about her."

"Let's call Thomas and ask him if he remembers the tour," said Lillian. She put her champagne glass down and reached for the phone.

"He won't be at the studio. He was leaving for New York immediately after he saw me." Sam moved away from the window and sat down in the other leather armchair.

"That's all right. We don't need him, after all. I just remembered something. Gus's sister was in town for several weeks before Eric was killed. Gus took us both to lunch one day shortly after she arrived. She really wanted to see the studio. Gus promised her he would arrange for a private tour. You don't think . . . ?"

"Renata Accardo Santori?" said Sam. "Could be. That would mean the Santori Chad works for isn't Tony, but his mother. Desiree definitely worked for the senator, though."

"You think she's the woman Eric took on a studio tour?" asked Archie.

Lillian nodded. "It makes sense. Eric was doing all he could do to impress Gus. If Gus's sister wanted a tour, Eric would have given her one. She must have killed him."

"You're doing it again, Lillian. Leaping to conclusions ahead of the evidence. Why would Renata kill him? The tour couldn't have been that bad." Shaking his head in mock disapproval, Archie winked at her.

Lillian smiled. "I'm not a professional. I'm allowed to jump to conclusions."

"You do more than jump, my dear. You take death-defying leaps."

"I still think she could have done it. Why else would she send Chad after me?" asked Lillian. "She wanted to shut me up."

"We don't know that she is the one who hired Chad. Even if she did, she could have done it for the same reason we thought Tony did—to stop you from reviving a scandal that might hurt her son's chances for election," Archie pointed out. "That doesn't make her a killer."

"Or she could be the murderer," Lillian stubbornly insisted.

Sam said, "Let's table this discussion until later. I don't know about anyone else, but I'm hungry. It's almost eight o'clock. Dinner, anyone?"

"I need to change if we're going someplace nice," said Lily. She wanted to go back to her room, crawl in bed and pull the covers over her head. But if it didn't bother Sam to eat a meal with a recently discarded lover, she refused to let it bother her.

"I'm already dressed for dinner," said Lillian. "I'll go with you, Lily. We have lots to catch up on. Archie, Sam, we'll meet you in the lobby in half an hour."

Lily and Lillian left the men in the suite and headed for the elevator. Once it came, Lily punched the button for the ninth floor.

"I thought you were on seven," said Lillian.

"That's Sam's floor," said Lily, getting off the elevator. She took her card key out of her purse. "My room is on this floor." Something in her voice must have alerted her grandmother.

Lillian gave her a sharp look. "You haven't been sharing a room with Sam?"

Lily inserted the card key in the slot and turned the handle. Before she'd decided how to answer that question, she felt something poke her in the back.

"Keep moving, Cupcake," said a familiar voice. "You, too, Granny." Chad shoved them both into the room and let the door close behind them.

"Chad!" said Lily, whirling around. "What are you doing here?"

"This is Chad?" asked Lillian. "I've heard a lot about you. None of it good. And don't call me 'Granny.'"

Chad took his hand out of his pocket. He had a gun.

"Where did you get that?" asked Lily, staring at the ugly weapon. "Joe Bones took your gun away from you."

"Isn't it lucky that I always carry a spare?"

"What do you want?" asked Lillian.

"To have a little talk. In private."

"I have nothing to say to you," said Lillian, using her haughtiest voice.

"Oh, I think you'll change your mind about that. Real soon." He put an arm around Lily's shoulders. "Between the two of us, me and Cupcake will have you begging to tell me everything. Cupcake knows, don't you?"

"Where's Desiree?" asked Lily, moving out from under Chad's arm. He let her go.

"Don't know. Don't care. Last time I saw her, she was wandering around in the woods in New Mexico, kinda in a daze. She got hit in the face with the air bag when we hit that tree. How'd you get away from Gus's goons?"

"They let me go. And they aren't goons. They were perfect gentlemen." Lily took a step away from him.

"Yeah. So. You both made it all the way to Hollywood. Did you figure out who killed the movie mogul?"

"No," said Lillian. "I've lost interest in that mystery. I have better things to do."

"You're working for Tony Santori, aren't you?" blurted Lily. "Why?"

"Tony Santori? Nah. Never met him."

There was a knock on the door.

"Don't answer it," said Chad.

Another knock sounded, this one louder. "Lillian? I've got your purse. I thought you might need it. Open the door, honey."

"It's Archie. He knows I'm here. If I don't open the door, he'll get suspicious." Lillian started for the door.

"Okay. Do it." Chad grabbed Lily by the arm and pulled her into the bathroom. He left the door open a crack. "Get your purse, but don't try anything funny."

Lillian opened the door a crack. "Hello, Archie." She looked at him cross-eyed and stuck out her tongue.

"Lillian? Are you all right?"

"Of course I'm all right," she said, rolling her eyes and wiggling her ears. "Why wouldn't I be all right? Lily is getting ready as fast as she can. Where's Sam?"

Sam was standing behind Archie.

Archie got it. He mouthed the words, "Is something wrong?" Out loud he said, "Sam's waiting in the lobby. Hurry it up, will you? We've got reservations."

Lillian nodded and mouthed, "Chad. Gun. Bathroom." She spoke, "Give me my purse and go wait for us with Sam." She took the purse and tried to close the door. Archie had his foot in the way.

Sam had moved down the hall. He was speaking into a cell phone.

"Well?" Lillian asked. "Are you going to give me my purse, or not?"

"Give us a kiss, first." Archie pulled Lillian into his arms. Against her mouth, he whispered, "Step into the hall."

Lillian broke away from him. "No. I can't leave Lily," she hissed. Louder she said, "We'll be ready in a few minutes. Don't be so impatient, Archie."

Lily wondered if Lillian was really having a hard time getting rid of Archie, or if she was trying to tell him what was going on. Chad had one hand over her mouth and the other—the one with the gun—around her waist. He had left the bathroom door ajar, and he was listening intently to Lillian.

This was the second time Chad had cornered her in a bathroom. After the first time, she had told Sam she'd be ready for him the next time, but she hadn't been. Joe and Fazio had saved her from him the second time.

Third time charm, Lily thought. Chad or Mick or whatever he called himself was going to finish the job he'd been hired to do. He intended to kill them. She couldn't wait around for someone else to save her this time. She had to do something, right now.

Lily bit down hard on Chad's finger.

He yelled. She twisted out of his grasp and picked up her hair spray. He raised the gun. She was quicker on the trigger, and she got him in the eyes with a blast of super hold.

Screaming obscenities, Chad dropped the gun and rubbed his eyes with the heels of both hands.

Lillian, Archie and Sam came rushing into the room.

Chad was sitting on the toilet, tears streaming from his eyes.

"What did you do to him?" Lillian asked, sounding awed.

"Hair spray. First I bit him. I drew blood. Do you think I need a tetanus shot?" asked Lily.

Sam picked up the gun Chad had dropped. "Move one muscle and I'll use this," he said. He sounded calm, and the hand holding the gun was steady.

"I'll call the police," said Lillian, grabbing Lily and dragging her out of the bathroom.

"I've already called hotel security," said Sam. "They should be—here they are."

Two uniformed guards entered the room, followed by a man in a business suit.

"What's going on?" asked the suit. He identified himself as an assistant manager.

Lillian pointed to Chad. "That man—his name is either Chad Boyd or Mick O'Neill—broke in here and threatened to kill us."

Archie and Sam pulled out their wallets and showed the guards their investigator's licenses. The assistant manager pulled out a walkie-talkie and ordered someone to call the Beverly Hills police department.

Lily's knees suddenly turned into Play-Doh. She sat down on the bed. Abruptly. Lillian noticed and sat down beside her. Putting her arm around Lily's shoulders, Lillian hugged her close. "You were very brave."

"He was going to kill us, Grandmother."

"Yes. He was. This is all my fault. I never should have started this."

Archie came to stand in front of them. "You did not start this, Lillian. Whoever killed Eric Winthrop started it. And they've gotten away with it long enough." He advanced on Chad. "Who hired you?"

Chad's only response was a sneer.

Sirens sounded, and few minutes later more uniformed men arrived. They identified themselves as Beverly Hills police and took Chad and his gun into custody. One of them said, "Somebody better come along and sign a complaint."

"I'll do it," said Lillian. "I'm the one he wanted to kill. My granddaughter just happened to be in the wrong place at the wrong time."

"I'm going, too," Lily insisted. "This isn't the first time Chad has attacked me."

Sam said, "You two need time to recuperate. Do you want a doctor?"

"No, we'll be all right."

"Sam's right, Lillian. You stay here. There are bound to be reporters and photographers waiting in the lobby. Sam and I will fill the police in on what we've learned so far. If they need you to sign a complaint, you can do it tomorrow."

"All right. We'll stay here. Don't worry about us. We'll be fine," said Lillian.

"I don't want to stay in this room," said Lily once everyone had left. "And I'm starving."

"Excitement does that. I'm hungry, too. Let's go eat. We can go to the hotel restaurant. I'll call the suite and leave a voice mail message telling Archie where we'll be."

The maitre d' seated them at a table for four in a secluded corner of the restaurant. Lily picked up her menu. "Archie and Sam may be at the police station for hours. Do you think Chad will talk?"

"Only if he thinks it's in his best interest. Which it may be. Isn't the first one to talk the one who gets the best deal? That's the way it always happens on *Law and Order.*" Lillian closed her menu. "I'm having the filet. And a baked potato. And a salad with bleu cheese dressing."

"That sounds good. Do you really think Chad was working for Renata Santori and not Tony?"

"Chad denied working for Tony Santori. Maybe I should call Archie and tell him that. Do you have your cell phone?"

"No. Sam has it. If Chad told us, he'll probably tell the police. Let's forget all about Chad and Santori and Gus and talk about something pleasant."

"Like what?"

"Like a wedding. I want all the details of your whirlwind courtship."

Giggling like a teenager, Lillian told her.

"He had a crush on you forty-five years ago?" asked Lily. Her jaws ached from keeping a smile plastered on her face.

"So he claims."

"Did you have a crush on him?"

"No. Sorry to say, I was too dazzled by the rich and powerful to pay attention to a studio guard. I did remember him, though. I thought he was cute. Still is, in my opinion. Now, enough about me. What happened between you and Sam?"

"N-nothing."

"Lily Redmond. Don't lie to me." Lillian put her fork down. "Or is that the truth? You're upset about something. But maybe it's not Sam. Don't you approve of me and Archie? I know it may seem sudden, but we did know each other before."

"That doesn't matter. If you'd only met six days ago, that would be long enough to fall in love. Wouldn't it?" Her face crumpled, and she burst into tears.

Reaching across the table, Lillian took Lily's hand in hers. "So that's what happened. You fell in love in six days—"

Lily held up three fingers.

"—three days—and Sam didn't? Are you sure? I would have sworn he cares about you. He was frantic when you ran away from him."

"Sam doesn't believe love happens that fast. He met his ex-wife on Tuesday and married her on Sunday. She left him six months later."

"Ah. Once burned—"

"—twice shy. Exactly. Sam has this idea that he has to know a woman for a minimum of six years before he can even begin to think about falling in love with her."

"Are you prepared to wait six years?"

"W-what?"

"I'm not saying Sam is right. Personally, I think it's quite possible to meet someone and know in that instant that he's the one. But if Sam has that in his head, are you prepared to wait him out?"

"Love him for six years? With him in Chicago and me in Mobile? He won't even remember me after a few weeks."

"Oh. I don't think you're all that forgettable. You're my granddaughter, and you take after me. Archie remembered me for forty-five years. So did Gus. It's more than likely that Sam will be thinking about you for years and years. The question is, will you be thinking of him? Will your love last for six years?"

Lily wanted to say yes. "I don't know. I think so. I never felt this way before. Not about Dexter. But for more than six years I thought what I felt for Dexter was love. I was wrong about that. What if I'm wrong about Sam?"

"I suppose you'll have to wait and see."

"Six years. Golly, Grandmother."

"Call me Lillian, dear. I don't feel like a grandmother."

"You don't look like one, either," said Archie,

leaning down to kiss her. He pulled up the chair across from Lillian and signaled the waiter.

"Well," said Lillian. "That didn't take long."

"We'll have to go back tomorrow—all four of us. They do want you and Lily to sign complaints. Right now, the Beverly Hills cops are talking to the LAPD about Eric's murder. Getting up to speed, as it were."

"What about Chad?" asked Lily. "Is he talking?"

"Only to ask for a lawyer," said Sam, sitting down on the remaining chair. "He'll work a deal later."

"He told us he wasn't working for Tony Santori."

"I'm inclined to believe that," said Archie. "I don't think Tony would hire a hit man. He may want to be governor, but I can't see him killing you just to keep you quiet about an old murder."

"The murderer hired Chad, I'm sure of it. As sure as I am that the murderer is Renata Santori," said Lillian.

"Why would she shoot Eric?" asked Lily. "I still don't understand that. They barely knew each other. Unless . . . Could Gus have talked her into doing his dirty work for him?"

"Why don't we ask him?" said Archie, looking over Lillian's head at the man standing behind her.

Lillian turned her head. "Gus. Hello."

He bent over and kissed her on the cheek. "Hello, Lillian. Long time no see. You're looking good. May I join you?" When Lillian nodded, he took a chair from the table next to theirs and pulled it up to the corner between Lily and Lillian.

"Thank you, Gus," said Lillian. "You're looking well, too."

"From what I just overheard, you've almost figured it out. I thought you might. You always were a smart one."

"Renata shot Eric?"

Gus nodded.

"But we haven't figured out why," said Lily.

"You do look like Lillian. Joe and Fazio said you did. After all you've been through, you deserve an answer, little Lily. My sister visited me here in '58. She was dazzled by Hollywood—had visions of being a movie star. Eric gave her a private tour of the studio, as a favor to me. They ended up in his office. Lillian, you can guess what happened there."

"The casting couch."

Gus nodded. "Renata kept quiet about it for several weeks—during which she continued to see Eric on the sly. But then she found out she was pregnant. She thought she could use that to get Eric to marry her. That, or me. She thought I would threaten to kill Eric if he refused. I might have done just that—if she hadn't killed him first."

"I can't believe Eric would have refused her," said Lillian. "He was a bully and a coward. He must have been afraid of you."

"Oh, he was. But Winthrop thought he had a way around that—he'd been taping our conversations. He was going to turn the tapes over to one of those Congressional Commissions investigating organized crime—his way out of paying off the debt he owed me and my associates. Winthrop told me about the tapes, letting me know he wanted out of our arrangement—I don't think he realized at the beginning what it meant to have me and my associates as partners."

"He thought he could use the same tapes to keep from becoming your brother-in-law."

"Exactly. When Renata told him she was carrying his baby, he laughed at her. Told her he wasn't afraid of me and said he was going to marry Madeline. That was all it took for her to realize that he had never cared for her. She lashed out at him, said she'd kill him herself if she had to. Winthrop panicked and pulled a gun."

"Eric kept a Charter Arms detective special in his desk drawer," said Archie. "That was the murder weapon."

"Yeah. Eric took the gun out and told Renata he guessed he'd have to kill her first. To save himself. He said he'd shoot her—his office was soundproofed—and bury her body in the back lot where they were getting ready to build the set for some ancient Rome epic."

"She would have been buried under tons of cement."

"Exactly. Not a bad plan. But for one thing. Renata started sobbing, told him she hadn't meant it and pretended to faint. When Winthrop knelt beside her, she got the gun away from him. There was a struggle. The gun went off. Eric died. Renata went straight from the studio to the train station. She left that night for Chicago. When she got home, she called and told me what she had done. I told her to keep quiet. No one knew about her and Eric. How did you find out, by the way?"

"Someone saw her leave the studio that night. But they didn't know who she was," Archie explained.

"What a terrible tragedy," said Lillian. "What happened to Eric's baby?"

"I know the answer to that one," Sam said. "He's a state senator in Illinois. Possibly the next governor. Right, Gus?"

"Right."

"Gus. You wouldn't be counting on having a governor beholden to you, would you?" asked Lillian. "It occurs to me that if the public knew Tony Santori's mother killed a man—a man who just happened to be his father—and got away with it . . ."

"Tony doesn't know. But if he did, he wouldn't want it to get out, you're right."

"So now you have to kill all of us?" blurted Lily.

"Red. Don't give the man ideas," said Sam.

"You may find this hard to believe, but I've never killed anyone. Personally. And my sister and I haven't spoken to one another for forty-five years."

"Why not?" asked Lillian.

"My sister wanted me to take the rap for Winthrop's murder. That's why she called me. She thought I could plead self-defense and get away with it. But by the time she called, Lillian had already given me an airtight alibi."

"I can understand why that would make you angry," Lillian said, nodding. "But what did Renata have to be mad about?"

"She doesn't like it that I know her secret. She's afraid I'll use it against her someday. Against her or Tony. Now I think she's more worried about Tony than herself."

"What do you want us to do, Gus? Keep her secret, too?"

Gus grinned wryly. "I think the chances of four people keeping a secret are slim to none."

"But if what Renata told you is true, she acted in self-defense," said Lily.

Sam added, "It would be her word against . . . no one. There can't be any physical evidence left that would contradict her story."

"The scandal would hurt Tony," said Gus. "Her son is her life."

"So. What are we going to do?" asked Lillian.

"There's only one thing to do. When you four go back to the police station tomorrow, I'm going with you," said Gus.

"You want us to help you rat out your sister?" Archie looked surprised. "You might get hit with an accessory after the fact charge."

Gus shrugged. "I've beaten worse raps. And I'm tired of keeping secrets. This one stayed hidden longer than most. It's time for it to come out. I knew that when I heard Lillian was going to look for answers. I also guessed that Renata would try to stop her. I'm going to tell the cops what I know and let the chips fall where they may."

Sunday the chips fell onto the front page of every newspaper in the country. "Fifties Femme Fatale Solves Decades-Old Hollywood Murder!" had been Lillian's favorite. After they all returned from the police station late Sunday afternoon, Lillian had ordered scissors from housekeeping. When Lily had left the suite, Lillian had been clipping stories about her escapade for a scrapbook.

Lily had excused herself, ostensibly to go pack. She did have to do that, since they were leaving for Las Vegas early Monday morning. But she had something more important to do first. She had to talk to Sam alone.

Lily walked to the elevator and punched the button. When the doors opened, Sam got out. "I was going to see Archie and Lillian."

"They're . . . busy right now."

"Oh." Sam held the elevator door open. "Well. I'll see you in the morning, then. What time are we leaving for Las Vegas?"

"At eight. Sam, I think we need to talk."

Looking uncomfortable, Sam gave a curt nod. "Okay. Let's go to the lobby bar."

"My room's closer." She got on the elevator and punched the button for her floor.

"Well. Lillian did it. She found out who killed Eric Winthrop."

"You helped," said Sam.

"So did you. So did Archie. Sam, we're going to be in-laws. Lillian's going to be your stepmother. Archie will be my new grandfather. What does that make us?"

"Friends."

"More than friends. Family."

"Lily—"

"Sam. I know you don't want to hear it, but I do love you."

"No. You don't. We went through some intense times together. I only wish I hadn't—"

"Sam Hunter. Don't you dare say you regret making love with me. Don't you dare! I don't regret it. I will never regret that. And I will never forget it. I'm glad that you were my first lover, do you hear me?"

"Yeah. It was my pleasure, Red. I'll never forget you, either."

"There's a but, isn't there?"

He nodded. "But. What you think you feel for me isn't love. It won't last. A few weeks, maybe a couple of months, and you'll be back to normal. These past few days have not been normal."

"Sam—"

The elevator doors opened. Dexter stood in front of her, his finger poised over the elevator button. "Dexter! What are you doing here?"

"I've come to take you home," said Dexter, reaching out a hand.

Lily put her hand in his and let him pull her off the elevator. As the doors began to close, she looked over her shoulder. "Sam . . ?"

Sam let the doors shut between them.

One look at Dexter B. Jackson, III, was all it took to convince Sam he had done the right thing. Lily's fiancé did not look like a nerd or a dork. Dexter did not look like a banker, either. He looked like a movie star, a rock idol, like Prince Charming come to life.

The next time Sam saw the prince and his consort was at the Chapel of the King in Las Vegas. Dexter had his left arm around Lily's shoulders.

Dexter stuck out his right hand. "You must be Sam Hunter. Lily's told me all about you. I want to thank you for taking such good care of my girl."

Sam nodded and shook Dexter's hand. "No problem," he muttered. Lily could not have told Dexter all about him. If she had, Dexter's hand would be at his throat, not giving him a firm, friendly shake.

A few minutes later, Arthur escorted Lillian down the short aisle. The service was short—other couples were waiting in the anteroom—and ended with the minister lip-synching a medley of Elvis's love songs.

Archie kissed Lillian. Lily kissed Archie on the cheek and gave Lillian a hug. Sam kissed the bride on the mouth with enough enthusiasm that Archie objected. Lillian and Archie ran outside and climbed into the Ford. Sam had spray painted "just married" on the rear window with shaving cream. Everyone waved frantically as the Ford pulled away.

Dexter looked at his watch. "We'd better get going," said Dexter. "We've got a long drive ahead of us."

Lily looked at Sam. She had tears in her brown eyes. Sam told himself that they were tears of happiness shed for Lillian and Archie. He didn't believe himself.

"Good-bye, Sam," she said, her voice a little wobbly. "Thanks for . . . everything. I'll never forget—"

Sam leaned down and kissed her one last time. "Good-bye, Red. Have a safe trip home."

Fifteen

A week later, Lily sat on the wooden dock behind her grandmother's house and dangled her feet in the warm water of Mobile Bay.

It seemed strange to have nothing to do on a Monday but watch the pelicans fishing, but she still had a week of her vacation left. Lillian and Archie had decided to spend their honeymoon touring every national park west of the Rockies. The last postcard had been from Yosemite.

She and Dexter had driven straight through from Las Vegas, with only brief stops for food and gas. They had taken turns at the wheel, sleeping when not driving. That hadn't left much time to talk, but it had been enough. Lily had told Dexter about Sam. Dexter had told Lily about Mary Alice McAllister. He confessed that he'd been in love with Mary Alice for years. Dexter said he'd tried to fight it, knowing full well what was expected of him.

His parents did not approve of Mary Alice. She had gotten a reputation—the boys had called her queen of the bleachers—in high school which she'd never lived down. Besides, Dexter had felt obligated to do what his parents—and Lily's—had wanted. He'd stalled proposing, hoping that Lily would fall in love with someone else.

The first thing they'd done when they got home was tell their parents that the engagement was off. Dexter's parents had been noticeably relieved—the supermarket tabloid stories about Lillian and her granddaughter and their part in solving the decades-old murder had made Lily undesirable as a daughter-in-law. Only that morning, Dexter had called to thank her for chasing after Lillian, confiding that her notoriety had made Mary Alice look like an angel by comparison. Mary Alice did sing in the church choir, after all.

Well. At least her escapade had made someone happy. Two someones, in fact. Dexter and Mary Alice had already set a wedding date.

Lily had asked her father to transfer the certificate of deposit back to Dexter. Then she had told her parents she was going to house-sit for Lillian, and that after that she would be getting her own apartment. If they thought she was being unusually assertive and independent, they hadn't mentioned it. They seemed relieved, in fact. Lily suspected that they had been afraid that they would be stuck with her forever, now that marrying Dexter was off.

She hadn't told them about Sam. Lily couldn't think of a way to explain what had happened that didn't make her seem foolish and Sam look like a cad. Her mother had given her a few odd looks, as if she knew *something* had happened that Lily wasn't ready to reveal.

Her father hadn't noticed. He had commented on her finally having had a Lillian-like adventure, obviously hoping that she'd gotten that out of her system once and for all.

He didn't have to worry about that. One adventure was enough for her. Her poor heart couldn't take another one of those. With a mournful sigh, Lily drew her feet out of the water, hooked her heels on the edge of the dock and wrapped her arms around her bent knees.

She was an idiot. She had been warned. Sam had told her he would not get serious about any woman he'd known less than six years. Phil had informed her that Sam's relationships only lasted a couple of weeks. He'd only spent a couple of days with her.

Then Sam had walked away from her without a backward look. Sam Spade Hunter was an idiot, too.

How could he have done that? He loved her. She knew he did. But he didn't trust what he felt because it had happened so soon.

Or maybe he didn't trust what she felt.

That thought had Lily almost falling off the dock. She couldn't blame Sam for leaving her. She'd let him go. What could he think but that her love for him had been nothing more than a flash in the pan, a blink of the eye, a—she was too excited to think of one more cliche. A woman in love didn't sit around and mope when things went wrong.

She'd learned that from Lillian's movies, too.

All of the ingenues in Lillian's films had won out in the end, defeating whatever had come between them and their men—the whatever being Lillian in her various seductive guises. Those women had succeeded by taking action, not by sitting around feeling sorry for themselves or waiting for someone else to tell them what to do.

Lily's heart began to pound in a go-get-him rhythm.

She could do that. She could go after Sam and convince him that she really, really loved him. If he didn't believe her, she would think of a way to stay close to him for six years.

Standing up, Lily slipped her wet feet into her sandals. As soon as she was back in the house, she headed for Lillian's study. She picked up the telephone and dialed Chicago information.

Sam stood at the window of his office, watching the sailboats on Lake Michigan. As usual when his mind wasn't occupied with anything else, his thoughts were about Lily. He thought about the first time he'd seen her, standing in the doorway of Lillian's bedroom, her mouth open and her brown eyes wide with shock.

He thought about the way her mouth had felt under his the first time he'd kissed her. About her sweet surrender the night he'd found her in Las Cruces. About her fierce pride when she'd saved herself and Lillian from Chad.

Sam tried not to think about the last time he'd seen her, the day she had walked out of the chapel on Dexter's arm. That memory hurt a little too much. His lips curled into a sneer. He was a wimp *and* a coward.

But on at least one occasion he had not been a selfish bastard. He had let Lily go. And if his heart ached and his insides felt hollow, he deserved it. He had broken the rules, after all. He'd fraternized. He'd grabbed. And he'd fallen in love with a woman he'd known for only a few days.

The door to his office opened. He did not turn around. Phil and Archie were the only ones who entered without knocking, and Archie was still on his honeymoon.

"Did you see the headline in the *Tribune* this morning?" asked Phil. "Santori's dropped out of the governor's race."

Sam sat down at his desk. "He had no choice. An uncle in the mob was hard enough to overcome. Having a mother who murdered his father—I could almost feel sorry for him."

"Yeah. But he crossed the line when he let his mother send a hit man after Lillian. He knew who Mick O'Reilly was. At that first press conference, when Santori said he had no knowledge of—how did he put it?"

"'The unusual circumstances surrounding his birth,'" quoted Sam.

"Yeah. That was a lie. He may not have known for sure, but he must have had suspicions."

"I thought so, too. He had to have known his birth date was only six months after Renata married Santori."

"I know how she managed that," said Phil. "I did some checking. Turns out Santori was on the hook for a loan from the Accardo family. His debt was marked paid shortly after the wedding."

"Well. That explains that." Sam didn't much care about Tony Santori's problems, but Phil liked tying up loose ends. "Anything in today's paper about how the extradition proceedings are proceeding?"

"No. But Renata will be extradited to California to stand trial for murder sooner or later. Besides Gus, Desiree's going to testify for the prosecution, too. She'll probably get off with probation."

"How come you're so up on the case?"

"Dad asked for an update on the whole affair last night when he called. I knew he would, so I prepared."

"Where are they now?" Sam asked.

"Somewhere in Colorado. But they're leaving today to go to New Orleans. They've got to pick up Lillian's car. They're going to stay there for a few days, then head on over to Fair Hope."

"Dad's really going to retire?"

Phil nodded. "Looks like. I can't believe he's going to move to Alabama. You and I will be on our own. I'm not sure now why we thought that would be a good thing. What if we screw up?"

"We can always call him if we need help." Sam knew Phil was more worried about him not carrying his weight than he was about Archie retiring. He hadn't contributed much to the bottom line since returning from Las Vegas.

"Yeah, you're right. Alabama's not that far away. We can call, and we can visit. What was Fair Hope, Alabama, like?"

"Green. Hot. Probably hotter now."

"I like heat," said Phil. "Beats cold any day."

"Only because you like to leer at women wearing skimpy clothes." A pastime he'd once enjoyed, too. Sam had a sudden vision of Lily in her white shorts and yellow tee, staring at him with her big, brown bedroom eyes.

"True. Speaking of women . . . There's an applicant for the secretarial job outside. I think you ought to interview this one."

"Why? If you think she's got the right qualifications, go ahead and hire her."

"Not this time. You're the one who needs her. You should do the interview."

Sam narrowed his eyes. His brother was up to something. "Why do you want me to do the interview? What's wrong with her?"

"Not a thing, as far as I could tell. But you're the one who will have to work with her. Come on, bro. Let me send her in. It will only take a few minutes of your time."

"All right. Send her in." Phil left. Sam swiveled his chair around and resumed staring out his window.

He heard the door to his office open. The hair

on the back of his neck rose, and he spun his chair around again.

Lily stood in the doorway. She looked anxious, but determined. Determined to do what? Tell him what an ass he was? He owed her that opportunity.

"Hello, Red. What are you doing here?"

"I'm applying for the job as your secretary. I called Phil last week and asked him if the job was still open, and he said it was; so I sent him my application. I suppose I should tell you that I don't type very fast, and I can't take shorthand. I'm not familiar with your word-processing program, but I'm sure I can learn. I'm a very fast learner." She stopped and took a deep breath.

Sam stifled a grin. Solemnly, he nodded. "Yeah. You are. I thought you had a job."

"I quit. It would have been awkward, working at the bank with Dexter."

"What about Dexter? Your engagement? Your parents?"

"The engagement is off. Mother and Daddy took it better than I expected. After living through Lillian's solving a murder mystery and getting married in Las Vegas—by an Elvis clone—a broken engagement was barely noticeable. Dexter is marrying Mary Alice McAllister."

"Dexter is an idiot."

Lily advanced into the room, blowing a stray red curl out of her eyes. "Maybe he is, but so are you. You should never have left me alone in Las Vegas."

"You weren't alone. Dexter was there. I thought you didn't need me."

"Well. You were wrong about that. I do need you. I love you, Sam. I can't help it that I fell in love with you so fast. That's your fault, too. If you weren't so lovable, people wouldn't fall in love with you."

"You think I'm lovable?"

"Of course you're lovable. Plus, you've got that testosterone thing going for you. You're so sexy you make my bones melt."

"You're sure you love me? I'm not just a passing fancy, a flash in the pan, an adventure, or an experiment?"

"None of the above. I love you. Why else would I have packed my bags, moved up north when I absolutely hate cold weather and applied for a job I'm not qualified for? Because you are lovable, that's why. Sam Hunter, you are so lovable, so sexy, so everything-I-ever-wanted-in-a-man that I had to find a way to stay close to you for six years. I called Phil, and he said you were still looking for a secretary, and so—"

"Did he tell you I wanted someone with at least twenty years' experience?"

"Oh. No. He didn't mention that." She stuck out her chin. "You can't do that. That's age discrimination."

"Ah. Well. I wouldn't want to break any rules." Sam couldn't hold back a grin any longer. "In that case, I'll overlook your lack of experience. And your lack of qualifications. You're hired. Take a letter."

Lily stared at him. She'd just made the best declaration of love she could think of, and all it got her was a job? And what did that goofy grin on his face mean? "Oh. I don't take shorthand."

"I know. You told me. I will speak very slowly."

Lily sat in the chair in front of his desk. "I don't have anything to write on."

"I've got a legal pad. Here." Sam took a pen out of the holder on his desk and handed that to her, too. "Ready?"

"I think so. Yes."

"The letter is to Lakeside Travel. Leave the address blank for now. You can look it up in my Rolodex later."

"Okay. Lakeside Travel. Got that."

"Gentlemen. I am returning the enclosed ticket for a full refund. Got that?"

" . . . full refund. Yes."

"Go back and change 'ticket' to 'ticket to Mobile, Alabama.'"

Lily looked up. Sam wasn't grinning any longer. He looked serious. Maybe even a little nervous. "You bought a ticket to Mobile?"

"Yeah. I did."

"Were you going there on a case?"

"In a way. There were some loose ends that needed tying up. But that's not the only reason. I have been having trouble concentrating on work lately. So I thought I'd take a trip."

"You just got back from a trip."

"Yeah. But it was too short. And not very relaxing."

"Oh. So you were going to Mobile on business and for a little vacation?"

"Red. I was coming to see you."

"You were? Why?"

Sam opened his desk drawer and took out a small velvet box. "I wanted to give you this."

Lily put the legal pad on the edge of the desk and carefully replaced the pen in its holder. She took the box from Sam and opened it.

"Oh, Sam." The box contained an engagement ring—a square cut diamond set in a yellow gold band. "It's exactly the ring I always wanted."

Sam walked around the desk, took the box from her and removed the ring. "I go with it, you know." He knelt beside her chair and slipped the ring on the third finger of her left hand.

"I certainly hope so." Lily held out her hand and admired the ring sparkling there. "How is it that you happened to have an engagement ring in your desk drawer? And a ticket to Mobile? You must have figured out that you love me."

"That was the easy part. Convincing myself that you loved me took a little longer."

"I thought that might be the problem. That's why I decided to come to Chicago. I love you, Sam."

"I love you, Lily Redmond. Will you marry me?"

"I'll marry you this minute."

"Illinois isn't as advanced as Nevada. I think it takes three days. That would give Archie and Lillian time to get here. Your parents, too. Or we could go to Las Vegas." Sam got up and pulled her out of the chair and into his arms.

"I can wait three days," Lily said, tilting her face up for the kisses she knew were coming. "I thought I was going to have to wait six years."

About the Author

Dixie Kane used to be a lawyer, but she got over it.
Now she is a writer, and she doesn't plan to ever
get over that.

Dixie's next Contemporary Romance, *Making
Merry*, will be published in October 2003.

Dixie loves to hear from readers. You may write
to her at P.O. Box 8523, Mandeville, Louisiana
70470, or e-mail her at <u>dixiekane@msn.com</u>